The Amazing Years

by

W. Pett Ridge

Double 9
BOOKS

The Amazing Years
by W. Pett Ridge

ISBN: 978-93-59950-19-8

Published by

DOUBLE 9 BOOKS

2/13-B, Ansari Road
Daryaganj, New Delhi – 110002
info@double9books.com
www.double9books.com
Tel. 011-40042856

This book is under public domain

ABOUT THE AUTHOR

William Pett Ridge was an English fiction writer who was born in Chartham, near Canterbury, Kent, on April 22, 1859, and died in London on October 2, 1930. He went to school in Marden, Kent, and at the Birkbeck Institute. He worked as a clerk for a while at the Railway Clearing House. Around 1891, he started writing funny sketches for the St. James's Gazette and other publications. His first book, A Clever Wife (1895), was released, but it wasn't until his fifth book, Mord Em'ly (1898), that he had his first big hit. This book showed that he could write funny portraits of life in the lower classes. Pett Ridge was a kind person who gave a lot of his time and money to good causes. In 1907, he started the Babies Home at Hoxton. He was also a strong backer of many groups whose goal was to help children. Because of his desire to help others and the fact that he became the best writer about London life and people, he was seen as Dickens' natural successor. He was a judge in the fake trial of John Jasper for killing Edwin Drood on January 7, 1914, in King's Hall, Covent Garden.

CONTENTS

CHAPTER I 7

CHAPTER II..17

CHAPTER III...30

CHAPTER IV 42

CHAPTER V..53

CHAPTER VI 64

CHAPTER VII..71

CHAPTER VIII...83

CHAPTER IX...93

CHAPTER X..109

CHAPTER XI..121

CHAPTER XII 132

CHAPTER XIII..142

CHAPTER XIV..149

CHAPTER XV 157

CHAPTER XVI..167

CHAPTER XVII 176

CHAPTER XVIII 192

CHAPTER XIX..198

CHAPTER I

Mrs. Hillier said something just before lunch that touched me more than she could have guessed. The family was to leave on the Saturday, and the elder of the two young ladies—Miss Muriel—had grumbled throughout the week because of the delay insisted upon by the master. The departure had originally been fixed for the twenty-fifth; Mr. Hillier, who seldom spoke at home, but when he did talk expected to be obeyed, announced that the party would not cross the Channel until the first. That would be two days before the Bank Holiday, and Miss Muriel foresaw discomforts arising from over-crowded compartments, carriages reserved for the incredible Polytechnic folk and the impossible Lunn trippers. Mrs. Hillier, as I managed with some difficulty to turn the key of a trunk, put her hand on my shoulder.

"Weston," she remarked, impulsively, "I wish you were coming with us."

"Ma'am," I said, "I don't like the sea, and I can't endure foreigners. Furthermore, a woman like myself, knowing only the English language, would be simply a hindrance."

"Wherever you found yourself," she declared, "you'd contrive to make yourself understood. Who is coming here to stay with you whilst we are away?"

"Thought, ma'am, of asking my young nephew. He's just got a scholarship, and the month's rest will do him good."

One of the maids knocked and came in to ask me whether she should sound the gong. Mrs. Hillier's manner altered at once. She gave definite instructions regarding the tying on of the blue labels that had been specially printed by a firm at Sidcup Hill, commented sharply on the condition of Master Edward's laundry, and mentioned that the working classes were becoming intolerably careless. When the maid had gone, she turned to me again.

"Weston," she said. "I'm worried about this trip. Before, I've felt confidence in your master to see us through any difficulty. He's been a sort of a dependable courier, and though he can't have relished the holiday, it's been at any rate a change for him. But lately—Oh I don't know," she broke off. "Perhaps I'm wrong."

Talk at lunch, I noticed, was devoted to the coming journey. The conversation could not be described as good tempered: it needed the presence of Master John to ensure anything like cheerfulness, and you might have assumed that the three, instead of going for a holiday, were about to engage upon one of the most trying and distasteful tasks of a lifetime. I had come into the family when it lived in Tressillian Road, Brockley, and Miss Muriel was twelve—that was ten years before—and Miss Katherine eight. A dear little soul Miss Katherine was too at that time, with her doll's perambulator, and her hoop, and a nursery not over furnished. There came Mr. Hillier's good luck in the City with the agency in Basinghall Street, and we moved to The Croft, where I was told to make no reference to Brockley, and to disclose to the maids of the house, or to the servants at any other house, no particulars of early days that had been imparted to me in confidence or gained by observation. It was little Miss Katherine's fault that I did not go from the family when Mr. Hillier went up in the world. It means a lot for a woman to be near a child—near any child—who can put its arms around her neck, and hug her.

"Dover and Calais," Miss Muriel was saying, as I directed the parlour maid to bring in the sweets.

"Folkestone and Boulogne," announced Mrs. Hillier.

"Dover and Calais is the shorter route, mother, dear."

"There's very little difference, darling, and one saves on the land journey."

"I shall tell father," declared Miss Muriel, "that unless we travel by way of Dover and Calais, I prefer not to go at all. Kitty, you agree with me, I'm sure."

"Your sister," said Mrs. Hillier, "has the good sense to take my view."

"I vote," remarked Miss Katherine, "for Newhaven and Dieppe, and I bet a large red apple that's the way we take." She hummed something about Yo ho, yo ho, a sailor's bride I'd be, and live for ever gaily on the bounding sea. Her mother requested her not to sing at table, and pointed out that the wives of seamen invariably lived on shore.

"Let Weston decide," suggested Miss Muriel. "Come along, Weston. This is where you come in, in the usual way, as peacemaker."

"'To foil their plans,'" said Miss Katherine, quoting from last year's pantomime, "'we now bring upon the scene, The villain's foe, our friend the Fairy Queen.'"

"If it was my case," I said, "I should wait until there was a Channel tunnel." It proved to be not the first time that I had managed, by disagreeing with all three, to check an argument.

Master Edward came home from Blackheath soon after six, and brought a new subject for consideration. He had enjoyed a good day in watching Kent play, and Kent had done well; in my room he rattled off the figures exultantly. Humphreys 45, Hardinge 86, Seymour 66, A.P. Day 55 and so on; three hundred and forty-nine in all. "Let's see Surrey beat that!" he remarked, defiantly. The boy took the brass shovel from the empty fireplace, and described some of the most important hits of the game. I reminded him of his own score of twenty-five, not out, performed on the ground of his boarding school at Westgate, and we had a serious talk concerning the wise life to lead: Master Edward thought mere education was very much overrated, and declared he would rather be Mr. Troughton, captain of Kent, than a science master at a college. I was unable to go all the way with him, and suggested, as a compromise, that games should be cultivated in moderation.

"But you see, my tall old bird," he said, persuasively, "you're only a woman. I don't say you can't throw a ball in straight, because, as it happens, it's one of the things you can just manage to do; but apart from that—Realise what I mean, don't you?"

Contention about the route came up again at dinner, when Mr. Hillier took the foot of the table, crumbling his bread in the absent-minded manner he had recently adopted. Sometimes the evening meal went through, I noticed, without a syllable from him, and when the savoury came he would give a nod of apology to his wife, and go off to his workshop at the back of the house. On this particular Thursday night he was cross-examined by Miss Muriel with severity concerning the question of tickets, and he admitted he had not yet secured them. Miss Muriel gave a picture of the rush, and tumult, and hurry-scurry at the station; the most cheerful detail seemed to be that father would undoubtedly be left behind. I was absent from the dining room in order to see that his two pipes were filled, that, in the study, the cigars set out in case any one should call; the liqueur stand had to be replenished, and I suppose ten minutes had gone when I returned. I found everyone talking—excepting, of course, the master—everyone shouting at the top of the voice, everyone begging the others to be silent.

"Weston," said Mrs. Hillier. ("Keep quiet, all of you. Impossible to hear oneself speak with all this din going on. Edward, I forbid you to say another word. Muriel, I'm surprised at you.) Weston, I want to ask you something." She rapped her forehead with her knuckles. "So much chatter that it's no wonder thoughts go out of my head." The rest declined to give the cue. "Oh, I remember. Have you heard any rumours about trouble on the Continent?"

"Only what I've read in the papers, ma'am."

"There!" she said, triumphantly to her husband. "Now perhaps you'll leave off throwing out these foolish suggestions that you have somehow got into your head. You speak before you think, James. I've warned you about it previously. You men in the City meet at lunch time, and over your chop, and your bottle of wine——"

"I always have a cup of coffee, and a piece of shortbread."

"And on that," she remarked, changing the subject, "you expect to keep well. Why don't you have a sensible meal at mid-day, the same as I do? It's very difficult," she said to the girls, "very difficult indeed to knock any sense into men."

Mr. Hillier rose, I opened the door. Miss Katherine followed him to whisper something consoling.

"Don't dare forget to see about the tickets to-morrow, father," directed Miss Muriel.

"I'll make inquiries," he said.

Colonel Edgington called later and I switched on the lights in the billiard room, took off the cloth, chalked two cues, and summoned the master from the workshop. I asked Mr. Hillier whether I should remain in the billiard room and look after the scoring board; he said, "Thank you, Weston, no. We shan't want to bother you this evening." As I was going, he called me. "Afraid," he went on, apologetically, "that we trouble you too much in this establishment. We get into the habit of depending upon you, Weston." I said, "Not at all, sir!" and left. At eleven, when Colonel Edgington had gone, I found that spot white had made four, and plain white had scored nothing. It looked as though the game had been interfered with by discussion. Home Rule probably. The Colonel came from the north of Ireland, and he held strong views on the subject; I knew from the papers that a four days' conference at Buckingham Palace had failed to settle the question. Apart from the condition of the scoring board, it was strange that the Colonel had not touched his tumbler of whiskey. I went over the house to see to the locking up, and encountered on one of the landings, the master: he was gazing out at the fine summer night and I expected he would make some casual remarks concerning the stars.

"Seven," he remarked, in a dreamy way. "Seven, Watson, seven."

"More than that, sir, surely."

"More later on," he agreed. "But seven is the number of Stock Exchange firms that failed yesterday."

The next day was cheerful, only in regard to the weather. Master Edward came home from the cricket ground to announce in a dismal manner that Hayward and Hobbs were doing astonishingly well for Surrey; I had to remind him that a match was not finished until the stumps were drawn on the last day. Several ladies had called during the afternoon, and they brought all sorts of wild rumours with them that Mrs. Hillier found extremely upsetting. One said she had heard from a bookstall boy at the station that the Bank of England was going to close its doors. Another had been told by her gardener that the Germans would probably land at Dover, after they had dealt with France, and march up through Kent, taking Chislehurst on the way, and this she regretted the more because her gladioli were very fine and likely, but for interference, to do well at the flower show. A third was able to give, as a more reliable piece of information, the announcement that her German governess, who had been with the family for years, and knew how to manage difficult children, had disappeared; it was found she had taken the train for Dover.

Mr. Hillier was bombarded with questions on these and other subjects so soon as he arrived. Generally he travelled from Cannon Street by the four forty-eight, which did the journey in half an hour, and his time for reaching the house was five thirty. He reached home on this Friday by a quarter past four.

"I don't know anything," he said. "I can't tell you any more than the man in the moon."

"Apparently you are able to tell less," remarked his wife.

"Perhaps," said Miss Muriel, "you can at least contrive to say, father, at what time we start to-morrow morning."

"Oh, that!" he remarked, calling the subject back to his memory. "Oh, we don't go to-morrow. I thought it was understood."

Miss Katherine stood by him, but the others raised their voices in indignant protests. Mrs. Hillier begged that he would, for once, listen calmly, and endeavour to understand that when trunks were packed, and preparations made, it was simply nonsense to say that the holiday was not to be taken; she implored him also to consider the talk that would go on in Chislehurst. Miss Muriel said that so far as she was concerned, she intended to go alone, and the others could follow when and as they pleased. Master Edward suggested it was rotten bad luck to be disappointed; he could not imagine the sort of tale he would have to make up on returning to Westgate after a blank and empty holiday.

"Besides," urged Mrs. Hillier, triumphantly, "there's John!"

"John I saw this afternoon," said Mr. Hillier. (You must understand that they all talked freely whilst I was about; if one of the maids put in an appearance, then, of course, they used more care). "John and I had a long talk. He expected to have a couple of songs out next month, and he's afraid all this trouble may delay them. Anyway, he wants to stay on, and see what happens. He's coming here this afternoon."

The elder son of the family had recently taken rooms in town; we all knew the songs he had composed, from myself down to the scullery-maid, and everyone in the house was looking forward to his next. I remember I felt more concerned at hearing the deliberate announcement of Master John's intentions than at anything else which was happening, and the others, too, seemed impressed by it. They left Mr. Hillier alone. The evening was very quiet, the grand pianoforte did not find itself opened. On the Saturday morning the master went up to Cannon Street, and came back before noon. He told me he heard the Stock Exchange had been closed an hour after it opened, and in regard to his own business in Basinghall Street, where he represented an important Austrian firm, nothing was being done.

"By the bye, Weston," he said, "there used to be something in the house that I don't seem able to find. You would know where it is if anybody does." I waited for him to explain. "I mean," he said, rather confusedly, "a revolver."

"Whenever Master Edward is home for his holidays, sir, I always take the liberty of putting that where no one but myself can find it."

"Very wise," he agreed. "But where is it exactly? You see," persuasively, "if we're going to be attacked, why we must be prepared to sell our lives dearly, eh?"

"We're not going to sell our lives, sir, and we're not going to give them away either. We must keep calm, and not do anything foolish, or even think of doing anything foolish, on the spur of the moment. If trouble's coming, we've got to face it."

"Quite so, quite so, quite so!" He looked at me for a while, and I looked at him. "Quite so!" he remarked once more. And began to hum. He had no ear for music, and the playing and singing of the young ladies were always endured by him with a pained air, but I never heard him or any other man hum a tune more incorrectly than he did on that occasion. It was a relief when Master John walked up the drive, and took his father at once for a run in the car. What Mr. Hillier required was fresh air, and sensible, male companionship.

We were more animated that evening. I had Master John's room all in order, and I told him I hoped he was going to stay for the week-end; he said he had not thought of doing so, but when I hinted that it would be a sensible thing to do, he nodded, and said, pleasantly, "Right you are, Weston. You always have your own way, somehow!" Even Mr. Hillier brightened in the presence of his elder son, and Master John was able to check his mother and Miss Muriel when they showed a tendency to go back to the grievance of the cancelled trip. Master John had been going about in some of the hard-up quarters of London, and recounted his experiences, described the folk he had met, the places he had seen. There was nothing very fresh to me in all this, but he made it attractive, and I had to speak rather sharply to one of the maids for laughing at a joke he told. The most difficult thing in drilling young girls is to convince them that they must keep a straight face when waiting at table.

"All the same," remarked Miss Katherine, "it must be a dud life for them. I mean to have two one double four Hell for a telephone number."

"They've been used to nothing different," argued her mother.

"I feel rather sorry," said Master John, "for the folk who come down to it from the heights."

"Even in those cases," said his mother, "they have only themselves to blame. Generally, it's drink."

"Sometimes sheer misfortune," he remarked.

"Rather than lead that sort of existence," said Miss Muriel, dramatically, "I would take a revolver and shoot myself." I frowned at her, and she said, "Don't make faces, Weston. It doesn't improve your appearance in the least." Her father glanced at me.

Master John had a theory, and proceeded to give it across the table. Many of the districts he had been referring to were, he pointed out, near the river. You would assume that nothing was easier for these people, when goaded by worry, and depressed by anxiety, than to stroll down to the edge of the water, and put an end to their existence. But, said Master John, this was exactly the course they did not adopt. It was not in their class you found men and women taking upon themselves a duty that belonged to a greater power, and deciding when life was to be terminated. These cases existed in other stages of society, where the crumpled rose-leaf, and nothing but a crumpled rose-leaf, was sometimes held to justify the act.

"An unpleasant subject to be discussing," said Mrs. Hillier. "Let's talk about the war for a change. What do you think Germany means to do, John?"

I have often, in recent days, wished I had written down all the views, and all the prophecies heard from different sources at that period. Likely enough, Chislehurst was not more fruitful in this than was other places, but we were just far enough from town to enable folk to go around, distributing new ideas between the arrival of editions of the London newspapers. Master John altogether refused to make any predictions. "Ask me again in a week's time," he said. He took his father along to the billiard room, and there kept his opponent concentrated on the game, and declined to talk of any other matters than that of how to deal with the red. Mr. Hillier made a break of twelve, and felt tremendously pleased about it. "Really believe, do you know, Weston," he said, cheerfully, "that if I had more practise, I'd be able to give people quite a decent game."

Master John astonished us by going to church on Sunday morning; he announced at the mid-day meal that prayers had been offered for the maintenance of peace. He ran up to town in the afternoon, and on his return, described an anti-war meeting held in Trafalgar Square, and a patriotic meeting held close by at the Admiralty Arch. An enormous crowd, he said, marched along The Mall to the Palace where folk sang the National Anthem, and the Marseillaise, and the King and Queen bowed acknowledgments of the cheering.

"Like looking on at history," he remarked.

"A good deal of preposterous fuss," commented Miss Muriel, in her superior way, "concerning absolutely nothing at all!"

It would save some trouble if one could ask you to accept Miss Muriel without explanation, and to judge her by the acts recorded of her, but this is perhaps making too great a strain upon credulity. At an entertainment given in aid of some Church funds at St. Mary's Hall I once saw a performance in which six characters took part: a highwayman, the landlady of a tavern, a Bow Street runner, a village maiden, an old Duke, and his elderly daughter; I observed that they came on separately, and so soon as one went off another entered, and I thought nothing special of it until I ascertained later, from the programme, that all the characters were performed by one gentleman. Miss Muriel had something of this ability. She was everything by turns, and nothing strong. At one time she determined to go down to posterity as a great musician, and during this period, she scoffed at her brother's efforts, and composed elaborate melodies that, without exception, sounded to me very like something I had heard before; the mantelpiece in her room was given up to small busts of Wagner and Liszt, and Beethoven and Mozart. There followed a rather serious attack of literature. Miss Muriel took literature very badly, and whilst it was on her, the house had to be kept perfectly quiet; any discordant sound, she declared, upset her writing for the day. She appealed to eminent novelists for their autographs (which they supplied with alacrity) and endeavoured to keep up the correspondence by asking their advice in regard to plots, to methods, and to publishers; the answers diminished in number, and Miss Muriel talked darkly of ring-bound fences, of the trials of new beginners.

"For two hatpins," she declared, "I would take up some other hobby!"

She did this, without the bribe suggested. At the time of which I speak, Miss Muriel was preparing herself for a brilliant career on the stage.

It was an epidemic that went around at intervals, started occasionally by an amateur performance, and the compliments given in the *Chislehurst and District Times*; in Muriel's case, it was due to the presence of a well-known actor who had returned from an American tour with plenty of money, and, taking a house near the Common, announced his intention of enjoying peace with dignity. Him, Miss Muriel encountered during the interval that followed convalescence from literature. It occurred to her that the stone cross which bore the inscription on one side—"Napoleon, Eugène Louis Jean Joseph, Prince Imperial. Killed in Zulu-land, 1st June, 1879," and on the other, "This Cross erected by the Dwellers at Chislehurst"—it occurred to her, I say, that this memorial was not receiving the attention it deserved. In placing her daily offering of a bunch of flowers inside the railings (the self-imposed duty lasted for nearly a week) she one afternoon met the great man. He was greatly touched by Miss Muriel's devotion.

"A beautiful act," he said, tears in his eyes. "A most charming thought. Dear young lady, allow me to offer you my sincerest compliments."

He called at The Croft later, and Mrs. Hillier was impressed by his manner, although Master Edward described him privately, as a white-haired fraud. Miss Muriel spoke of her wish to assist the stage by her presence, and he received the announcement with enthusiasm, promised to give any help that might be necessary. But he went off in a state of crimson-faced indignation, and I found that, in my absence from the drawing room, Mrs. Hillier had been so incautious as to offer a casual and approving remark concerning one of the younger members of the profession. Miss Muriel asserted that her bright anticipations had been marred by this carelessness, and it did prove that the promised help failed to come. A Sunday journal announced that the gentleman had been induced, by pressure from his countless admirers, to return to the boards, and to give a series of "those brilliant impersonations with which his name, and his name alone, will ever be associated." Miss Muriel's letters to him were not answered, but she told me this circumstance would have little or no effect on her plans.

"Even this absurd war business won't stop me!" she declared.

CHAPTER II

Guard Richards called at The Croft on the Monday afternoon, and brought a newspaper which he said contained little that was fresh and nothing that could be reckoned as jolly; before entering into any conversation with him, I took it to Master John.

"The governor requires careful handling," he mentioned. "You understand, Weston, I'm sure. He mustn't get too many whacks all at once."

"He can scarcely have anyone near him better than yourself, sir."

"The others are not helping a great deal," he admitted. "I foresee how much we are going to rely upon you, Weston." I expressed the hope that he would stay as long as was possible, hinted that, in the circumstances, he might perhaps feel disposed to give up his rooms in town. "It will depend upon—" he began, and searched for a word. "Circumstances," he added.

William Richards I had known since the country days when I tried to be a school teacher and failed in the examination, and my mother, considerably annoyed, packed me off to service, and he, too, disappointed his people by refusing to be educated with the view of becoming a Wesleyan minister, and ran to London, and joined the railway. By the time I returned to the hall, Master Edward had found him, and Richards, with coat off in the field near the house was sending down a swift ball at a single stump, where Master Edward in gloves and pads endeavoured to imitate the methods of his favourite wicket-keeper. For some reason, the spectacle annoyed me. In the case of the boy it was easy enough to understand, but William was forty if a day, and at a time when everyone about the place seemed more or less worried, it was irritating to see a big hulking chap playing at games.

"But it's Bank Holiday," he argued, when I had given my opinions.

"You're nothing but a kid," I declared. "In everything but years."

"Neither you or me, Mary Weston, can reckon ourselves as mere chicken. But that's no reason why we should go about with a face as long as a fiddle."

"It's a reason why we should set an example to those younger than ourselves. Are you aware that your country is likely to find itself in the biggest difficulty it's ever encountered?"

"A lot of passengers," he remarked, "have been telling me about it, but I never take much notice of rumours. Up at Charing Cross, one of the inspectors said the railways was going to be taken over by the Government; but, there again, I don't place much dependence, for the simple reason that it comes from a man who has give me more wrong tips in regard to 'orses than I've had from all the rest of the staff put together. Who's this coming up the road?"

A woman in my position cannot possibly think of everything, especially at a time when there is more than usual to be thinking about, and I had clean forgotten to write to my young nephew to tell him the Continental trip was cancelled. Here he came, looking taller than ever, but slightly round shouldered; his leather case in one hand, and in the other a book that he read as he walked. Herbert Millwood was never one to waste a single moment in his studies, and we watched him as he by chance avoided collision with other people, and by luck escaped contact with a lamp-post. He was going past the second gate of The Croft when I called to him. He came out of his dreams, dropped the book. Master Edward, impatient to resume play, ran out and picked it up whilst Herbert gave me a kiss, and offered his hand to William Richards.

"Are you reading this too?" cried Master Edward. "I've just finished it. Isn't it a ripper."

"I found it," said my nephew, in his careful way of speech, "extremely interesting. It appears to me a most accurate description of cowboy life in Western America."

I recognised one of the twopenny volumes with which the house was always strewn during the period of Master Edward's holidays. Coming on the top of Guard Richards's behaviour, the discovery did not lessen my resentment.

"Herbert," I said, shortly, "you can take yourself off home again. I meant to have written to you. William Richards, perhaps you've got sufficient intelligence to tell us when the next up train goes?"

Miss Muriel came out of the house, walked down the steps, and along the broad gravelled space. "Weston," she said, authoritatively, "arrange something for me to do. The tennis party I ought to have gone to has been put off. It's most annoying." She stared at Herbert.

"My nephew, miss," I said, presenting him, "who was to have stayed here if you'd all gone abroad."

"Do you play?" she demanded.

"Haven't a racket," he answered. "It's been sent up to Cambridge with my luggage."

"One can be found. And do you play?" (To William Richards.)

"No reason why I shouldn't be learnt, Miss."

They took the whole business out of my hands. Herbert and Miss Muriel decided to be partners against William Richards and Master Edward. The two visitors remembered, at the last moment, that their shoes might damage the grass. "It doesn't matter in the least," said Miss Muriel, with a touch of bitterness. "The general impression I gain is that we shall be leaving here before the end of the week."

"You don't mean that!" exclaimed my nephew.

"Really don't know what I mean," she retorted, irritably, "or what anybody else means. There are so many riddles about that I have given up all attempt to answer them. And Weston, here, whose business it is to cheer us up, and who is paid to cheer us up, has apparently gone on strike. Just as though," addressing Guard Richards, "just as though she were a railway man."

"Miss Hillier," said Master Edward, "having made herself pleasant and agreeable to most of the company present, will now show us her celebrated imitation of Mrs. Lambert-Chambers at the net."

"I am not a crack player," she remarked condescendingly to my nephew, "but I have my good days."

It appeared, later, that Miss Muriel was put off her game by the marching by of Territorials, an insect in her eye, rays of the sun, and one or two other discouraging incidents. Nevertheless, the game improved her temper, and she was in a gracious mood when I sent two of the maids out with table and trays; she admitted the victory had been a narrow one, and that Herbert was as good as Master Edward, whilst she was but a shade better than Guard Richards. William Richards improved his position, and caused himself to be reckoned an efficient member of good society by juggling dexterously with four tennis balls. "If I could do that," declared Master Edward, "I should never trouble to do anything else. How did you get the knack of it, guard?" William explained that on long journeys, when parcels had been sorted, and letters arranged, an official of his rank had plenty of time for practising the art. He tried to make a further impression by essaying a trick he had seen at a popular entertainment; this necessitated the providing of a leather hat case, an open umbrella, and a cigarette, and all these articles were readily discovered and furnished. William Richards threw the cigarette in the air, and failed to catch it with his mouth, the leather hat case fell upon Miss Muriel, and the open umbrella came down upon me. William said he thought he had better catch the next train, but Master Edward, declaring that he, too, did not always succeed in his experiments, begged him to stay.

I was afraid Mrs. Hillier, when she came out, would be annoyed at the sight of the mixed group, but she was so eager to obtain opinions concerning the war that she seemed ready to forgive the presence of the two visitors, and to overlook the fact that one of them was in a uniform. My mistress, at that period, always accepted and repeated the views of the last person consulted, and the effect of this was that sometimes she felt certain we were not going to be involved in the war, sometimes that France, with one hand tied behind its back, could beat Germany, sometimes that the Kaiser would be at Buckingham Palace by the end of August. William Richards took care from her shoulders by alluding to the numerous occasions, within his knowledge, when inaccuracies had appeared in the journals of the day.

"If they spelt your name wrongly in the Board of Trade inquiry you are speaking of," she said, "why it stands to reason that the newspapers are capable of making even greater blunders in regard to more important subjects."

"Exactly my argument, lady," he said.

"I must get you to talk to my husband, guard."

"If the gentleman has made up his mind, perhaps it wouldn't be much use."

"That," she said, addressing the group, "is just what I complain of in regard to Mr. Hillier. He's obstinate. He's self-willed. He won't listen to reason. He doesn't understand as I do that no reliance can be placed on what one reads. I wonder whether we shall get an evening paper?"

I mentioned that Guard Richards had brought one, and went in search of it. On the way back I glanced at the stop press column, which William apparently had over-looked. It seemed a pity to spoil the comfort of the party, and I tore the portion off, and held it in my fist.

"This time next week," said Mrs. Hillier, after glancing at the head lines, "we shall be laughing at the way people have allowed themselves to be upset over trifles."

My dodge did enable them to enjoy an hour of composure; I regretted, in a way, that the others were not present, if only to see how well my nephew could comport himself when he encountered his betters. William Richards was telling the old story of the flustered young woman passenger, who on the platform kissed the guard, and gave her husband threepence, when Colonel Edgington came along the drive, flourishing a newspaper.

"The bounders have invaded Belgium," he shouted.

"I don't believe it," declared Mrs. Hillier at once. "It's probably a misprint."

"Weston," he said, ignoring my mistress, "where is the governor?" I hurried towards him, and explained that Mr. Hillier was out with Master John and Miss Katherine; I hoped that if Colonel Edgington happened to meet them he would be careful to soften down any bad news he had to communicate. "War is a man's business," he retorted. "All that you women have to do is to just stand outside the ropes, and look on."

"I think you'll find us doing a lot more than that, sir."

"Ah," he said, "you mean nursing. Well, we may allow you to take a share in nursing, but nothing else, mind."

"It probably won't rest with either you or me, sir."

"It certainly won't rest with you, Weston. If I miss the governor, say that I am going up to the War Office to-morrow morning early. I shall most likely catch his train. But I daresay it will slip your memory. Never met a woman yet who could be depended upon to do as she was ordered."

"Perhaps your experience of them has been limited, sir."

"Weston," he said, rolling up the newspaper, and pointing it at me, "I've often heard it said about here that you were treated as one of the family. I've denied the statement. I've always pointed out that you are treated as the head of the family."

There was telephoning to and fro, and the local shops were kept in attendance on the instruments, town establishments were harried and badgered by the same means of communication. I looked through the stock room, and at first decided that no great additions were necessary; if the worst came to the worst, The Croft could stand a siege of reasonable length, and the kitchen gardens would furnish supplies. But the shop-people at Sidcup alarmed me, and another housekeeper I met there induced me to believe I was failing to take wise precautions. The shop folk spoke of the immense orders they were receiving from customers who had the fear that either prices would go up with a tremendous jump, or that articles of food might be unobtainable; my friend assured me, with gleeful confidence, that whatever happened to other households in the neighbourhood, her's, at any rate, was safe.

"They made me pay cash for everything, Miss Weston," she went on, "but that was only reasonable. Paper money is not of much use at times like this. What I'm anxious about is the number of hands that will be thrown out of work. I told my girls, only to-day, they'll all be starving before the month is up."

"That ought to have pleased them."

"We've got to face the facts," she declared, earnestly. "There's not the slightest use in burying our heads in the sand. Everyone will be getting rid of servants, and what the poor souls are to do doesn't bear thinking of. I suppose your people are like the rest, talking of cutting down expenses."

"Hints. Nothing more!"

"Fortunately," she said, "I have been able to put by, just as you, no doubt, have managed to do. Eh?"

"I didn't say anything."

"And my notion is that when it becomes too hot, I shall rush off to a quiet place I've got my eye on in Wales where the Germans won't trouble to come, and if they do, all my money will be safely buried in the flower garden, and I shall pretend I'm too silly to understand anything that's said to me."

"You'll find that easy enough."

"You wouldn't care, I suppose, Miss Weston—I've always had a great respect for you—to join forces with me, so to speak, and — — "

"No," promptly. "Got work to do here. Folk to look after."

"The time will come," she prophesied, in going, "when you'll want to kick yourself for not having listened to friendly advice."

It occurred to me that even if there existed little risk of a shortage in supplies, the fact that so many people were making large purchases might have serious results, and I resolved to concentrate my thoughts on the subject of flour. Flour became an obsession with me. Flour, for the space of at least one morning, was the one article that I desired. I had, the previous night, dreamt of flour; sacks of it, cellar-fulls of it, and the dream finished with the perturbing discovery that the bags on being opened contained nothing but wooden shavings. It is easy enough now to look back upon those very early days of the war, and to smile at the flurried anxieties and the nervous agitation; I can say truthfully that, being ordinarily as calm as most people, I nevertheless caught the epidemic and came as near as I have ever been to losing my head. My most extravagant act was to induce William Richards, by wire, to make himself responsible for bringing, whilst off duty on the Tuesday, two hundred-weight of flour from London; he conveyed it from the station to The Croft on a luggage trolley.

"Your thanks, Mary Weston," he said, "amply repay me, they do, for all the trouble. Came in, I did, for a fair amount of chaff on the way down from humorous colleagues of mine, and it's been a warmish business getting the stuff here, on a day like this, but this glass of cider, and your kind remarks—"

"When I wrote off in a hurry to you last night, I never thought you'd be able to do it."

William finished his glass, and appeared to be forming words in his mind. Altering the intention, he hummed the first lines of "Auld Lang Syne."

"There's a good deal of extra work going on," he remarked, "with the railways, and I can't always call my hours my own. But anything I can do for you, Mary Weston, I'm prepared to do. If I may offer a suggestion it is that your next orders should be such as not to make my uniform look quite so dusty."

I found a brush and dispersed the white marks. As I went up and down the sleeve, he took my hand and kissed it, and, at once, rushed from the kitchen, leaving the second glass that had been poured out for him. Going down to the tradesmen's gate, I caught sight of William Richards sprinting along the tarred road, more as one under the impression the Germans were after him than as though he had given an impetuous sign of affection.

My housekeeper acquaintance was not the only person who held the view that the war would throw folk out of employment. Everybody seemed to be furnishing everybody with the same idea. The most cheerful anticipation was that there were always the workhouses, and in any case the Government would have to do something. The disturbing fact that, as my acquaintance hinted, cheques were not being accepted, was, in itself, enough to startle and to alarm. Master Edward went on his bicycle a dozen times in the course of the day to pick up news at the station, and never returned without something like an arm-full; the trouble was to sift the correct from the undependable, and to keep one's mind clear of inaccuracies, but appetite for particulars was so keen that nothing was refused. Our old gardener with whom, owing to his partiality for alcohol, I had hitherto been on remote terms, appeared flattered to discover that I listened to his muddle-headed rumours with an attentive ear.

"They do tell me, ma'am," he said, confidentially, "that these 'ere foreigners drink a kind of beer that don't have no effect on you, like what our stuff does. Nice cheerful sort of prospect, ain't it, for those on us that are what you may call settled in our 'abits? Dang my old eyes," the gardener went on with vehemence, "if it ain't nearly enough to induce a man to turn teetotal!"

Mr. Hillier made no attempt to catch his usual train. Instead of doing this, or cultivating his hobby in the workshop, he walked up and down on the lawn, tweed cap at the back of head, and when I sent Miss Katherine out to him, she returned with the announcement that he wished to be alone; Master John was similarly repulsed. My nephew had been asked to stay the night, and he and Master John were consulting together with serious countenances. Two of the maids came to me with telegrams, and asked to be permitted to leave at once. In one case a father belonging to the Naval Reserve had been called out, and the mother wanted her daughter's company at home; in the other, the girl wished to say good-bye to her sweetheart, a Territorial who was leaving with his battalion for a sea coast town. I allowed them to go, and went to mention the circumstance to Mrs. Hillier. She never objected to any decision of mine, but I generally kept her informed of anything that happened.

"I was just going out," she said, "to liven your master up, Weston. If you have a few minutes to spare, you might come with me. I've got rather a good idea, and you will come in handy to support it. Get the rose basket, and my leather gloves, and the scissors."

No pretence that my mistress adopted would have taken in a fly, and when she affected to be surprised at discovering her husband on the lawn, he glanced at her without speaking. She submitted the good idea, without delay. Mr. Hillier was to take advantage of the brief holiday from Basinghall Street, and start upon the task of learning to play golf. "I'd sooner walk about on my head," he declared. She begged him not to come to a hasty decision, and pointed out first, that no one walked about on the head; second, that a great many folk did play golf, and if one could judge by their conversation, found enjoyment in it.

"You want something, James," she argued, "to take you out of yourself. You're getting into a habit of brooding and that never yet did any good to man, woman or child. Try to follow my example, and take cheerful views. Think of the people who are worse off than yourself."

"I wouldn't mind so much," he said, "if I were twenty years younger."

"Now I appeal to you, Weston," she remarked, looking up at me. "Isn't that a foolish thing to say? Why, if he were twenty years younger he wouldn't be living in this large house, and these fine grounds, and with plenty of servants about to do everything that's wanted." The under-gardener came across to ask some question; I signalled to him to stay where he was.

"The large house," said Mr. Hillier, with deliberation, "and the fine grounds, and the plenty of servants, will soon be nothing but a memory."

"Wandering in his speech," she whispered to me.

"It's time," he went on, speaking carefully, "that you knew the truth, and there's no reason why Weston should not hear it. If it hadn't been for this war, I might have pulled matters round, but as it is—Well, I'm done for!"

"You've been smoking too much."

"My pipe is the only real comfort I have left."

"James," she cried, expostulatingly, "you forget me!"

"There was a time," he said, "when you were my good companion, but that takes me back a long, long while ago. And the children are not children now, and altogether—I beg pardon, my dear. I ought not to be saying anything likely to hurt."

"If matters are so bad, we must try a little economy." Mrs. Hillier had a sudden inspiration. "I've sent off a couple of the maids already."

"You'll have to do more than that."

"You don't mean," she cried, alarmedly, "that we shall have to do without Weston?"

He gave a half smile at me; I waited anxiously to hear what he would say. "We shall have to do without everybody," he said. "It's like this. I've been working all these years to make money for you and the kiddies. I've never saved, partly because you gave no help in that direction, partly because I wanted to look on and see everyone having a capital time."

"How selfish of you, James!" I touched her arm reprovingly.

"The sooner we get away from here," he said, "the better for my good name. I want to keep that because—because it's about all I shall have left. The only question that's worrying me is this. What sort of a part are you going to play?"

"I shall go," she replied, with an air, "wherever destiny calls me."

"Well then," rather doubtfully, "that, I suppose, is all right then. If you set an example to the children, they'll follow on. Explain it all to them—or perhaps Weston here will do that, as one of her last jobs before leaving—and make it clear to them that I'm sorry. And she might contrive to hint that it isn't altogether my fault."

I gave the two gardeners their notice at once. The younger one, it appeared, wanted to leave and was ready to go instantly; the other who always made a grievance of everything, took it very ill. "Me just in the middle of a lot of clearin' up, and now I'm called upon to go and look for another situation! Hard lines; that's what I call it, miss." I pointed out that he was not the only person who suffered. "I'm the only one that interests me," he said, doggedly. "People don't seem to remember that I'm getting on in years. Be rights, I ought to be pensioned off, or dumped into an almshouse, or some'ing of the kind." I reminded him that he was fortunate in having no wife or children. "There's some advantage in being a bachelor," he agreed, "because there's no one to nag at you when you reach home at night a bit late, and a trifle comfortable. On the other hand, you've got no one to 'elp earn your living for you. And that reminds me. I shall chuck work for a hower or two, and go along, and take a glass o' beer. Just in order to stiddy my nerves." He came back later singing, and told one of the dogs that there were many worlds inferior to this, and that he proposed to celebrate the occasion by arranging a good old hang-it-all bonfire. Master John and my nephew had gone from the house (without mentioning where they were bound for), otherwise I should have asked one of them to order the elderly chap to go home. I might have done this myself, but I never care to argue with men when they are in drink. It is impossible to tell whether they are going to be extremely abusive, or aggressively affectionate.

The master seemed more like himself now that he had made a full statement of the position. At his request, I went over the house with the two of them, and we made something like an inventory; I estimated the prices, and Mr. Hillier was quite cheered when he eventually reckoned up.

"Might have been worse," he said. "The money we've spent hasn't all been wasted."

"I've never bought any furniture," remarked Mrs. Hillier, "without first taking Weston's advice. She's an excellent judge."

"It's hard to be treating her as a criminal," he mentioned, "after all these years."

"Don't you trouble about me, sir," I said.

"I foresee," he remarked genially, "that a certain official on the railway will shortly send in an application for holiday leave, and passes for himself and wife."

"If Richards has got any such idea in his head," I declared sharply, "he's in for a big disappointment. My intentions are entirely different."

"I must go and find a good auctioneer," he said, "And at once."

In this way it happened that when the fire at The Croft broke out, there were women folk only in the house. For over an hour there had been a smell of burning, and when I spoke of it, one of the maids said the old gardener had set light to rubbish, but that the flames were now out; in the quiet summer evening air the scent remained. It was at about eight o'clock when the alarm came that the garage was on fire. Dinner was half over; the ladies were wondering at the delay in the return of Master John and of Herbert, and hoped they would soon appear with the latest news. Directly I caught sight of the blaze I recognised that here was a serious matter, and I ran off to the telephone, and called up the Brigade. Then I beckoned from the doorway of the dining room to young Master Edward, told him what had happened, and begged him to rush around and get together all the able-bodied men he could find in the neighbourhood. Downstairs the maids were hysterical, and one had fainted; I spoke to them with an abruptness that made them come to their senses, and gave directions. I collected hats and coats belonging to my mistress and the young ladies and, saying that there was no danger and that the fire would soon burn itself out, told them to go on the lawn, and to watch for the engine. Miss Muriel began to talk excitedly and protestingly; her sister and mother interposed.

"Weston knows best!" they said.

Even if there had been a man about the place, I doubt whether it would have been possible to save the car. The bemused gardener had set his mound of rubbish near to the wooden doors, and these were the first to catch alight. The billiard room was overhead, and when an explosion came from the garage I knew that nobody would ever play on that table again. There was not much wind, but all that existed was blowing in the direction of the house. The master's workshop, where he had spent many Saturday afternoons, was the next to go.

Master Edward (enjoying it all tremendously) ran up the drive with his party of a dozen men, Colonel Edgington amongst them and clearly determined to take charge, and to extinguish the fire in his own style; he gasped out orders that no one could understand, and no one felt called upon to obey. The men rushed through the dark path at the side of the house, where Colonel Edgington had the misfortune to step upon a rake that instantly—as is the habit of rakes when thus treated—instantly sprang up, and gave him a blow in the face which put him temporarily out of action. His language included several words quite new to me.

"Pails, Weston!" shouted Master Edward.

We had a number of pails but, despite the efforts of the helpers, they were of little more use than a soda water syphon would have been. For one thing, the fire was now so scorching that the men could not get near; the water when thrown fell with a slight hiss and had no other result. I called them into the house, disregarding Master Edward's appeal, and asked them to do their best to save the furniture. Their best, I am willing to admit, was very good. Colonel Edgington came up the staircase and again endeavoured to assume command: I told him to go down, and look after the ladies, and keep them out of the way of the articles that were being flung from the windows. It was no time for being civil, and it was no time either for careful and delicate handling of furniture. A cheval glass came down on the sun dial, and cracked in all directions. Articles in silver from dressing tables rained upon the grass; a jewel case danced about on the gravel, distributing its contents. I felt glad to see two constables inside the gate, keeping back folk who wanted a good view.

The house was alight when the fire engine came, and everyone was out, and gathering up the property that had been strewn around; Mrs. Hillier and the two young ladies worked as hard as the men, and with the maids— the early fright over—I had no reason to discover any fault. Master John and my nephew Herbert arrived when the hose was playing on the flames; the supply of water, owing to the recent fine weather, was not too good, and the pond, that might at other times have assisted, was almost empty. The two young men accepted the condition of affairs without a word; threw off jackets, and dashed into the task of salvage. Despite all the efforts it was not a great amount that could be saved: the fire chased the men from room to room. A drizzling rain came on, and the lads found tarpaulins and canvas to serve as protection to the rescued furniture. Colonel Edgington had vanished, and I was congratulating myself on this, when he returned with his car.

"Come along now, Mrs. Hillier," he said, authoritatively. "And the two girls. And the small boy. And any of the servants who can find room. I'm going to take you all over to my place, and you'll stay there as long as you like. Weston," he said to me, "I'll come back for you."

"Sorry, sir, if I was rather rude to you, just now."

"Rude?" he echoed. "Bless my soul, that was nothing. I'm rather rude to everybody. But I mean well, Weston: indeed, and I mean well!"

The brigade superintendent, making his way across pools of water, at the finish, asked me whether the house and the fittings were insured, and I said, "Why, of course!" The men assisted in returning furniture to the two or three rooms that had not been touched by the fire. The beer cask in the cellar was safe, and I told them to find tumblers and help themselves. Master John and my Herbert came up to me, so begrimed that I kissed Master John by mistake; he declared it was a full sixteen years since I had thought of paying him such an attention.

"Wish we had been here at the start," he remarked. "We should have been, only that there were so many others waiting to enlist."

"Others?"

"We've both joined," he announced. "Is that the governor out in the road?"

Mr. Hillier was gazing at the damaged house. We went across, and I put the question to him that the superintendent had put to me. He mentioned that he had experienced a difficulty in finding the auctioneer, and was describing this at some length when I repeated the inquiry.

"I wish you'd tell me, sir, about the insurance," I begged. "Just yes or no."

"The answer is no, Weston," he replied, in a quiet voice. "I allowed the policy to lapse at midsummer in order to give the job to a hard-up man who was starting as an agent. I heard last week he had disappeared."

"You don't seem very much upset about the fire."

"Dreamt that it happened," said Mr. Hillier, "these three nights past." He turned to his son. "Anything fresh about the war, my lad?"

CHAPTER III

I had at times complained about the folk of the neighbourhood; some made money rather suddenly and appeared anxious to persuade the residents that they belonged to aristocratic families; a few took up an attitude of reserve that could be easily mistaken for contempt. But, in the misfortune which had overtaken my people, their behaviour left no room for criticism. It was not only Colonel Edgington who showed kindness. I stayed the night in Miss Katherine's room, which was amongst the apartments that had escaped, and when I went out in the morning and walked along to the Colonel's house I found, even at that early hour, cars outside and messages being delivered, and all sorts of hospitality tendered. If we had cared to accept them, we could have put up at a dozen houses.

"Thank you ever so much," said Miss Katherine, taking the duty of answering. "It is really sporting of you, but we shall be perfectly all right here for a few days. And then we shall have to find a new house."

"At Chislehurst?"

"Not at Chislehurst. I think my father intends to butt in at some other neighbourhood."

"Quite natural in the circumstances. Be sure to let us know if there is anything we can do."

Under her breath Miss Katherine said, "Oh do push off!"

The old gardener, in a sobered morning mood, had given himself up at the police station, but Mr. Hillier declined to take any proceedings. (We heard, later, that the gardener, acutely disappointed, again tried the remedy of beer, and was eventually fined ten shillings for being drunk and disorderly; a tame finish, so far as he was concerned, to the whole incident.) Mr. Hillier wished to make another effort to discover the auctioneer, but I told him there was not enough of property remaining to justify a public sale, and that if he determined to get rid of everything, I could arrange with my brother-in-law at Greenwich to make a valuation, and to give a fair price.

"See to it, Weston," he directed, cheerily. "I have been talking it over with Mrs. Hillier, and we agree that we want to begin afresh. We're going to make a new start."

"Very glad, sir, that you are all taking it so well."

"I've an idea that the fates have used their last cartridge. It's a relief, Weston."

"Afraid you haven't yet heard what Master John has done."

"But that," he declared, "is the best news I have had for months. It's good to think he joined up without advice or encouragement. To tell you the truth, I was afraid that he might be afraid. And that would have been, not so much the last straw, as a whole truss of it to carry on my back all through the war."

"Don't know what Herbert's father will say."

"I can guess," said Mr. Hillier, confidently. "Everything depends now on what our lads do for us."

The two young men left directly after breakfast. They had passed the medical examination, it seemed, at the schools near St. Martin's Church, Trafalgar Square, and although Master John was rather short for a guardsman, they urged their desire to be in the same regiment, and it had been arranged they should join the Coldstreams at Wellington Barracks. We all came out to wish them good luck, and Colonel Edgington took off his straw hat, and, waving it, led the three cheers. I mentioned to him that to see the two going away side by side—my mistress's son and my own nephew—was one of the proofs that a war existed. "You'll see mightier changes than that," he remarked. "People who know nothing whatever about it are saying it'll all be over by Christmas." I expressed the hope it would not last so long. "Indeed," he cried, explosively, "and you're as big an idiot as the rest of them. In this respect, I mean," he added. Later, the Colonel took me aside, and spoke in confidence. He asked me to believe that his house was at the disposal of the family for an indefinite period, but he knew it would be better for the Hilliers if the move which had to be made were effected quickly, and whilst the excitement of recent occurrences was still about. "Do just what you think is best," he said.

Herbert's father kept a second-hand furniture shop in London Street, Greenwich, and whilst my sister was alive the business had been prosperous; on her last day, she gave such precise instructions concerning the boy's career that Millwood had never attempted to depart from them. I took an afternoon train to New Cross, and the tram-car from outside the station there, and found Millwood setting up a map in the window of the shop and adjusting small flags upon it; a crowd stood watching interestedly. Children, free from school (their holidays were afterwards cut short) marched along banging toy drums, and wearing paper hats. The newspaper placards gave the information, "Kitchener at the War Office." Groups were talking and arguing on the pavement.

"Knowed my boy'd be one of the fust to offer hisself," said Millwood. My sister improved his manner of talking a good deal, in her lifetime, but when she left, he dropped back into his earlier methods. "I says, soon as ever I heard about the war being started, I says to myself, 'Mark my words. Young 'Erb'll be in this. Right in the very thick of it.'"

"Good to find you accept it like this. You being such an out and out Radical—"

"How could I accept it otherwise?" he demanded, warmly. "And can't a Radical be as partial to his country as what the bigoted dunderheaded Tories is? I remember hearing Bradlaugh say once—"

"I haven't called to talk politics."

"Because you know very well, Mary Weston, which of us comes the best off when you and me do have an argument."

"I do know. And I must say you generally accept your beating in very good part."

"I never get beaten in no discussion," he shouted, "and if I did, I shouldn't accept it in the way you describe. Often feel uncommon glad that I didn't pick out you instead of your poor sister. I might ha' done, but for what I may term the intervention of Providence. You was better educated than her, and to tell you the truth nothing but that saved me from making the blunder of a lifetime."

"I should perhaps have had a word or two to say in the matter."

"Can't imagine any subject on which you wouldn't."

I had to talk him round because there was a favour to be asked. He declared, at first, that he had no wish to add to his stock or to his responsibilities; of the second, I knew nothing, but I could see that the contents of the shop had scarcely altered since my previous visit on the occasion when the funeral took place. There were dilapidated writing desks that no one seemed to require; a suite of chairs with red plush that had nearly lost colour from exposure to the sun, a cabinet out of the perpendicular owing to partial failure of one leg, an easy chair with broken springs, engravings in mottled frames of events in the life of Queen Victoria, a tipsy-looking music stand, a bookcase that ought to have revolved but had lost the trick. It was but necessary to hint at the misfortunes that had overtaken the Hillier family, to secure Millwood's aid. He was ready to see the furniture, to offer a good price for it on my behalf, to attend to the removal and the storing. Two young women came in whilst we were arranging this, and asked Millwood for the address of the local newspaper. He gave the directions, and they mentioned that they wished, by means of an advertisement, to let their furnished flat in Gloucester Place. "We are going off nursing," they mentioned, animatedly. I came forward, and put some questions, and within five minutes I was looking through the rooms in their company, and inside of a quarter of an hour I had come to an agreement with them. The rooms were old-fashioned in build, and pleasant to look upon; Gloucester Place, with The Circus, bow shaped, opposite had, in their day, been the society part of Greenwich; a large railed garden was set between the two rows of houses; a broad roadway led in from Royal Hill, and a narrower one went out to Crooms' Hill, and to the Park. To Gloucester Place a touch of modernity had been given by the conversion of one house into County Council offices. At the very top of the residence I inspected were two rooms, not occupied, and not furnished. Before I left, I saw the agent, and took these for a quarter at a rent I could well afford. The ground floor, I ascertained, was occupied by a quiet, elderly couple.

"Depend upon me," said Millwood. "And as you're coming to live in my neighbourhood, mind you drop in whenever you have the opportunity, Mary Weston, or the wish to do so. I foresee that with both political parties coming into line over this fighting business, life for a public man like myself is going to be jest a trifle monotonous. I shall get stale if I don't find someone to have a few friendly words with."

It pleased him when I gave him an order to pick up one or two articles of furniture I indicated from a sales room with which he was acquainted.

I went home and announced the result of my journey. I settled with cook and the two housemaids and sent them off in a good temper. I rang up the agent for the owner of The Croft, and advised him to give notice to his insurance people. I took the two young ladies to the house and found old trunks in the cellars, packed some of their clothes that the fire had not damaged; Miss Muriel appeared inclined to be sentimental over the task, but Miss Katherine chaffed her out of this, pointing out that the verses composed by her sister that morning, with, for opening lines,

> "Home of my childhood, oh where art thou gone,
> The fire has consumed thee, thy loss I bemoan"

had, if looked upon as poetry, certain merits, and if considered as a statement of facts, many inaccuracies. It was not, she declared, the home of Miss Muriel's childhood, unless that period could be reckoned to start at the age of seventeen. The house had not gone, and it could not be said with truth that the fire had consumed it, for here it was, requiring only the aid of a builder and carpenter to make it habitable for new tenants.

"And that's that!" she said, summing up briskly. "You chuck poetry, my beloved sister. There's no money in it, and you never use it except as a medium for grousing."

"I mean to write some verses about the war," said Miss Muriel, resolutely.

"If it gets known, peace will be arranged without delay. Besides, I thought you were going on the stage. Weston, can we give you a hand with your packing?"

"Couldn't think of asking you to do that, Miss Katherine."

"Which, being interpreted," she said, "means that even you, with all your common sense, have not yet realised all that has occurred. Tell me: you have money put by, haven't you?"

"A trifle, Miss Katherine."

"So that you are now above us. You are better off than we are. You are a plutocrat, Weston. At any moment, some gay spark may come along on his motor cycle, wed you for the sake of your riches, take you off in his side car."

"A pity," I said, to change the subject, "that neither of you young ladies had contrived to get married before all this happened. It would have simplified matters a good deal."

"Perhaps," she remarked, "we have hitherto been too ambitious. In the new circumstances, I shall be ready to listen to any honourable proposal from a baker. No," correcting herself. "Let me not sink too low. A confectioner. A confectioner, near a school. And over military age."

"There won't be many young men left if this fighting goes on for long."

"'How happy,'" quoted Miss Katherine, "'is the blameless vestal's lot, The world forgetting, by the world forgot.' By Pope, my dear Muriel, Pope. A gentleman who was in the line of business you have recently taken up."

We managed to finish the task, and a greengrocer undertook to convey the packages to Colonel Edgington's house. I was under the impression that everything was going well and smoothly, when a telegram came from the two young women at Greenwich. "Find course of lectures indispensable. We remain in flat for a time."

The delay which ensued became one of the most trying details of the whole affair. If I had been able to whisk the family off as I intended to do, if it had all been done whilst the excitement was upon us, if we had been able to give a hurried good-bye to Chislehurst and then disappear, why, I do believe the job would have proved easy enough. There was the alternative of finding other rooms, but I had fixed my mind on the arrangement at Greenwich, and when it was suggested to me privately by Colonel Edgington that this might be done—

"Not a word to the others, mind, Weston. Don't want them to think I'm tired of their company."

Then I talked about contracts, and represented the two impetuous girls at Gloucester Place as square-headed, obstinate women of business; I hinted that to argue with them or plead to them was like contending against a brick wall. So the Hilliers stayed on, and each day brought for me some discouraging occurrence. Mr. Hillier, with nothing else to do, went back to his habit of mooning about: the Colonel was very good, and always endeavoured to give him his company, but the master seemed to prefer solitude, and whenever he could manage it, contrived to slip away for a lonely walk. Mrs. Hillier, dismissing all thoughts of the immediate past, allowed herself to be taken up by her friends in the neighbourhood, and readily agreed to take positions—for which she was in no way fitted—in the charitable work that had been started with feverish and excitable energy. The idea was, at the time, that there would be an enormous amount of distress in London, and meetings were held, and speeches made, and Mrs. Hillier when asked to take any part, succeeded in making just about as big a fool of herself as it was possible to do. I told her so. I told her so plainly, and we came very near to parting from each other on account of this. I suppose I was becoming irritable over the postponement of my scheme, and I certainly did not like the notion of all of us staying on at Colonel Edgington's for an indefinite period. One word led to another, and I happened to use a phrase without giving due consideration to it.

"Imposing on good nature?" she echoed, amazedly.

"We'll call it sponging, if you like."

"Weston," she said, with dignity, "you are, and you have been for some weeks past, free to leave my service. The wages due will be paid so soon as Mr. Hillier has had time to look about him."

"He's doing that now. And precious little of anything else."

"It is not for you to criticise your master. That is one of my privileges, and I think I may say that I have never failed to take advantage of it. For the moment, my powers in this respect are directed against yourself. You are forgetting, Weston, the position you hold, and unless you think fit to remember it, I shall have to ask you to go."

"You know as well as I do, ma'am, that I can't leave you all like this. You'll be lost without my help, and I should have it on my conscience for the rest of my life."

Master Edward rushed in. He had been down the hill to the station, seeing train loads of soldiers go through, and, with the assistance of other boys, cheering them. He began to tell us of his experiences but, recognising an unusual tension in the air, dashed off at once to find his sister Katherine. When she came, the trouble was soon adjusted. I apologised to Mrs. Hillier, and Mrs. Hillier apologised to me, and we both said it was all a misunderstanding, and one that would not happen again.

But I went over, that afternoon, to Greenwich, and waited there until the young women arrived home from their lecture at the Polytechnic. Millwood had carried out my instructions very well; the two rooms on the top floor needed only a few more bits of hay to make them into a comfortable nest. The two came in, tired with study; all the animation they had shown at our first encounter seemed to have vanished.

"Of course," said the elder, desolately, "we are sorry for the inconvenience that is being caused, but you have no idea how much there is to be learnt before one can be reckoned a capable nurse."

"Have you considered the advisability of trying anything else?"

"We most particularly want to tend wounded soldiers."

"But," I argued, "wounded soldiers don't want to be tended by people who can't tend."

"Seems a pity."

"Now, if you care to leave it to me," I said, "I'll find out whether there's anything else you could start upon. What do you say?"

"It must be something we can do at once," they urged. "We appear to be wasting time."

I hurried along to the Miller Hospital, and consulted a Sister there whom I had known for years. She told me that hospitals in London, and at other places, were on the defensive owing to the strong attacks made by unqualified, but well-intentioned ladies. For example, a society woman attended one of the classes and said, at the end, to the lecturer, that she had gained a considerable amount of knowledge by the afternoon, but that as she was going abroad with an ambulance party, she thought it would be advisable perhaps to come to a second afternoon. The lecturer retorted that she herself had been learning the business of nursing for ten years, and still felt she had much to learn. "Ah, yes," said the society woman, "but you see, I'm exceptionally quick." The Sister told me other anecdotes of the period, and then considered the problem set before her.

"Let them become gardeners," she decided. "Gardeners at a convalescent home I'm acquainted with."

A reply paid telegram was sent, and, before I left the hospital, the answer had been received. Taking it to Gloucester Place, I used the best argumentative qualities at my disposal. Here was a noble chance of taking— in all likelihood—the places of two men who would thus be released for the purposes of the war. Good, healthy out-door work, and later, when soldiers came to the home, there would be a splendid opportunity of instructing them in arts connected with the land. "An opening of a lifetime," I urged. They confessed they had been brought up on a farm, and knew something of agricultural tasks, but it was dear the attraction of becoming second Florence Nightingales was too great to be relinquished hastily. I mentioned that, if they insisted on becoming nurses they would probably find themselves at a hospital in London; the chances of being sent abroad were small, and I furnished details of the hard labour probationers were called on to perform.

"If we did accept this offer," asked one, "do you think we should be allowed to wear some kind of uniform?"

"Sure you would," promptly. "And when the War Office takes over the home, why, of course, you will be under Government control."

This settled the matter. I found an A.B.C. and selected a train; sent a wire announcing the time of their arrival; fetched a cab from the station yard, helped the driver with their trunks. They shook hands with me gratefully, and alluded to me as a treasure, and a perfect dear.

That evening, my people arrived at Gloucester Place, and even Miss Muriel could discover no fault in the new surroundings. Mr. Hillier took Master Edward down to the riverside whilst we were arranging the different rooms; they came back enthusiastic regarding the shipping, the London steamboats, the College, the view from the Observatory. For the first time since the Saturday before the Bank Holiday we made no reference in conversation to the war, and I abstained from mentioning that a placard of an evening journal bore the words, "France fighting for its Life now." Nor did I repeat a scrap of talk I heard near the station between two Deptford women. "And ain't it a shame," said one, "to think that all this trouble has been caused by the Germin Emperor." The other shook her head. "It ain't the Germin Emperor what's to blame," she said, correctly. "It's the Kayser." Boys ran around The Circus bawling news, and we took no notice of them. Master Edward came out strongly on historical subjects, and told us of all the Royal folk who had lived at Greenwich, from King Henry the Eighth, onward; it seemed to make us feel that we had really gained in social position by the removal. Mr. Hillier mentioned that history was interesting enough to look back upon, but trying to live with; Master Edward expressed sympathy for the boys who came after him and would have to learn all about the present war. The master and Mrs. Hillier conferred with each other near a window that looked across at The Circus. I heard her say, "You must tell her, James. If I try to do so, I shall simply break down." He beckoned to me, and we went out on the landing.

"Weston," he said, clearing his voice rather nervously, "I've shut the offices in Basinghall Street, and it wasn't pleasant to say good-bye to men who have worked for me and with me during past years. And now a duty has been imposed upon me that I should very much like to escape. But someone has to do it, and I suppose—The fact is, we are very grateful to you for all you have done for us in this trying and exacting predicament, and we are obliged to you for piloting us safely to this new—er—harbour." He hesitated, and went on again. "You have, I take it, made your own plans, Weston?"

"Yes, sir."

"Very well, then. It only remains to say good-bye, and to give you this small envelope that contains the wages due. I ask you to believe that the sum in no way represents our indebtedness—"

"Look here, sir," I interrupted. "I know all about the finances of the establishment, and if I take this money I shall be taking nearly the last penny you have. You just let it stand over. Any time will do for settling with me."

"Good of you."

"And as regards future arrangements, I'm going to live on the top floor, and I shall be in and about in a friendly sort of way whenever I'm wanted. The mistress and the young ladies have been used to plenty of help and attention, and I don't wish all that cut off suddenly at the main, so to speak. My wages stop from to-day, and when matters get brighter—and that may not be long ahead—why they can start again."

"Weston," he declared, "the State ought to be making you, just now, a generous allowance. You should be put in charge of the ray of sunshine department. You are a mascot. You're a sheet anchor. So long as you are with us, we shall feel ourselves safe. God bless you!"

In the morning, I went down early to answer the milkman's knock. Content to gain new customers, he told me an important item of information which had come to him direct from no less an authority than the pier-master at the end of King William Street. Russian troops, in enormous numbers, were on the way *via* Archangel, and would shortly pass through England on the way to France. The pier-master's idea was that this would settle the war in less than no time.

"But don't give it away, miss," begged the milkman, urgently. "Don't mention it to anyone, because it's a secret, and only a few of us, who can be depended upon to keep it dark, are supposed to know anything about it."

We were all of us to blame, more or less, for the circulation of rumours, but the chief responsibility in my own immediate district had to be placed upon Arthur. Arthur was—it sounds like an extract from a French lesson book—the brother of our greengrocer's wife; the lady professed to be suffering from nerves in consequence of the war (she had no relatives engaged in the struggle, and felt, I think, that it was necessary for her to take up a distinguished attitude in order to avoid the pain of being reckoned of no account) and Arthur had previously been spoken of by her as a West End club-man, one who mixed with the aristocrats, not so much on equal terms as on terms of high superiority.

"Great shock to him when I went and married a tradesman," she confided to me. "I recollect so well the words he said to me at the time. 'Julia,' he said, 'promise that you'll never on any account do a hand's stroke of work in the shop.' And," triumphantly, "I've kept my word, even on Saturday nights." Her husband, instead of being annoyed, and rating her for indolence, took great pride in the aloof attitude thus taken up; he was in the habit of referring to her, in conversation, as his little Queen of Sheba.

It appeared—when a doctor had been sent for and admitted, after he had cross-examined and investigated, that he could not give a name to her ailment (the greengrocer's wife was enormously conceited over this, counting it as a victory for herself), and when the oft-mentioned brother called and asked me to keep an eye on her—that the description of West End club-man was exact, but not complete. He was, in point of fact, a hall porter at a club, where he described himself as second in command, and his hours were from eight o'clock in the evening until three in the morning or earlier if there happened to be no member remaining in the establishment.

"And you'll easily understand," he said, with an effort at modesty, "that in my position, I get to hear about a large quantity of matters that under the present arrangement of keeping nearly everything out of the newspapers, won't be mentioned in print, for months to come, perhaps not at all. So in return for the kindness you are going to show to my sister Julia, I shall make it my business to bring down to you, miss, any little tit-bits of information that come my way, because, with a nephew in the army you must feel specially interested. Do you follow what I'm driving at?"

I take some credit to myself for making a selection from the particulars brought, later, by Arthur. When he prefaced an announcement by—"Looked in at the club, I did, on me way, and the last thing in on the tape machine was to the effect that——" then I felt justified in assuming that the news had association with truth. But when he said, "Overheard one of our gentlemen, I did, talking to another in the lounge last night, after dinner, and he said, as distinctly as ever he could speak that—" then I knew that here was something which required a good deal of salt before it could be accepted, something it would be wise not to pass on to other folk. Apparently there was, in the West End, all the keen desire to be early in the field with news, that existed in minor districts of town, with an added gift for invention. At times Arthur brought a double load, and one was called upon to take a share in a perfect orgie of rumours. Of notable public men (alive to-day) who had been rushed off to the Tower, and shot, without trial or any unnecessary fuss—

"They tie him to a chair in the Range," said Arthur, exultantly, "six Guardsmen come along from Wellington Barracks, their rifles are loaded, the party in the chair is blindfolded, the sergeant gives the word of command, and then—shoot, bang, fire!—and there's no more headaches for him! Do you follow what I'm driving at?"

Of members of the Government in the pay of Germany, and making money hand over foot; Arthur said darkly that their names were known to him, and they had best be careful. Of the utter and complete uselessness of these Zeppelins that Germany was bragging about; Arthur explained to me a means of bringing down an enemy air-ship, so simple that it appeared to be within the capacity of any boy of ten. Of a remark made by the wife of a Cabinet Minister to her lady's maid, and transferred by many and devious routes, and losing nothing, it was certain, on the way. Of optimists who knew for a matter of absolute fact that Germany's finances would not allow her to continue the struggle for longer than six weeks from now, and of pessimists who said (as the old lady remarked when she heard that Spa Road Station was to be closed), "This war is really getting beyond a joke!"

Until the greengrocer's wife—finding that people were ceasing to inquire after her health and discovering too that, on one occasion her brother called on me without visiting her—until she announced that by exercise of strength of will she had cured herself, where doctors proved of no avail, we were well supplied with rumours, and could have sold them, at a profit, at two for three half-pence. For the rest, came throughout the day, and every day more reliable news on the posters, and often these announcements were staggering blows that made one feel as sick and as helpless as a defeated team in football; sometimes the punishment was followed by a cheering and encouraging smile from the fates, and for the moment, disasters were forgotten. Take it as well as one might, it was a trying period and one cannot pretend any desire to live through it again.

Arthur, on his last call, said that he had found my company very soothing, and assured me that but for the existence of a wife and six children, living at Fulham, nothing would have prevented him from making me a definite and honorable proposal.

"Wish I'd met you earlier," said the hall porter, speaking tremulously, "but there it is, and it's little use grumbling about what can't be remedied. Do you follow what I'm driving at? All the same, I wish you every prosperity, miss, and when the right man comes along—he's a trifle late, if you don't mind me saying so, but he may have been detained—why, I'll trust you'll recognise him, and that you'll both live happy ever afterwards!"

CHAPTER IV

It was all very well to accept the compliments that Mr. Hillier had paid me, but as a matter of fact, whether a ray of sunshine, or a mascot, or a sheet anchor, I felt as much disturbed by all that was going on out in Belgium and France as anybody; if I woke up at night, I was so anxious and depressed about it that I could not get to sleep again. Looking back, it is possible to see how greatly one was helped by the milkman's Russians. He never wavered from his first announcement, and I am sure that at the present time he is confident he was right, and official statements were wrong. Indeed, one was receptive for any encouraging news at a time when a journal, on a beautifully bright and summer-like Sunday, gave the question on its poster, "Can the British Army be Saved?" and the thick black line on the daily war maps bent lower and lower in the direction of Paris. And at the fishmonger's, plaice was a shilling a pound. I tried to bargain with the man, and he said bitterly that I could take it or leave it, or, if I knew how, do both. Belgians were coming over, he added, in their thousands, bringing no money, and we should have to keep them. In a short time, he prophesied, the French people would arrive.

"We shall be eaten out of 'ouse and 'ome," said the fishmonger, dismally, "and I 'alf wish the Germans were here now, and that it was all over and done with!"

Master John and my Herbert wrote that they had been transferred to Caterham for drill. Their letters were common property, and if I received one I read it aloud, and if the family had one, I was called in to listen. Miss Katherine began to take lessons from me in cooking; Miss Muriel joined a sewing society and, clumsy enough at first, and quite incompetent when put in charge of the cutting out, did keep on at it, and showed herself ready to learn, willing to be reproved for blunders. Master Edward I took off to the Council school, and that disposed of him for five and a-half hours from Mondays to Fridays; at first, he came home extremely contemptuous of what he called the blighters, but in a few weeks he was bragging of Wilkinson, and Perrett, and Moore, and other great lads of the educational establishment. It was the subject of income that worried me. Money was going out, day by day, and a ten shilling note seemed to vanish in no time; not a penny was coming in. So soon as the amount representing the sum due to me was exhausted, there would be left nothing but farthings in the pillar box on the kitchen mantelpiece. Mr. Hillier looked through the advertisements carefully, and occasionally wrote letters; he became a special constable partly for the sake of filling up time. Mrs. Hillier alone declined to make any change other than those which circumstances forced upon her; now and again I was tempted to take her by the elbows, and give her a good shake.

"I find Greenwich very soothing," she would say, complacently. "Ideal, really!" The first cold day, and the falling of brown leaves out in the park, made some impression on her, and she shivered slightly in making any comments upon the fighting.

Master John, home on Sunday, gave us a description of his drill at Caterham. He had experienced a fall at the gymnasium, and made light of it, but his mother was concerned, and offered the view that Mr. Asquith ought to be told. Master John said that turning out time in the morning was half-past five; on the previous day he was on duty until a quarter to ten at night. Nearly eight thousand men down there, all Guards, and the Senior Medical Officer examined everyone, although the men had been passed in London for general army service; Master John said that about ten per cent. were rejected, and was content to announce that he himself had gone through safely. Food rather poor at times; occasionally it had to be taken without the assistance of plates.

"Your father must write to the papers about that," decided Mrs. Hillier, warmly. "Gross carelessness on the part of somebody."

Master John said that everyone was eager to get out to the front. Now that the Germans had been turned back from the Marne, and were on the run northwards, the fear at Caterham was that it might not be possible to arrive at the fighting district in time to take a share in the lark. Mrs. Hillier said this would be scandalous.

It was soon after this that the milkman told Mrs. Hillier of the imminent reduction in lighting; she declared that other people could, of course, do as they pleased but she, for one, intended to take no notice of the order. I argued with her, the young ladies argued with her, but she was obstinate until Mr. Hillier took the matter in hand. He gave a hint to the most serious of his colleagues who paid a call one evening at Gloucester Place, and talked to Mrs. Hillier in a way that she had probably never been spoken to before. After pointing out the risks and the penalties, he remarked that neighbours would have no alternative but to assume that she was in sympathy with the Germans. Upon that Mrs. Hillier gave directions, and blinds were drawn, lights carefully shaded. As I let the special constable out at the front door, he said to me:

"A difficult lady to deal with, your friend upstairs."

And I had to agree with him. I sometimes wondered whether any occurrence would effect an alteration in her.

She proved to be greatly annoyed by Miss Katherine's announcement. Miss Katherine had told me of her intentions, but under the bond of secrecy, and when she disclosed the fact that she had obtained a position as clerk in a bank, you might have thought, from Mrs. Hillier's deportment, that a lasting and intolerable disgrace had come upon the family. Nothing ever upset Miss Katherine, and even in our palmy days, she had always been the one to keep a serene temper; she listened now to her mother's severe criticism, and explained that the matter had been kept quiet for the reason that it was possible a failure might have occurred over the examination.

"The news is bound to reach Chislehurst," bewailed Mrs. Hillier. "And when we eventually go back there, I can't see, for the life of me, how it is to be explained."

"We must put it down, mother, to temporary insanity on my part."

"That wouldn't answer," she declared seriously, "because everyone is aware that there have been no signs of it on either your father's side or mine."

"Hadn't thought of that," admitted Miss Katherine.

"Weston," said Mrs. Hillier, appealing to me, "is it, or is it not a fact that in many cases a girl behaving in this way would, by some parents, simply be cut off with a shilling?"

"If you wanted to do so, ma'am," I said, "you'd have to borrow it."

"Not very tactful of you, surely, to throw my misfortunes in my face."

"Has to be done, now and again, in order that you should be reminded of them."

"Because I preserve calm," protested Mrs. Hillier, "whilst all around me are losing their heads and behaving in a hysterical manner, it does not mean, Weston, that I am indifferent to the events which are happening. Katherine must write a letter to the authorities at once, and say circumstances prevent—"

"You can't do that with a bank, ma'am. A bank has powers that a lot of other firms don't possess. People never dream of arguing with a bank."

"I didn't know, Weston," she said, weakly.

"High time you did," I declared.

I was glad to have the prospect of some money coming in to the household, and when Miss Katherine arrived home, after a day at office, I took care there was a meal ready, saw that she went off each morning in good time to catch her train to the City. I think the work must have been trying, exacting probably for any young lady brought up, so to speak, in cotton-wool, and I encouraged her to talk about it to me and to her sister; Mrs. Hillier declined to listen to any reference to the occupation. Miss Katherine, it appeared, reached the bank at ten minutes to nine, and engaged sometimes on the work of entering up pass books; occasionally she was given the task of writing up the waste book where the cheques paid in, on account of other banks, and sent out, were recorded. For the first time in her life, the girl discovered the necessity of being exactly precise, completely correct. Mistakes were not permitted. Miss Katherine described to me the machine called a totalisator that reckoned any figure you gave it up to ninety-nine thousand pounds.

I began to feel anxious again in regard to Mr. Hillier. He managed to catch a cold whilst walking on his beat during the early hours of a night, and thought of the expenses of a doctor worried me. I nursed the cold, and made remedies, and whilst attending upon him there occurred the opportunity of talking over his own prospects. He said, at the start of the conversation, that these could scarcely be discussed at any great length for the very sound reason that they did not exist; I assured him it was his indisposition which forced him to take this view.

"But I am simply not wanted," he argued. "That's the long and short of the matter, and when you have said that, there's nothing more to be said." Mr. Hillier gave a movement of the shoulders that indicated hopelessness. "The fact is, Weston, I was suited for one job in this life; fairly well suited for it. If it had not been for the war, I should have pulled round, and contrived to go on making an income. But there seems nothing else that I am capable of doing."

"Surely you could be a clerk, sir, in some office, and earn thirty shillings or a couple of sovereigns a week. You've got to pocket your pride, you know, at a time like this."

"All the pride I have," he said, "could go into my waistcoat pocket. The one that used to hold my watch. But it's impossible for me to go and beg a situation from the men I used to know, and the men I don't know just give a glance at me and shake their heads."

"But look here," I argued. "You're talking as though your's was a singular case. There must have been many others who came a cropper last August in the same way that you did. What are they doing now? They're not all moping about, surely, and wearing a hump on their back!"

"I have met only one or two. And they pretended they hadn't a care in the world, and I did the same."

"Oh, you men!"

"Face the difficulties of your position, Weston," he counselled, "and recognise them, and don't commit the blunder of attempting to perform impossibilities. The women of this family you may be able to manage, and in doing that you are achieving more than I have ever been able to do. But the men must go their own way."

"Trouble about some of you is that you don't know your own way, and you are too independent to ask. Why, bless my soul, there's work just now for everybody. Somewhere or other there's a job waiting for you."

"Wish it would give me a call," he said, earnestly.

I visited Millwood's shop in London Street, to settle for the articles of furniture he had bought for me; I had looked in for this purpose two or three times before, and discovered no one but a boy who appeared to have few other qualifications but that of impudence. On this occasion I noticed a small bill, lolling so carelessly in the window that it was with some pains I made out the announcement, "This Business to be Sold. Enquire Within." London Street was a thoroughfare where, since I had known it, there had always seemed to be establishments closed or on the point of closing; shutters were up at places, and, at others, announcements of selling off. The cheeky boy said the governor was not in, and would not be at home to receive company until six o'clock; he added that the governor was a widower and preferred to have nothing to do with ladies. "Me," explained the lad, "I'm just the reverse. Never 'appier than when I'm in their company. Always able to get a smile out of 'em." I made it clear to the youngster that he was dealing with an exception to this pleasing rule: he affected terror, and begged me not to be cross, or to do tricks with my features. He spoke of one or two remarkably good films at the local picture palace where the characters exercised this art with greater success, and illustrated his assertion by depicting for my benefit, hate, acute anxiety, murderous intentions, foiled villainy, triumphant love. I sat in the least dusty of the arm chairs, and my interest gained the boy's confidences: he told me that the occupation on which he was engaged did not satisfy his wishes, and that he had some thought of making his way to the interior of Germany, and there playing the part of an ingenious and successful spy, worm out all the enemy's most important secrets, and bring them back to be laid before our War Office. "One shake of the hand from Kitchener," he declared, with emotion, "and I sh'd feel I'd been amply repaid for my trouble." He was describing further magnificent projects when my brother-in-law came in. He gave a curt nod to the boy, and the young gentleman, after smoothing his hair with both hands in front of a cracked looking glass, put on a roller skate, and, uttering a piercing scream that conveyed satisfaction at the relief from business duties, vanished.

"That's all right, Mary Weston," said Millwood, in taking the money. "Glad you was satisfied with what I picked up for you. You're not a easy one to please."

"I find you looking a deal brighter than when I saw you last."

"That remark, coming from the quarter it does, is scarcely intended to be in the nature of a fulsome compliment. I know you mean it. And if you want to know the reason, it is that I am working 'ard."

"About the last thing, Millwood, I should have expected you to do."

"A justifiable comment," he agreed. "I admit I was getting slack. Loafing about in a business like this, and only moving when somebody stopped outside to have a look at the furniture, was enough to make anyone become blassy, as our friends across the water would put it. I showed a card, I did— 'Don't hope for the Best: come inside and get It'—but it didn't stimulate matters. Now I'm at the Arsenal. A mechanic at the Arsenal: that's what I am. Getting good money, and earning it. I come back here of an evening, jolly well fagged out, and uncommon pleased with myself. And now there's the chance of you making one of your sarcastic snacks that you're reckoned pretty good at."

"Millwood," frankly, "you have every reason to feel pleased with yourself."

"Thank you, Mary Weston. Wanted to get the idea, you see, that I was doing something useful."

"There are one or two matters I'd like to talk to you about, but, first of all, there's this shop. It's no use to you."

"It's a incubus," confessed Millwood.

"You are trying to get rid of it."

"Anyone can have it as a free gift, if they'll only let me go on living over'ead."

"I'll take it off your hands."

Directly I had said this, and Millwood had recovered from his surprise, he began to hedge; I expected this. He explained that the phrase "a free gift" was used in a metaphorical sense, and that if he had realised he was talking to a likely purchaser, he would, of course, have selected his words more carefully. Millwood was a haggler from long practise, and I was something of a bargainer by habit, and we spent a very pleasant hour in coming to terms, with, on the one side, an amount quoted at first above and beyond all expectations, and, on the other, a sum low enough to provide a margin for increase. In the end, we agreed, and Millwood said that, so help his goodness, I was a hard nut to crack if ever there was one, and I said of him that he was as artful as a waggon load of monkeys.

"I'd nearly forgotten something else I wanted to speak of," I said. "This Arsenal work. Do they want more hands there?"

"They're nearly full up, but there's still a chance. If it's any working man of your acquaintance, get him to hurry along."

"And I suppose if he has some skill in engineering, it makes a bit of difference."

"Makes all the difference," said Millwood. "The difference between being a mechanic like myself, and something a good deal better paid. I know a fitter there who's earning close upon four quid a week. The work is indispensable to the Government, and the Government doesn't mind paying for it. But it's no child's play, mind you!"

Millwood, in regard to the shop, suggested a letter should be written agreeing that he could retake possession when the war was over, or earlier.

From that moment I was as fully occupied as one desired to be; perhaps a trifle more. There came first the business of getting Mr. Hillier free of his cold, and here I missed the assistance, by day, of Miss Katherine; meanwhile I threw out hints concerning the Arsenal, and he showed interest in the description of some of the tasks performed there. He confessed that in leaving Chislehurst the greatest wrench had been the loss of the workshop. "The one place," said Mr. Hillier, "where I could forget everything else. It was drink, and golf, and smoke to me. If Mrs. Hillier nagged, or the girls bothered, or matters went wrong in the City, I had only to go down beyond the garage, and put on a yellow over-all, and, for the time being, I was someone else. Those experiences can never come again, Weston."

I provided some additional information regarding the Arsenal, spoke of the convenient train journey. You left Greenwich, and passed Maze Hill, Westcombe Park, Charlton, Woolwich Dockyard, and there you were at the Arsenal station. Fifteen minutes in the train.

I knew Mr. Hillier well enough, and I understood his temperament sufficiently to be aware that the idea would seem much more attractive if he had the impression that it was his own, and that it had not been forced upon him by anyone else. Later, he put some questions about Trades Unions, and I promised to make inquiries.

"There is no hurry," he remarked. "I asked only out of curiosity."

Master Edward arriving home from school, made an announcement that astonished me, and furnished a new task. I ought to have remembered that a boy leaves the County Council schools when he reaches the age of fourteen, but I had so much to think of that the fact escaped my notice; Mrs. Hillier, on hearing this excuse, said it seemed to her my intelligence was decaying. Miss Muriel had been invited to pay a visit to friends at Chislehurst, and I was relieved from the task of looking after her: Mr. Hillier was making a good recovery, and I hoped my scheme in regard to him might be successful; the shop in London Street was in the hands of a firm of decorators who had promised to be out of it within seven days, from the start, and had already been pottering about there for three weeks. And here came Master Edward thrown back from school upon my hands; it appeared to be understood at Gloucester Place that it was for me to arrange the launching of him into business life.

"What would you like to be?" I asked, sharply.

"Really don't know, Weston," he answered.

"But haven't you any bent, or inclination, or——"

"I fancy the pater's notion was that I should go in for the law."

"You'll have to do something useful," I declared. "Something that will bring in a few shillings a week, without delay."

"Most chaps have a holiday when they leave school."

"Not in these war times. Just now, the country wants everybody to work. Don't let me hear any nonsense talk of that nature."

"Wish I were old enough to do as John did, and join the army."

"My dear lamb," giving up my manner of severity, "you ought to be thankful that you're young enough to be out of all this terrible business. Haven't you seen the poor wounded soldiers limping about in the Park, and on Blackheath?"

"They look happy," said the boy.

I sent a postcard to William Richards, and he hurried down from Charing Cross so soon as he was off duty. We met at the station, and I first took him along to the shop, where the elderly workmen were startled by the fact that I had brought a companion; William Richards supported my arguments with some determined words that they seemed to understand better than the milder language which I used. He said they were a dashed lot of adjective mikers. He declared his intention of calling on their adjective governor, and dashed well taking the adjective job away, and giving it to some other adjective firm. He assured them they had every reason to be dashed well ashamed of themselves. William Richards wore a bowler hat to indicate that he was free of railway service, but underneath an overcoat was his brass buttoned uniform, and I think the decorator's men were impressed by the sight of this. The foreman urged they were doing all that mortals could be expected to do; contended that a job, to be carried out well, should be carried out with nothing like undue haste. William Richards waved these arguments aside, and used some more of his resolute denunciations.

"Look here, sir," said the old foreman. "We don't wish for no unpleasantness. All we want is to live and let live. In regard to this job, we'll get a move on, and I promise you we shall be clear and away by Friday evening."

"Friday noon," directed William Richards, "and not a minute later."

"Friday noon it shall be," agreed the other, "and it's been a pleasure to meet a gentleman who can express himself so clear as what you have done. Mind that pail as you go out, and see that your lady friend don't take off any of the wet paint on her skirts!"

We walked around the old-fashioned market off Nelson Street, where the names—Underwood, Austin, Gladwin, Goulding, and others reminded one of country days—and considered the case of Master Edward. William said that so many railway men had left to enlist, and so many more wished to go, that it was an easy matter for a lad to obtain employment. All the same, William shook his head in a doubtful way, and happening to discover as he talked the phrase of *infra dig*, used it liberally. He remembered the family as it existed at Chislehurst, and declared it would be *infra dig* for any member of it, however youthful, to join the railway service. He could scarcely imagine that a gentleman who had once been a first class season ticket holder would become so *infra dig* as to allow his son to go in for railway work. The railways were not intended for *infra dig* people. In his opinion *infra digs* ought to offer themselves to loftier occupations.

"Go back at once to headquarters at London Bridge," I ordered. "Get a form of application, and send it to me by this evening's post. And thank you very much, William Richards, for being kind enough to help."

"I'd do more than this for you, Mary Weston," he said. "And well you know it."

Master Edward was sensible over the business, and rather pleased to be engaged on something like a conspiracy. We said no word about it to any of the others, and on a day when Mr. Hillier had gone out with the remark that he did not expect to return until late, I obtained permission to take the boy to London on the pretence of seeing the recruiting on Horse Guards Parade, and listening to any bands that might be playing. The application form had been endorsed by the head master at the schools, and by Millwood. At the head offices, Master Edward was told that he could start work on probation the following morning in a booking office at a suburban station: wages ten shillings a week.

"Bright looking lad, that son of yours," remarked a senior clerk, as I was waiting.

"He's not my son."

"A nephew, perhaps."

"Not a nephew."

"I see," he remarked. "You're just a friend of the family."

It occurred to me there were some grounds for hoping that this was not altogether an inaccurate description.

The announcement was made to Mrs. Hillier that evening and, fortunately, Miss Katherine arrived home from the bank in good time, and ready and willing to support the action taken. Mrs. Hillier complained that she was being treated as though she were a mere nonentity in the household, declared that it was high time Weston learnt her right place, and was made to keep in it, and to refrain from assuming responsibilities that, correctly speaking, belonged to others: Master Edward had described his own satisfaction with the arrangement, and Miss Katherine was inviting her mother to recognise the facts of the case, when Mr. Hillier came up the staircase, taking two steps at a time, and whistling as he entered the room.

"I've obtained a berth at the Arsenal," he announced, cheerfully, "and I feel as happy as a sand boy. Give me your congratulations, my dear."

"No," said his wife, distantly. "No, I cannot do that. That, James, is impossible. But I willingly extend to you my most earnest sympathy."

The last post brought a letter from Chislehurst which induced her to regard events with a slightly diminished amount of gloom. It gave the news that Miss Muriel was engaged. "I hope the man has money," said Mrs. Hillier. "I think we can trust Muriel for that. And, at any rate, it saves her from the peril of going on the stage!"

CHAPTER V

I paid little attention to the news from Chislehurst, although one was, of course, interested in Miss Muriel as in the others; the opening of the shop at London Street occupied in truth a good deal of my time and care. Mrs. Hillier, answering my invitation to look over the establishment, said that in view of my incurable habit of embarking upon adventure without consulting her, it was impossible for her to give any sort of countenance to the business, or make purchases there. I retorted that I had no desire to ask for her patronage, and I might have added—but did not—that in the circumstances, it was not much she could afford to buy. But the good lady appeared to find one of her rare joys in pretending that her money resources were as large as they had been before the war, and it seemed a pity to be always destroying the notion. Miss Katherine was the one who sometimes took me apart, and said:

"Weston, dear. How much do we owe you now?" It was to Miss Katherine alone that I showed the penny memorandum book in which I entered the accounts. The girl had given up her manner of talking slang; she said it was not approved by the best City authorities.

I gave Saturday to the new shop, and a part of Sunday (better the day, the better the deed) and on Monday morning, was there again so soon as I had prepared breakfast at Gloucester Place for the three working members of the family. Mr. Hillier left the house at six o'clock, Master Edward, being at present on middle duty, caught the train at half-past eight; Miss Katherine did not have to go until rather later.

The cheeky boy, at London Street, had been paid off by Millwood, and his mother called to beg me to take him on again. She was one of the helpless parents that London sometimes cultivates.

"I'm sure I don't know what'll become of him," she declared, rubbing eyes with the hem of her apron, "if you refuse to take my Peter in hand. He only wants looking after; nothing else. And hearing you talked about, Miss, as a rare good manager, why, it struck me that I couldn't do better than get you to look after him. You've got a chance of doing a good action, and I'm sure you'll regret it if you don't take advantage of the opportunity. It'll be on your conscience."

"If he comes back here, he will have to work. And work hard."

"Break that news to my Peter," she urged, "as plainly and as forcibly as ever you can. Give him a good nagging. He takes no notice of anything I say. I'd very much like," she added, tearfully, "that he should grow up a credit to me. It's hard on mothers when their sons turn out badly."

I took Peter back, but did not deliver to him anything like an address, or a lecture, or a heart to heart talk. Instead I provided him with a duster, and a bottle of polish, and other articles constituting an outfit, and gave him brief instructions. Ten minutes later, I found him behind a leather screen, and resting on a settee; he was concentrating his attention upon literature that dealt with the Adventures of Gideon Smart, Detective. I placed the journal in the fire, and Peter supported the argument of heredity by weeping; I allowed him to cry, and, when he had finished, pointed to the tasks which awaited his consideration. Used to the companionship of words and plenty of them, my silence impressed him, and so soon as he had finished one job, I provided him with another. Peter submitted later some brass candlesticks for my approval, and was honoured with a guarded sentence for which he seemed acutely grateful.

"Excuse me, miss," he said, respectfully, "but you're not much of a conversationalist, are you?"

"I'm a worker."

"Couldn't it be managed, do you think, to run the two, so to speak, at one and the same time?"

"Work comes first," I said. Peter gave the sigh of a man who regrets the eccentric rules concerning business deportment.

Neighbours looked in from shops hard by, and told me that their own trades were doing badly, and would, in their opinion, do worse ere they did better. Having said this with much cheerfulness, they endeavoured to assume a compassionate air in giving the view that of all the trades none could expect to fare so ill, in these exceptional times, as that which dealt with furniture; they spoke of the condition of affairs in Shoreditch and Bethnal Green. Their knowledge was never first hand, but had come from a cousin of a friend who knew a person whose brother-in-law was something of an authority on the subject. Certain of the older ones spoke of the days that were prosperous at Greenwich, when visitors came to the Ship and the

Trafalgar, and climbed the ascent in the Park, and strolled about the town, and bought mementoes and souvenirs.

"Fifty year ago," said a watchmaker to me, confidentially, "you might have made a do of it. Now, it's like throwing your money down a sink. Besides, you women-folk always get swindled right and left when you barge in to affairs of this kind. By the bye, I've got a couple of grandfather's clocks you might care to have a glance at when you're passing my way. They're almost genuine!"

A proportion of Millwood's stock was useful only as fire-wood, and the covered yard at the back received these articles, making a pile to be drawn upon during the winter months. The mere eviction of these improved the look of the shop; the greatest change was perhaps effected by the linoleum covering of the floor which gave a fair imitation of parquet, and received the care of Peter when there was nothing else for the lad to do. Folk, hurrying past on their way to the station, observed the altered appearance and stopped to give a few moments of inspection, and I hoped some of them would come in, and at least inquire the prices, or make an offer where the amount was exhibited. Not until three o'clock on the second day did the first customer enter. He was young, and I wondered why he was not in khaki. He seemed pressed for time.

"You a judge of furniture?"

"I am," I said.

"Able to tell whether it's good or not?"

"Rather!"

"Care to take on a sort of a contract?" he demanded.

"If I can make anything out of it."

"How long have you been engaged in this work?"

"You wouldn't believe me if I told you," I answered.

He appeared satisfied with my replies, and, taking off his silk hat, explained his wants. He was a doctor and had to join the R.A.M.C. the following week. Before that date, he proposed to get married. The lady had remarked, in agreeing to the hasty procedure, that the drawing room and the dining room were to be set out with articles that possessed the quality of age; she drew the line at the accession of Queen Victoria.

"Now," he said, rapidly, "I've no time to go about searching here, there and everywhere, and, apart from that, I haven't the necessary knowledge. I may have hinted to her that I possess it, but as a matter of fact I don't know Chippendale from Wensleydale, or whatever they call the stuff."

"What is the limit, sir?"

"Two hundred and fifty," he said.

"Give me some references."

"Rather give you a cheque."

I set ink and pen before him, and he, demanding my name, filled in the slip.

"There you are," he said, preparing to run off. "I've made it three fifty. Now, I'm depending on you. Don't fail me, whatever you do."

It occurred to my mind that although he was trusting me, there appeared no reason why I should trust him. The cheque was drawn on a local branch, and leaving Peter in charge, and giving him enough to do to keep him out of mischief, I went along and saw the manager. He said the cheque, if paid in at once, would be met, and he suggested I should open an account of my own. I did this.

The milkman—an uncertain person so far as concerned rumours of large events—proved useful and reliable here. He knew, as not many knew, the financial position of establishments in the neighbourhood; his information, most likely, was gained from news collected in areas, and corroborated by promptitude or delay in settlement of his account. Also, he was able to tell me of houses where the furniture was old and valuable. By a stroke of luck, it happened that the very first door in Crooms' Hill I knocked at proved to be a place where my call was welcomed, and indeed expected. The three ladies there, facing serious reductions in dividends, had resolved to leave Greenwich, and go off to a cottage owned by them and already sufficiently furnished in Buckinghamshire. (When the transaction ended, one of them admitted to me that fear of air-raids and nearness to the Arsenal had something to do with the decision.) Terrified by the idea of a public sale, they had, the night before, made an appeal on their knees that some other means should be supplied.

"Providence has sent you," said the eldest, contentedly, "and, knowing that you have been selected to help us at this moment of trouble, we are willing you should go over the house, choose what you require, and name your own figure. Of course, it's a wrench for us to part with the furniture, but it brings with it the consolation that we are taking our share in the war. And it is such a relief to find that we are not called upon to deal with some man, with a smell of tobacco about him."

Their simplicity disarmed me, and their genuine piety forced me to deal with them in a more straightforward manner than I might otherwise have adopted. One or two of the articles were particularly good and valuable: there was, for instance, a Chesterfield sofa that would have fetched forty pounds in the open market, and I told them so, and advised them to take it, with some of the rest, away to Farnham Common. In the servants' bedroom I found three Queen Anne mirrors. I made up an inventory that included four-posters, cupboards, dining tables, suites of chairs, an Adam cabinet, two escritoires, some remarkably fine glass, and a few mezzotints.

On these last I was not qualified to put an exact value.

"I'll give you three hundred pounds for the lot," I said, handing over the list.

"No," remarked the eldest firmly. "Dear me no!" I prepared for the duel of bargaining. "Two hundred and fifty will be ample. We cannot think of taking advantage of one who has come here in answer to our prayers." The sisters nodded an emphatic endorsement, and I realised it was useless to argue with them. They asked, as a great favour, that the van which took the furniture away should attend at an early hour in the morning, before Crooms Hill was awake. "We don't wish," they pleaded, "to be the subject of gossip." They gave me a new prayer book, and I came away with the feeling that one had peeped into a world too good for a business person.

The young doctor was well satisfied with the transaction. He told me his fiancée said she had always known that his taste and selection could be depended upon, and he thanked me warmly for my assistance. To the milkman I presented five one pound notes signed by John Bradbury, Secretary to the Treasury, and when he realised that the notes were genuine and that he was not being made the target for a practical joke, he declared I was a lady well worth knowing, assured me that any information he possessed concerning the inside of residences at Greenwich would always be at my disposal.

The telegram informing us that Master John and my Herbert were leaving for the front arrived one morning when the working members of the family in Gloucester Place had gone off to their respective duties. A few hints had come before, but this information was definite.

"We shall have to hurry, ma'am." Mrs. Hillier was taking breakfast in bed. "There's no time to lose. Bustle about!"

"You are asking me to do something, Weston, altogether foreign to my nature."

"I very often wonder, ma'am, what can happen that will rouse you up thoroughly. There seemed a possibility that it was going to happen at Chislehurst but it passed off."

"With so much turmoil and excitement," she said, serenely, "going on around me, I feel it my duty to give an example of—"

"We must be out of this house in half an hour's time."

"But why on earth—"

"I'll tell you," I interrupted. "We're going to see the dear boys off for the reason that we may never catch sight of them again!"

"You always look on the dark side, Weston," she complained.

In the tram-car, on the way up to Westminster Bridge, she made it clear to other travellers that my position was that of a dependent, and this would have been continued throughout the journey, only that at New Cross Gate two jovial factory girls came in, and these, appreciating the situation, at once began to imitate her voice and her manner. Mrs. Hillier was silent after this, and when I explained to the two girls the task on which we were engaged, they stopped their raillery, and, apologising, told me that their chaps were abroad fighting; they insisted upon showing me the latest communications which had reached them. Our half of the car became friendly on this; other notes and cards were produced, photographs were handed around. A woman possessed a letter from the King's secretary, congratulating her on the circumstance that she had a husband and four sons in the army, and this broke down Mrs. Hillier's attitude of lofty reserve. She counselled the owner to have the document framed, lest, by frequent passing about, it should become creased and torn; the woman said this was a rattling good idea, and promised to act upon it. The factory girls left at the Elephant, and Mrs. Hillier shook hands with them; when we alighted at the Boadicea corner the passengers gave us a message of good luck to be tendered to the two boys.

"Some of these people, Weston," she said, tolerantly, as we went in the direction of Birdcage Walk, "are, after all, very human." I thought to myself that the same could be said of her whenever she cared to show herself at her best.

We found an enormous crowd outside the barracks. Inside the park, hobbled horses were at the sand place marked "This Space is for Children only"; the lake was empty. We stood on the high walk near the park railings, and could see the Guards drawn up on the parade ground; it was impossible to identify Master John or Herbert.

"Why didn't you think to bring the field glasses, Weston?" complained Mrs. Hillier.

"Because they were sold," I answered. "Sold with everything else that would fetch money. And try to recollect, ma'am, that this isn't a moment for asking silly questions; you're looking on at something wonderful. Something that you'll want to keep in your mind's eye for the rest of your life. Don't let me have to speak about it again."

The soldiers were allowed to stand easy for five minutes: their comrades ran forward to have a last talk. Orders were shouted. The men marched out four abreast through the open gates. The crowd cheered, and began to move eastwards; we followed and went at a good pace, but not good enough to keep up with the foremost ranks. There was no music, but the soldiers sang, and called out facetiously in unison, "Is the canteen shut?" and gave a shouted answer of "No!" Each carried his full equipment, and a tin of thick sandwiches. In Great George Street, when I had begun to think we should have to give up, Mrs. Hillier caught sight of Master John and they exchanged waves of the hand; encouraged by this she walked faster, and we crossed the bridge at a rate I had not experienced since competing in running games at school.

"Aunt Mary!" cried a voice, as they swung around into York Road.

"God bless you, Herbert, my lad," I panted. "And bring you both back safely."

"Don't forget to ask Him to do so," said my nephew. Some of his comrades thought this was meant as a joke: I knew quite well the dear lad was in earnest.

We went home by tram-car, too full of our thoughts to exchange a word with each other. That night, in my rooms at the top of the house, I obeyed my boy's directions. It made me think of the three ladies of Crooms' Hill, and I could not help wishing I had some of their placid and simple faith.

It seemed possible the departure of the lads would have a lasting effect upon Mrs. Hillier, and this, I believe, might have happened but for the arrival of her elder daughter. The others of the family were in good working order. Mr. Hillier returned at night, comfortably tired, ready for the meal prepared for him, willing to talk of the incidents of his new life, the men he encountered and the tasks he was called on to perform; all the satisfaction he had gained from his hobby at Chislehurst he was now securing at the Arsenal. Mr. Hillier often pointed out to me that the fighting had sent us back to a condition of affairs where the man of brains occupied a position inferior to that of the man of hands.

"It will take the conceit out of some people," he remarked.

"It's taken a certain amount out of you, sir."

"Agreed, Weston. It has improved all of us. Excepting—" He did not finish the sentence.

Miss Katherine came into the flat of an evening, justifying her father's assertion, eager to chat vivaciously of everything that had to do with banks, and her own progress in type-writing and shorthand. The first of these came to her easily enough; the second presented greater difficulties. Sometimes I read aloud a speech from the parliamentary reports and Miss Katherine took it down, with appeals of "Please, please, not so fast, Weston, dear," and then, apologetically, "You always are a bit of a sprinter in conversation, you know, and I expect it's not easy to get out of the habit." When it was finished, she took her meal, and then transcribed the speech from her shorthand notes, and read it aloud. Often, she had to admit that the result was incoherent, and not to be understood: I tried to comfort her by pointing out that the same might be said of the original, but Miss Katherine shook her head. "I shall never be any earthly good at it, Weston," she declared, hopelessly. It seemed that the qualification was not needed in the department where she was at present engaged, but Miss Katherine had hopes of promotion.

Master Edward, too, had been changed considerably by his railway experiences. His hours when on the early turn were from five o'clock, and when on the late turn from one o'clock; every other Sunday he had to give sixteen hours to duty, with three hours off for the mid-day meal. Later, he hoped to be transferred to a London station where the figure of wages was said to reach as much as £90 a year. The early turn was the one that troubled him, and indeed it was not easy or comfortable to turn out in the dark of a January morning. At times, when I knocked at his door, he would reply in a bright active voice as though he were fully awake, but I knew boys too well to be deluded by that trick, and I waited and knocked again until he came to the door and assured me that he would be ready for his cup of hot coffee within ten minutes. One of the compensating moments of pride came when I gave him on his birthday, a case of safety razors that I had picked up at a sale; he accepted it gratefully as a tribute to his age, and impending requirements. For the rest, Edward had to tell us of agitated passengers who came with a rush demanding tickets for the station which they wished to leave, of attempts on race days to ring the changes or tender notes of home manufacture, of the dislocation of time tables to permit of trains being run for Government purposes, of the cancelling of all excursion fares and cheap tickets, of economical parents whose long-legged children refused to admit to any age above twelve, of the head booking clerk who always began the day in the worst possible temper, and invariably ended it with perfect geniality. I daresay Master Edward lost some of his refinement of manners, and I confess I was shocked when I first heard him allude, one morning to "these blasted shoe laces."

"Oh," he said, answering my reproof, lightly, "you're old-fashioned, Weston. You belong to the antiques. By-the-bye, how is London Street doing? And who, just now, are you doing?"

I want to speak of Miss Muriel, but whilst I think of it, I must set down some reference to the collection of glass that I came across in a large house at Vanbrugh Park, where an old lady, the daughter of an Archdeacon who knew something besides Church matters, had recently died, leaving her property to a certain benevolent society, "because," her will said, "it has never asked me for a donation." Sales were not being well attended just then, and at each one that I went to—sometimes nodding frequently to the auctioneer, and sometimes keeping my head still—there were fewer of the agents, as they liked to call themselves, to be seen. A mixed crew, these, and inclined, at first, to resent the presence of a woman dealer; they tried, on one occasion, to pinch my fingers by running up the price of a fine horse-hair settee for which I had a purchaser ready, and I stopped just in time to compel a syndicate to take it; one of the members came to me later, and made a deferential offer that involved a loss on his side of two pounds ten. In the matter of the glass referred to there was little competition; a few private buyers were willing to bid for certain articles, but the fact that it was all comprised in one lot compelled them to refrain from making any offer. I have rarely been so pleased in all my life as when I took back to the shop in London Street that set of glass, cleaned it well and arranged it on dark wooden ledges. (In the result, I disposed of every piece, but I never parted from one without feeling regret for myself, and something like animosity towards the buyer.)

Let us come to the topic of Miss Muriel. She had been away at Chislehurst for some time; she and her mother had corresponded regularly and her letters, since the announcement of her engagement, seemed less querulous. Miss Muriel wrote, in one, a description of the gentleman's house, and this ought to have prepared me for the facts; as it happened, it was not until Miss Muriel brought him over one Saturday afternoon to be formally presented to the family, and I heard him below in Gloucester Place giving directions to the driver of his car that I gained the first hint of his age. He was speaking in curt, loud, and ejaculatory manner, and—just as well to admit it—I made up my mind at once that I was not going to regard him favourably. And this intention was confirmed when Miss Katherine ran up to my rooms at the top of the house, and said through the half-opened door—

"Weston! Weston! He's a bounder. A bounder from the village of Bound. One of the worst ever. Come down, and have a peep at him!"

I had to go back to the London Street shop, and ascertain whether Millwood was able to take care of the establishment and to look after Peter for a few hours; my brother-in-law proved quite ready to do this, and I fancy he took some pleasure in sitting near the window, and observing the interest shown by passers-by, listening to their comments, and, if they entered, to say, "You must call again when Miss Weston is here, unless you're prepared to give what's marked on the tab that's tied to the articles. I've got no power, mark you, to accept a farthing less!" In Gloucester Place, could be heard now the middle-aged gentleman's voice at the balcony, explaining how the trees in the garden ought to be cut down. Miss Muriel came out to the landing.

"Ah, Weston," she said. "Haven't seen you for ages. I expect you have missed me."

"In a sense, yes."

"Never a flatterer," she remarked, indulgently. "You might, at least, though, offer your congratulations."

"I've not seen the gentleman yet. But if you've quite decided, miss, to change your name, there's nothing more to be said about it."

"Your assumption is wrong. I don't propose to change my name."

"The engagement is off, then."

"Once more," she said, complacently, "error has crept, Weston, into your calculations. Mr. Schloss intends to take my name. He will become Mr. Hillier, and I shall be Mrs. Hillier. And he has an income that will enable me to live in the comfort I was once used to."

"Your handwriting, miss, is so bad that I never guessed he was a German."

Miss Muriel reprimanded me for the criticism of her pen, and for the suggestion concerning her gentleman. Mr. Hillier came out of the room.

"We don't talk to Weston in this manner," he ordered, closing the door behind him. "Weston is one of us. We owe a great deal to her, Muriel, in more ways than one. In fact, we are only just beginning to pay off the indebtedness. Kindly treat her in a proper way."

"She had no right," protested Miss Muriel, "to suggest that he is anything but English."

"I ascertained a while since," said her father, quietly, "that he was naturalised, rather hurriedly, in August of last year. And he has just admitted the circumstances to me."

"Nothing," she declared, in a tragic manner—"not even the extraordinary behaviour of my own people—shall ever part us from each other!"

CHAPTER VI

Miss Muriel went back in the car to her friends at Chislehurst, with the air of one who, for the sake of romance, was prepared to defy the world. She had always been spoilt by her mother (it is fair to myself to mention that the treatment was started before I entered the family) and Mrs. Hillier now took her side against the rest of us, declaring that a girl had to obey the instructions of her own heart, that love was something which could not be directed by those outside its influence, and that, moreover, it was a comfort to think there was likely to be an establishment available which would enable one to escape from the surroundings of Greenwich.

"Apart from all that," she argued, triumphantly, "a man can't help the country he was born in."

"He ought to help it," said Master Edward. The lad was the most strenuous of us all on the opposition side. "This chap should have gone back directly the war started. He has no business here."

"Pardon me," said his mother, "he has a business here. And a very good one, I am happy to say."

"I mean that when two countries are fighting each other——"

"You don't know what you mean," she asserted. "And, besides, you are much too young to have an opinion on a subject of this kind. If your father, sitting over there by the window, and saying nothing, had a proper control over his children, he wouldn't allow you to talk in this way."

"Do you want my view of the matter?" asked Mr. Hillier.

"Oh, no," she answered quickly. "No. It's all settled, and there's nothing more to be said."

"My view is," he announced, "that I'd rather see her cleaning doorsteps."

"I daresay!" said Mrs. Hillier, coldly. "That is because the Arsenal work has coarsened your outlook. Vulgarised your mental attitude. Twisted your sense of proportion."

Miss Katherine went to her father: Master Edward crossed the room to his mother. I left them as Mr. and Mrs. Hillier were beginning to offer apologies for hasty words. The day was Sunday, and upstairs—having the time to spare—I wrote the drafts of two notes; one begging Miss Muriel to come and see me and have a long talk, and the other asking her to think of the way in which her brother John, out in France, would receive the news of her engagement. I am supposed to be handy with my pen, but neither of these communications satisfied me, and I decided to take a few days to consider the matter. Instead, I wrote a long communication to Corporal Herbert Millwood, and sent in it an affectionate message to Master John. I tried to make the letter cheerful. "If you come across the Kaiser on his birthday, please wish him, for me, many unhappy returns."

William Richards called at London Street one afternoon. Whenever he had happened to say anything of a specially friendly nature—as he had done on his previous visit—William always stayed away for a considerable time, as though desirous of allowing the memory of it to fade, and he now seemed rather nervous; to conceal this, he told me three war anecdotes, which, so far as I could see, had no point whatever. I mentioned this, and he admitted that a story never improved in his hands. He gave compliments to the shop, remarked that Peter seemed a decent sort of lad, spoke of the large amount of traffic which was being dealt with by the Southern railways. He had heard excellent reports of Master Edward, and told me that the boy's appearance, speech, and behaviour had, by good fortune, been noticed and commented upon by the wife of the superintendent. After this interval of sanity, William again went blundering in and amongst tales from the fighting line.

"Now that one," he remarked, rubbing the top of his head with the peak of his uniform cap, "that one, I'll swear, appeared funny when I first heard it. And now it sounds simply chronic." He glanced at his large watch. "By Ginger," he exclaimed, "but time does fly when you're in pleasant company. There was something I wanted to tell—" He gave a fair imitation of a puzzled look. "I've got it," he said, triumphantly. "Piece of news I heard at Charing Cross. The Major of that lot that your nephew, and your Master John was in: he's been took prisoner. Good-day to you, Mary!"

The news was confirmed by a brief paragraph in the evening journal; I said nothing of it at Gloucester Place because it is rarely wise to go out of your way simply in order to shake hands with trouble. Far better to wait where you are, and let trouble, if it cares to do so, come to you. (Afterwards we discovered that all of us had seen the announcement, and each determined to make no allusion.)

The first information of a definite nature came in a letter from a Quartermaster-Sergeant. Addressed to Mr. Hillier, and written in pencil it said, "I regret to tell you that your son, Corporal Hillier, has been missing since the twenty-fifth January. He may be a prisoner, but we do not know for certain. He asked me, should anything happen to him, to let you know."

There followed a brief letter from my nephew, Herbert.

"We were surprised in a dug out," he wrote. "We ran in single line for cover, with machine firing coming across. John had no rifle. That was the last we saw of him. Tell his people to hope for the best. I was one of the few who escaped, but I am in hospital. Nothing serious. Love to my father, and to you."

There came a month of suspense during which we gathered scraps of news but nothing that re-assured us. The good Quartermaster-Sergeant, in another letter, said there were no further particulars; they could not say what had really happened; directly the battalion obtained definite information he would write again.

I went up to town, and called at Wellington Barracks; Mr Hillier paid a Saturday afternoon visit to the War Office; Miss Katherine communicated with a girl friend at Geneva, begging her to make inquiries of the Red Cross Society. During all this time, I noticed that Mrs. Hillier, eager as the rest of us, showed no tears, but she became more active in the work of the small household, and took duties that had hitherto been performed by the rest of us. She rose each morning to see her husband leave for the Arsenal, and kissed him before he went: kissed him again when he returned in the evening. No complaining came from her now. If she spoke of Master John, she referred to him hopefully.

An envelope arrived with the postmark of Cricklewood. We recognised the handwriting, and waited anxiously for Mr. Hillier to come home and open it.

"I am having this letter posted," wrote the Quartermaster-Sergeant, "by a comrade who is off to England, so as to avoid it being censored. Well, to tell you as much as possible, sir, about your son. We were in the forward trenches on the morning of the twenty-fifth of last month, when the enemy made an attack. Their trenches were not a hundred yards from our own. They had under-mined our forward trenches. They threw up some smoke bombs as a signal, and to blind their attack. At the same time, they exploded their mines. The result was that part of our trenches were blown up, and before you could look sideways they were upon us in thousands. The Right Flank and the Left Flank of our regiment stuck to their ground until overcome by sheer weight of numbers. Then, those that possibly could, retired to a brick field about eight hundred yards back which the remainder of the battalion (two companies) had turned into a miniature fort. This was known as The Keep. The Germans made violent attacks, all without any material advantage to themselves, on this position, but were unable to take it. And it was not lost when matters quietened down. Our trenches have now been regained, and our boys, I am pleased to say, managed to steal some of the German trenches.

"I am very sorry to say I can give you no good news of your son. I have made inquiries of the regiments who held the position after it had been regained, and one of the sergeants told me they buried over two hundred of our men. Some of them were found dead at the 'present,' ready to fire at the enemy, so you see it is no good telling you anything that might build up very great hopes.

"The strength of the companies going into the trenches was two hundred and seventy-six. Of these forty-six returned. Of course, we held a position where we did not dare to lose ground, and although it was a terrible business, it was a great victory for the English and French troops. At any rate, the enemy did not score much on their Emperor's birthday.

"You can understand how deeply I sympathise with you as none of us knows the minute when our own people will need the same. I have a father and mother living at Lewisham."

Mr. Hillier read this out to us, in a voice that broke now and again. His wife took his hand when he finished, and patted it sympathetically.

"I could hug the man who wrote that nice letter," I declared.

Herbert sent a note later from the hospital at Boulogne (where he found himself, after treatment at a dressing station) saying that he was nearly well, and ready to go back to the fighting line. "Have you any news of John?" he asked. "We were real good chums." The official communication came to Gloucester Place from the War Office, stating that Corporal Hillier was reported missing. His mother, showing greater industry in domestic work every day, and relieving me of half my duties, argued that the use of this word by the authorities proved that they were not without hope; the rest of us abstained from contesting this opinion. We knew that all the two hundred and thirty mentioned in Quartermaster-Sergeant Cartwright's letter would be reported in the first instance under the same heading. Mr. Hillier ventured to allude to the question of Muriel's engagement as regarded in the new circumstances.

"I have already written to her, dear," said Mrs. Hillier. "Don't you let that worry you. I've told her the engagement must be cancelled. After the way his people have treated our boy—"

"I was sure," he said, gratefully, "you would see the matter in that light."

"You can consider it as settled," she declared. "Weston," turning to me, "I'm going to cook supper this evening. And you are to sit down with us, please."

I was not at all certain that I wanted to join the family party at table, and I had my doubts concerning Mrs. Hillier's abilities to prepare a meal. As a fact, the dish she served up was excellent, and when we offered our congratulations she disclosed a circumstance that had been kept from everyone but Mr. Hillier; in her early youth, it seemed, she had been compelled to take charge of a household, and run it with economy. "But, mother dear," protested Miss Katherine, amazedly, "why in the world didn't you tell us this before?" Mrs. Hillier considered for a moment before replying. "I can think of no other excuse," she said, "than that of foolish pride." From that moment, I began to feel a new regard for Mrs. Hillier. It needed some courage to make an admission of the nature before her own children, and in front of me. We were very cheerful that evening (partly, I think, because we had resolved to keep each other's spirits up) and Miss Katherine, recalling a comment of mine when the letter from France was being read, sketched out a romantic episode in the life of the Quartermaster-Sergeant to take place after the war, with a wedding at St. Alphege's, and the bride offering a charming appearance in the latest confection from Dover Street. She suggested that business could be combined with sentiment if all the gifts were purchased at the bride's establishment in London Street.

"But I've never set eyes upon the man," I protested.

"The moment he sets eyes upon you, Weston," prophesied Miss Katherine, "his fate will be sealed."

"He may be married already."

"If he has, which I very much doubt, for he spoke of parents at Lewisham, but said nothing about a wife—if he has, I say, she is suffering from a nervous affection that will take her off in the nick of time."

"None of your widowers for me," I declared.

The affair of Miss Muriel's engagement was not settled so easily as we had hoped. She wrote expressing regret at the absence of definite news concerning her brother; she was also sorry to find that her mother had allowed herself to be impressed by occurrences which had no real bearing on plans agreed upon earlier. Her marriage was to take place on the twenty-seventh. Mr. Schloss had decided to set up a new home in the West of England: this, owing to prejudices which were being shown by folk of the neighbourhood who ought to know better, but were seemingly unwilling to listen to reasonable argument. Miss Muriel enclosed some verses of hers beginning, "True love knows no barriers."

My brother-in-law met with a slight accident whilst on the way to his work, and came home to London Street, depressed by the thought that he would be prevented for some time from assisting in munition tasks, discouraged by the knowledge that his wages would cease. I set him right on this second question by engaging him to look after the shop which he had once owned, and I gave Peter instructions to look after him and to see that he did not over-exert himself. Peter had joined the Boy Scouts, and had become such a dependable lad and so well spoken that Millwood announced he was prepared now for miracles of all sorts. (Peter's mother called one day at the shop and denounced me, up hill and down dale, on the grounds that I had marred and spoilt her views regarding the boy; she intended, it seemed, that he should follow the example of her two other children, and qualify himself for being sent by a magistrate to an Industrial School where the State would have accepted the responsibility of making a man of him. "And all my plans set aside," she lamented, "owing to your clumsy interference!") Millwood was glad to be able to go with the aid of a couple of sticks to his club again of an evening, although he complained that with Radicals and Tories working in hearty agreement over philanthropic matters, all the pepper and mustard had gone out of the institution. Millwood had given up alcoholic beverages for the duration of the war. "Really," he explained to me, confidentially, "I did that because I fancied it might please young 'Erb. I'd rather like the boy not to be ashamed of me."

It was near the end of the month that I went to town to see a customer, recommended to me by the doctor who set up the home of old furniture. He lived in North Street, behind the Abbey, and on the way back I looked in at Whitehall, and made inquiries. The officials there, although badgered by anxious folk, answered me politely. No news of Corporal Hillier. I returned from Charing Cross, where I happened to see William Richards.

"Hope on, hope ever!" said William, encouragingly.

I told myself in the train for Greenwich that I had come to the limits of my optimism, and that Master John was to be henceforth only a memory. I thought of his early days when I had first come into the Hillier establishment; thought of the pride we all took, later, over his first song; wondered whether there was perhaps some young girl, not known to us, who sorrowed for the loss of him. Crossing by the subway at Greenwich station, and coming up the steps I caught sight of Master Edward, on his way to late duty, and, to my pain and astonishment, dancing on the platform. His train came in before I could reach him, and give him a word of reproof.

At Gloucester Place, Mrs. Hillier waved gaily from the balcony; I assumed this was but a part of her new and improved method of conducting life. She disappeared, and a few minutes later came running—actually running—along to meet me.

"Sorry to say, ma'am," I remarked, "that I have no good news."

"But we have, Weston," she cried, exultantly. "The dear boy is safe. The dear boy is wounded, but he's alive. Come indoors, and see the card for yourself!"

It was a beautifully clean, white card, headed on the front "Field postkarte. Kriegsgefangenen—sendung," and endorsed "Geprüft pass zentrale, gouvernement—Lille." On the back the words, "Envoyez directement à la Famille." Underneath, the entries filled in with Master John's own handwriting.

"Je me trouve à.... Lille."

There followed Nom et prénoms, Regiment, Compagnie, Escadron. Then this message under the word Notices.

"Painfully wounded left leg, and rather weak."

I observed that, for the first time since the beginning of the war, Master John's mother had tears in her eyes.

CHAPTER VII

We all went slightly off our heads that evening at Gloucester Place. At first, there was a misapprehension on my side to be removed: I had forgotten that Lille was in the hands of the Germans, although the superscription of the card ought to have made this obvious; explanations made it clear to me now that Master John was a wounded prisoner, and that we should probably not see the dear lad again until the war finished. Master Edward, when he came home, was still so greatly excited that he omitted, for an hour, to tell us that he was about to be transferred to the head offices at London Bridge, where his hours would be fixed and regular, and escape effected from hot tempered and argumentative passengers. The recommending word of the superintendent's wife and his own engaging manner had to be thanked for the swift promotion. We regretted the absence of Miss Muriel; if she had been with us our party could have been reckoned complete.

"Really didn't think we should hear of him again," admitted Mr. Hillier. "With every desire to hope for the best, I had come to the conclusion John was lost to us."

"It will be something to tell the girls at the bank," mentioned Miss Katherine. "They have been inquiring every day, and they meant it well, I know, but it only seemed to remind me of—Anyhow," brightly, "the suspense is over. Let us be musical. We haven't lifted up our tuneful voices in song for a long time past."

"There's no piano," I remarked.

"Unaccompanied," directed Miss Katherine. "Edward, my laddie, if you have gone past the stage when you didn't know whether you were going to give out a high note or a low one, you make a start. Anything, except Tipperary."

We were joining in a chorus when a rap sounded at the door. I answered it, and, seeing the old lady and gentleman of the ground floor, assumed at once that they had come up to protest against the noise.

"Beg your pardon," said the elderly gentleman, "but—my wife and myself—we're rather quiet people."

"The singing shall be stopped at once, sir."

"By no means," he cried, urgently. "Pray do nothing of the sort. We are here to ask you if you would kindly leave your door open. Our sense of hearing is not so good as it was, and we want to learn the words of some of the popular songs of the day."

"Are you serious?" I asked, incredulously.

"Bless my soul, no," he chuckled. "We're not serious. We enjoy life. We're rather lonely, it's true, but apart from that you can look upon us as the most frivolous young couple this side of the river." He turned to his wife. "Always have been, haven't we, my sweet?"

"We married for love," whispered the old lady to me, nodding her head.

They had the appearance of people in fancy dress—she with ringlets and a lace cap, and a silk dress that, as my mother used to say of a remembered costume of the same quality, could have stood by itself, and he with large collar, black stock, heavy watch chain and fob, velvet jacket, shepherd's plaid trousers.

"Our compliments to your young folk," he said, with a bow, "and our apologies for interfering."

"You, like ourselves," she remarked, "are fortunate in having no relative engaged in this terrible war. Few have such cause to be thankful. We wish you good evening."

Mrs. Hillier came forward, and, breaking the rule which she had laid down regarding communication with neighbours, joined in the discussion, gave the news concerning Master John. The old gentleman, greatly interested, offered congratulations, and excusing himself, left his wife to go on with the talk. She with many antiquated protests—

"But I shall be discommoding you, I fear."

"I hope you will not look upon it in the light of an intrusion."

"Pray do not fail to tell me when to go."

Accepted the invitation to enter the sitting room, and giving a curtsey, felicitated Miss Katherine upon her singing, spoke of Madame Jenny Lind, Mario, Grisi, Sims Reeves. We were in the sixties, and forgetting all about the current year and its troubles, when she stopped suddenly. A jingling sound was heard from the landing.

"Do you mind," she said to me, "helping Captain Winterton? He is not quite so active in household duties as he used to be. I myself am just the same that I always was, but I perceive a change in him."

Captain Winterton had brought up a large silver tray that I coveted the moment I caught sight of it; the tray bore decanters of cut glass that would have looked well on the shelves at London Street; a cigar case had a flourished inscription announcing it was a testimonial from the passengers of sailing vessel *Magnitude*. The old gentleman wore now an embroidered smoking cap with a tassel.

"Sir," he said, giving up the tray to me, and addressing Mr. Hillier, "this is a great liberty, and no one knows it better than I do, but the circumstances must be held responsible. A few beverages, selected by me on my many travels, and I want you, sir, and the ladies, if they will be so good, to favour me with their opinion on them."

I went off to cut sandwiches. When I returned he was near the fire-place, making a speech. Old Mrs. Winterton beckoned to me. "Remarkably gifted," she whispered. "So much experience, you see, on board his ship. This is the only time I've heard him speak about the war." She laid a finger on her lips to enjoin perfect silence.

"—Goes off to fight for his country's welfare," Captain Winterton was saying, in the full enjoyment of oratory, "and fights, I'll be bound to say, like a gallant and determined Englishman. And although he appears to be now suffering from his honorable wounds, and is detached from his comrades, and his friends, I am sure he has the consolation of knowing that they are all thinking of him with affection and sincere regard, and looking forward to the joyful day when he shall again find himself among them. I drink to the elder son of this estimable family. I wish him a quick recovery, a safe and a glorious return."

I think Captain Winterton was slightly disappointed to find that he had succeeded in making no one cry but his wife: he assured Mrs. Hillier that in his happiest moments and his most successful efforts on the last day of a lengthy voyage, you might look around at the tables when he had spoken after dinner, and fail to discover a single dry eye.

"I may be out of practise," he suggested, wistfully. Mrs. Hillier assured him that she felt more touched by his remarks than she cared to show. He said that as time went on, one was bound to recognise alterations and differences; as to himself, he could perceive no great change in the last thirty years, but he feared Mrs. Winterton was exhibiting some of the marks of age.

"My sweet," to his wife, "we mustn't outstay our welcome."

"My dearest," she agreed, "there is your beauty sleep to be remembered."

"You are not going to hurry away like this," protested Mr. Hillier. "Recollect that we so rarely get visitors, nowadays."

Mrs. Winterton spoke of the period when she mixed in the best society that the neighbourhood afforded. Greenwich, she said proudly, was Greenwich in those times, and held up its head, bless you, and saw the aristocrats coming down to dine at the Ship; carriages arrived from London bringing the finest in the land, and the railway was still something like a novelty. Master Edward had seen at the head offices an aged picture of the earliest trains leaving London Bridge to the music of a band; the old lady said very precisely that this she had heard, but she had no personal knowledge of the occurrence, and Captain Winterton rallied her good-temperedly on the question of her age. "My sweet likes to be thought," he remarked to us, "as on the sunny side of eighty, but I can remember that when I first met her she called herself seventeen, and that was in the year of the great Exhibition in Hyde Park, and I could tell you what she wore at the time. She'd got on the prettiest little poke bonnet—you don't see anything so attractive in these days, if this young lady here will forgive me for saying so—a full flounced skirt and a waist so small that I could nearly go twice around it with my arm—" Mrs. Winterton took her husband off, and returned for the tray, and to explain that her husband's memory was failing, especially in regard to dates.

A few weeks earlier, and Mrs. Hillier would have resented the call from the elderly pair of the ground floor; now, she made friends with them, running down sometimes to have a chat with old Mrs. Winterton, and delighted when the Captain made a visit, bringing daffodils, "With respectful inquiries, ma'am, and hoping you continue to have good news of your boy." The best service they did to my mistress was in taking her mind from the war. It seemed that they were too advanced in years to give their mind to events of the day, however important and enormous these might be; they lived in the past, and to them we were all nothing but children with memories covering a brief period only. To Miss Katherine they became specially attached, although Mrs. Winterton could not approve of the idea of a girl engaging herself in commercial affairs; she spoke with pride of the days when no young women of good position had any other prospect or hope but that of marriage. To me, she confided a secret which I was not to disclose to a soul, or ask whence the information had been obtained; it was that on the day that the first woman was entrusted with, and exercised, the power of voting, on that day the world would undoubtedly come to an end.

"A great pity, of course," she said, nodding her ringlets and dismissing the topic, "but it can't be helped, and there you are, and that's all about it!"

Miss Katherine followed Master Edward's success by gaining a transfer to the correspondence office, where figures were less intrusive, and the work more varied. The weekly income at Gloucester Place was now as follows:

Mr. Hillier	£1 17 6
Miss Katherine	1 10 0
Master Edward	15 0

We were able to settle up tradesmen's books promptly; there was some talk of a holiday to be taken, months later on, but economy had to be observed, and one of the improvements in Mrs. Hillier was noticeable in the fact that she now heartily supported my efforts in this direction. No more cards arrived from Master John. We wrote to him regularly to the care of the Information Bureau at Berlin, taking pains to give nothing but domestic news, and we hoped he was receiving these communications. At the Post Office I was told it would be useless to send parcels until he came out of the hospital; I was also assured it was unnecessary to do so, and from other quarters we gained that the hardships over there did not begin until the wounded men were away from medical treatment. Herbert sent me a cheery letter saying that he was back in the trenches, and mentioning that there was a chance that he might get his third stripe. Answering my question, he said that he knew Quartermaster-Sergeant Cartwright, and described him as a chap who thought a good deal of himself. My own estimation of Cartwright was not diminished by this, and I began to forward *Punch* to him each week, and the Quartermaster-Sergeant occasionally sent me one of the printed cards with everything crossed out excepting the line,

"I am quite well."

And

"Letter follows at first opportunity."

By asking Herbert what Cartwright was like, I meant that I wanted a description of his appearance. In the absence of particulars, this had to be left to the imagination. Miss Katherine pictured him as a tall man, florid and stout, with an enormous moustache, and using language at which she could but hint.

"Dismiss this particular romance from your thoughts, dear Weston," she counselled. "Concentrate your mind, instead, upon your railway guard."

"You and your nonsense!" I exclaimed. "There's precious little chance of me getting married to William Richards or to anyone else. My opportunities never have been great, and now they are less than ever. And it doesn't matter so much, for some of us, but I do feel sorry, when I look at the casualty lists each morning, for young ladies like yourself. Luckily, in your case, there is no one out there that you're especially fond of."

Miss Katherine said something in regard to the latest fashions. Hearts, she mentioned, were no longer worn upon sleeves.

There were several matters, and many views, and some fears, in those days which we kept from each other; the young people had long since given up at Gloucester Place the old habit of reciting dreams at the breakfast table. In my own case, I found that, awaking at three o'clock in the night, it was possible to consider the most dismal and gloomy aspect of everything. At that hour, all the good news was forgotten, and nothing but disaster could be anticipated. By day, there was generally some encouraging placard to be seen, and the announcement given, though not always based on fact, was undeniably cheering. ("Only two forts left in the Dardanelles," was one of these, I remember.) But in the small hours, Dreadnoughts were sunk by the dozen, U boats were doing as they pleased, German forces again came near to Paris; the enemy's navy was steaming up the Thames, and bombarding the college at Greenwich; my nephew Herbert had been killed by a hand grenade, and Master John was being kicked and starved. When these pleasing incidents ceased to dance about in my brain, there was always the business in London Street to offer a possibility of disaster. The number of times that, in my imagination, I saw the name of Mary Weston, spinster, figuring amongst the names in the list of receiving orders from the London Gazette, cannot be reckoned.

Water carts came out, and the green chairs were set in Greenwich Park, spring flowers made their bow, Gloucester Place brightened itself, children at the L.C.C. schools behind The Circus played their games more shrilly, and the river took on a cheerful air that had been absent throughout the winter. My brother-in-law Millwood, at the shop, complained that Peter's industry left him with no scope for exercise of the mind or body, and I sent him, with his walking stick, on a hobbling tour around the neighbourhood, and invested him with a task which I described precisely. He was to make a list, in no case was the sum to be higher than ten pounds, and in most instances the amount was to be less. Then I inserted an advertisement in a Woolwich journal that had a circulation amongst the Arsenal workers; a well displayed advertisement with a note to the effect that it would not appear again. The Chance of a Lifetime, it was headed, and it announced that Weston's had been fortunate enough to secure some Magnificent Bargains in the shape of Second Hand Pianofortes by Well Known Makers. Satisfaction Guaranteed. Do not Delay. A Rare Opportunity for Lovers of Music.

I have no wish to exaggerate the results of this notice, but I can say with truth that Millwood, and young Peter, and myself, had a busy time. There was plenty of money being earned in Woolwich, and all of it did not go in wastefulness, as some folk suggested: there were many families where the desire was to improve the interior of households. We became a sort of clearing house for pianofortes, exchanging them from establishments affected adversely by the war, and passing them on, by pantechnicon vans, to those where incomes had been improved. I remember an Arsenal man and his wife and young daughter called one day to make a purchase: they examined the cases only, and made no attempt to try the keyboard. They were puzzled which to buy of two that seemed to them equally attractive.

"Look 'ere, old gel," he said, at last to his wife. "One will look rather lonely. We'll take both." And this they did, paying the money down.

There was one attractive baby grand that Millwood picked up at rather above the limit fixed, and I arranged to have it delivered at Gloucester Place. It arrived there just as daylight was going, at seven o'clock. Miss Katherine had received but few tokens to call attention to her birthday, and one could not help guessing that she might be comparing it with previous anniversaries. A welcome card had come from Master John; she declared that this, in itself, was the best present any one could require. "Still in hospital," he wrote. "Leg progressing slowly. Am fairly cheerful."

The men with the van had done so much work on my account that they tackled the difficulties of the job in a determined and breezy way; they reached the landing of the first floor watched by the old Captain, who gave advice in seafaring terms that they did not pretend to understand. Miss Katherine came out.

"Weston, my child," she exclaimed, "they will never manage to get that beautiful instrument up to your rooms."

"They'd better not try, miss. It's for you, wishing you, with all my heart, many happy years."

"But," she stammered, taken aback, "you really mustn't, you know, do extravagant actions like this, dear soul, in war times."

"There's no one, Miss Katherine, in a position to dictate to me how I shall spend my money." She tried to conceal her emotion by making some reference to the Quartermaster-Sergeant.

There could be no doubt that the new pianoforte—new to the Hilliers, anyway—did manage to cheer and brighten up the establishment. Now that Miss Katherine and Master Edward were exempt from the direction of music teachers, they practised and played of their own will instead of being driven to the keyboard. The family began to talk of other additions in the way of furniture, to be exhibited as a surprise and a gratification to Master John when he returned. Mrs. Hillier admitted to me that she was becoming as house-proud as she had been in the early days of her married life.

And into the comfortable group suddenly arrived Miss Muriel. Miss Muriel, fresh from the large house of her friends at Chislehurst, and losing no time in complaining of the want of room at Gloucester Place, of Weston's position of equality at table, of her father's appearance when he returned from the Arsenal, and indeed of everything that lent itself to criticism. She was allowed a free tongue at first, but when she returned to the grievance that concerned me, her mother interposed. Miss Muriel followed me out of the room, and offered a kind of defiant apology.

"What's wrong, miss?" I inquired. "You were always rather difficult, but I should have thought that this war—"

"I am under no obligation to the war."

"Few of us are, but we can't help being influenced by it. People who, before it started, had good expectations, find themselves with none, and folk who used to be on their beam ends, so to speak, are now doing well. It's all according to whether a person is of any real use, or not."

"I can't pretend," said Miss Muriel, "to be greatly interested in the fortune of others. To compensate for that, I am enormously interested in my own."

"We are all hoping, miss, that your engagement has been cancelled."

"An amiable wish," she retorted, "that has been anticipated by events. Mr. Schloss is interned. Interned by the astonishing authorities of this country."

"Very glad to hear it," I said, genuinely. "And now that you are amongst us again, I trust you'll make yourself as amiable as possible, and we, on our side, will try to recognise that it's hard on you, miss, to have been disappointed in love."

"Not disappointed in love, Weston. Disappointed in money would be a more correct phrase."

"Upon my word!" I exclaimed warmly. "I can't make it out at all. I'm sometimes inclined to look on you as a bit of a freak."

"At last," said Miss Muriel, "I have achieved a notable success. I have contrived to make our Weston really angry. No one can say now that I have lived in vain."

The others, as has been hinted, had adopted the habit of looking after themselves, but Miss Muriel exacted from me all the attention to which she had a right in the old days. I found myself doing lady's maid work. She did not do a hand's stroke in any of the domestic tasks. She bewailed the circumstance that her friends at Chislehurst, answering her appeal, wrote that they regretted it was impossible to offer a fresh invitation; I pointed out to Miss Muriel that it was always an error in tactics to remain at people's house for an undue length of time. In her trunk, I found a packet, carefully sealed, and I put a question regarding the contents; she recommended that I should mind my own business. Later, she mentioned that the parcel held documents which she believed were of high importance, and asked whether at London Street there happened to be a fire-proof safe.

"I can get one," I said. "Been thinking about purchasing one for some while past. After our experience at The Croft, we can't be too careful."

"Take charge of the packet now, Weston," she begged. "The responsibility will be off my mind."

"Do I understand that you don't actually know what is inside?"

"I can trust you," she said, after a moment's pause. "You are queer, but you are reliable. Mr. Schloss gave this to me just before the police called on him. I promised to look after it until all the trouble was over. And that cannot be long now."

I bought a good second-hand safe, and Peter took a leather, and polished up the brass handle, and the cover of the lock; set in a corner of the shop it would give a solid, business-like look calculated to impress people who came to inspect furniture. Whilst the lad was engaged on the work, my attention was taken by a group from Charlton who had called to see about a pianoforte; the woman who desired to buy had brought with her half a dozen experts made up of female relatives and neighbours. When they had gone, I turned and found Millwood and Peter endeavouring to move the heavy safe to the place chosen for it.

"Mind that packet on the floor!" I cried.

The safe, in moving, crunched over the parcel entrusted to me by Miss Muriel, smashing the seals. I contrived to make the two understand what I thought of such clumsy behaviour; Peter offered to obtain a stick of wax from the shop not far off, and declared confidence in his ability to repair the damage. Millwood said it was a good job the parcel contained nothing of a breakable nature.

It was sheer curiosity that induced me to look at the papers inside; I found little to repay me, for the letters were all written in a language I did not understand. Millwood was prepared to take his oath that the language was German.

"You'd best be careful, Mary Weston," he said. "You mind out what you're a doing of. Otherwise you'll find yourself at the Tower. They don't make no bones about shooting nobody, not nowadays, they don't!" Millwood was giving more advice, when William Richards looked in. The two men never liked each other; in earlier days they always wrangled on political subjects, and now, in view of the truce agreed upon regarding these topics, Millwood, with the comment of "Hullo! Not dead yet, then?" went into the back room.

William Richards wanted news of Herbert, and of Master John. He hoped the Germans would deal with Master John fairly, but admitted he could not trust them in this or in any other particular. When we had discussed the subject, I told him about the parcel, submitted the documents. William shook his head gravely. "If only Dickenson was here!" he said. It appeared that Dickenson was a uniformed interpreter, known to William, and for the number of languages with which Dickenson was acquainted you needed the fingers of both hands, and the thumbs as well.

"Look here, Mary Weston," he said. "Hand 'em over to me. Just as they are. You shan't be dragged into the affair. I shall tell Dickenson I found the parcel on the floor of a second-class smoking. If they're nothing more than love letters, or business communications, you shall have 'em back!" Peter arrived with the sealing wax, but we decided that the present condition of the parcel should remain.

Mr. Schloss was tried a few weeks later on a charge of attempting to deal with the enemy, and he received a sentence of twelve months hard labour. Miss Muriel, terrified and penitent, begged me to destroy the parcel she had confided to my care, lest the contents should have any bearing on the matter, and, in promising her that she might depend upon me, I gave her about the straightest talking to that she had ever received in the whole course of her existence.

"It will be a lesson to me," she declared penitently.

"But some of you," I remarked, "want such a lot of teaching!"

Old Captain Winterton, in his determination not to discuss war news, fell back on reminiscences, and if he sometimes told these more than once, the Hillier family nevertheless gave him their attention; although he talked in an elaborate manner, they made no attempt to interrupt. I could not help comparing their Greenwich methods with those adopted at Chislehurst. He had three anecdotes and to these his wife listened eagerly and expectantly, sometimes whispering to me, after the twentieth or so repetition,

"You'll like this, Miss Weston."

And.

"This is new to you, I expect."

She joined in the expressions of amusement with great heartiness. The first story was of the lady who feared that if the storm continued she might find herself in Heaven, and wanted to be re-assured. ("Depends on the life you've led, madam.") The second was of the sailor who reported that Jim Bates had been blown overboard. ("And that ain't the worst, cap'en. He's took my pail with him!") The third was so long and so much involved, and required such an amount of preliminary description that the old fellow never reached the point of it, and we, at times, wondered if any point existed. I liked him best when he described Greenwich, at Easter, in the old days at the period when Richardson's Fair was held at the end of what is still known as Tea-pot Row, although its proper name is King William Street, and all the tag, rag and bob-tail came from far and near, and to carry a watch in one's pocket was to make a present of it to somebody with light fingers, and the taverns did a roaring trade; all this, it appeared, came to an end in '57. Of the time when London folk drove down in hackney coaches, and the men wore veils to their white top hats, and the ladies wore crinolines, and they had joyous hours at the Ship or the Trafalgar, and gave incredible tips to waiters, and started for home singing "Slap bang, here we are again!" Of more demure parties of statesmen who came, once a year, by steamer, from near to Westminster Bridge, and were reported to chat over the table of other matters than Cabinet secrets, and to consume quantities of old port, and, at any rate, returned in a sleepy condition, ignoring the cheers raised by their local supporters, and the groans given by their opponents. Of crime connected with the borough—

"Love," interposed Mrs. Winterton, "be careful not to shock the young ladies!"

"I will be most cautious, sweet!"

And, in particular, of one Charles Peace whose real name, it seemed, was John Warne, and who on a night in October shot three times at Constable Robinson in an avenue leading from St. John's Park to Blackheath; shot with a revolver that was strapped around Peace's wrist. Captain Winterton had learnt, word for word, the statement made by Peace when Mr. Justice Hawkins asked him whether he had anything to say why sentence should not be passed upon him, and the old chap spared us nothing of this, from—

"I have not been fairly dealt with, and I declare before God that I never had any intention to kill the prosecutor—" to "So, my Lord, have mercy upon me; my lord, have mercy upon me!" Peace lived for a time at Greenwich, in a well-furnished house where he sometimes gave musical evenings.

"I always give myself the satisfaction," said Captain Winterton, with relish, "of gazing at the dwelling whenever I happen to pass that way."

If he began to tell the story of the murder of Jane Maria Clousen— discussed and debated at Greenwich to this hour, because no one was hanged for it—Mrs. Winterton placed hands over her ears. Miss Clousen it seemed was, in '71, a domestic servant in the employment of a Greenwich printer; she was found in Kidbrooke Lane, Eltham, on the edge of death, murmuring, "Oh my poor head, oh my poor head!" and the acquittal of a young man, charged with the crime, was followed by noisy and disorderly gatherings outside his father's house, and proceedings at law for libel.

Captain Winterton had, too, political reminiscences of the borough, and of the time when it was notably represented in Parliament, and we had excerpts from Mr. Gladstone's speech on Blackheath, and from Mr. Gladstone's farewell address at the Ship Hotel, and a description of the wonderful moment when Mr. Gladstone said to Captain Winterton, "And what, pray, is your view in regard to the future of our mercantile marine?" and did not wait for an answer, but instead furnished his own opinions on the subject. And we listened (none so eagerly or so absorbedly as Mrs. Winterton) to the Captain's account of the *Princess Alice* disaster of '78 at Becton Reach near Woolwich, and in the technical details—was the *Bywell Castle* to blame, or did the *Princess Alice* starboard her helm, when she ought to have done something else?—in all this, I found myself at first bewildered, then semi-detached, and finally my thoughts went to London Street, and prices of the articles of furniture stored there.

CHAPTER VIII

I should, perhaps, have given more attention to the case of Miss Muriel, but for the demands upon my time made by the business: it appeared that many of my Woolwich customers were well satisfied with their dealings with me, and they handed my cards around, with the result that the shop was rarely free of callers, and sometimes Millwood, and Peter, and myself would be all engaged in answering questions, quoting figures. Once the visitors had made up their minds that they wanted a certain article—a cheval glass, a sideboard, a card table, or anything else—there was little haggling about price: from a well-filled purse they produced one pound notes and ten shilling notes, and settled the account; their chief difficulty came in an urgent and feverish desire to get the articles of furniture home with the least possible delay. I once saw two women, customers of mine, who had bought a music stool, and a settee, and a brass fender with fire-irons, endeavouring to board a tram-car with the burden of these possessions. They told the conductor, after argument, that he would undoubtedly come to a bad end.

Apart from the business, I had some anxiety caused by a letter from the Quartermaster-Sergeant. Written, as usual, in pencil, and mentioning, as always, that he was in the pink, it said that he hoped to be coming home on leave soon; his first call would be given to his parents, and he then proposed to look in at Gloucester Place and thank me for the journals sent to him each week. I wished the man further. I felt sorry I had ever hit upon the idea of posting the illustrated newspaper, or of writing. I had some thought to going away to escape him, but one did not know where to go. The postscript to the letter offered some hope: it said that leave was a doubtful thing in these days, and I was not to be disappointed if it happened that he could not get away. And I was beginning to think I had worried myself over nothing at all, when a telegram signed Cartwright came from Folkestone. I showed it to Miss Katherine.

"But, my dear soul," she protested, "you're trembling. In your own words, you're all of a fluster."

"The mistake I made was in not telling him my age at the outset."

"That would have been an eccentric course to pursue. It is one that I, myself, rarely adopt in these situations."

"You're young, Miss Katherine, and it doesn't matter what they imagine your age to be. I'm getting on towards the forties, and it matters a good deal to me. I've always tried to write to this blessed man in a cheerful style, and if he has got the idea that I'm twenty-two, and look less, one can't blame him."

"There are beauty specialists in Bond Street."

"And there are foolish women who patronise them."

"If he comes along," said Miss Katherine, "when I am home from the bank, I could—pardon the conceit in the suggestion, for which I am sure Heaven will forgive me—I could pretend to be you, Weston."

"That wouldn't do at all," I declared promptly. "I want to see him. Want to find out what he is like."

"The next best idea that occurs to my inventive brain," she remarked, "is that I should take you in hand to-morrow morning before I leave, and by all the dodges known to my toilet table, subtract a few years from your appearance."

"No making up," I bargained.

"I will do nothing," she agreed, "to bring the artificial blush to your cheek, dear woman. The game we are going to play is, believe me, not rouge et noir."

Compliments have sometimes been offered to me on the length and the colour of my hair, but they mostly came from maids at Chislehurst who wanted the afternoon off to go and meet their sweethearts; for the rest, people troubled very little about my looks, and I suppose I had not paid an extravagant amount of attention to them. Certainly Miss Katherine, when she assumed management and command, did effect some notable improvements. She persuaded me not to look in the mirror whilst the task was in progress, and when I was allowed to take a glance, I gasped with astonishment, beamed with satisfaction.

"That's it!" cried Miss Katherine. "That's exactly the right kind of smile we want. Ah," regretfully, "it's slipping. And now it's gone!" She imitated the tricks of the photographer when he is taking portraits of defensive babies; I assured her the ability to grin was not in my line. "Practise, Weston dear," she counselled. "Remember that with hair like yours you need never say dye."

Miss Muriel offered no remark upon the alteration, but Mrs. Hillier gave compliments, and declared she was reminded of the time when we first met;

she advised me not to mar the effect by wearing one of the hats I usually pinned on before leaving the house. Noticing that I wavered, she insisted on accompanying me to a milliner's establishment near the Chatham and Dover station. When, later, I entered the shop in London Street, Millwood came forward, without first putting on his spectacles, and not recognising me, said:

"Well, lady, and what can we do for you this morning?"

Subsequently, he delivered a lecture on the impossibility of regarding women-folk as anything like sensible beings so long as they devoted nearly all their time, and the whole of their thoughts, to fashion. "You don't find me spending money, and going to shops, and fussing about, just in order to make myself better looking than I really am." I answered that, more than once, I had been tempted to call his attention to the fact.

Quartermaster-Sergeant Cartwright dashed in soon after mid-day. He had called, it seemed, at Gloucester Place, and had been sent on to London Street.

"A flying visit," he announced to Peter. I was in the back room, looking once more at my reflection in the mirror. "Tell the lady to hurry up. Only five days leave, and a thousand and one urgent matters to see to. Mention that I'm pressed for time, will you."

He was tall, broad, and middle-aged; very smartly set up, and with, apart from his quick deportment, the air of a man accustomed to give orders, and expecting them to be obeyed. This I gained from the first sight of him over the curtained glass of the door.

"Miss—Miss Weston, I believe," he stammered.

"Quartermaster-Sergeant Cartwright, I think." We shook hands.

"You'll excuse me," he said, confusedly. "I'm rather taken aback. I had the notion—forgive me for saying so—that you were somewhat older than—. What I mean to say is—"

"I am old enough," I said, "not to tell you how old I am. This is my brother-in-law, Mr. Millwood. This is my assistant, Peter. What do you think of the shop?"

"Fine," he declared, with enthusiasm. "A1. Top hole. First class. Anyone can see, with half an eye, that you've got good taste. You know what to select, you do."

"I may point out," chuckled Millwood, "in regard to Mary Weston that no one has yet taken the trouble to select her." He looked around for approval of this remark. Nobody laughed.

"Oversights will happen in this world," said the visitor. "We find them even out in France."

"In my view," contended Millwood, "this war isn't being conducted in the manner that it ought to be carried on. Blunders have been made which seem to me most 'ighly reprehensible. Mistakes occur which ought to have been foreseen."

"I can tell you the reason," said the Quartermaster-Sergeant. "The reason is a very simple one. It's mainly because you are not out there. And now," to me, briskly, "what about lunch? Can you spare half an hour to come and have something to eat with me?"

"I can spare an hour and a half," I answered, "to take you along to the Ship, and get you to take a meal with me."

"But my motive for calling on you was to repay you in some measure for—"

"You're wasting your breath," interposed Millwood. "I've knowed her longer than what you have, and I can tell you, in strict confidence, that when Mary Weston has made up her mind, dynamite by the ton won't move her."

We walked towards the riverside, and the Quartermaster-Sergeant congratulated me on the fact that I was one of the few women he had met who could keep in step with him; he called my attention in Nelson Street to the difficulty encountered by tall soldiers who walked with short girls, and never succeeded in coming to an agreement concerning gait. Cartwright was a shade taller than myself, but I noticed, by the reflection in shop windows that my new hat made us appear to be of almost equal stature; two women, near the entrance to the market, gazed at us and said in duet, "Them's a fine-made couple, and no mistake."

It is not for me to dictate or advise other members of my sex who may find themselves in like circumstances, but I do feel sure, in looking back, that I did the wise thing in providing Cartwright with a good meal, and one served up in environments calculated to impress him. He had some doubts whether a N.C.O. would be allowed to enter the dining room; I interrogated the head waiter who said, re-assuringly, that, bless his heart, all the old nonsense had long since been dismissed; he pointed out a couple of brothers seated at a corner table, one a Staff Officer and the other a Private in the H.A.C. So I piloted Cartwright to chairs near the window where we faced each other, and could gain a view of the river with its bend towards Woolwich, and there gave orders in a manner intended to show composure, and no doubt exaggerated into sharp authority.

"I can see with half an eye," said Cartwright, admiringly when he had placed his cap on a hat peg, "that you're well used to this sort of thing. I'm not. I'm new to it. And if I make any blunders, you must just give me a quiet reminder to think of what I am doing."

"Providing you don't think of what you're doing," I declared, "you won't find the leastest trouble. For my part, I wish I knew what to call you. I can't say 'Mister' to a soldier, and Quartermaster-Sergeant seems such a mouthful."

"What about calling me 'George?'"

He discovered, half-way through the meal, that our first names were those of the King and the Queen, and we pretended that we lived at Buckingham Palace, and talked of giving a few days to Sandringham. The boy waiter, attending upon us, dropped a plate to the floor on hearing us speak of our eldest son, the Prince, and the fine work he was doing out in France; he later induced some of his colleagues, relieved from distant tables, to come and listen, whereupon we spoke of ordinary matters, such as increase in the price of vegetables, and reductions in the motor omnibus service, and an Aunt Maria at Stepney; our juvenile waiter was told by his elders that over clever kids who tried to play practical jokes invariably obtained, sooner or later, the reward of a thick ear.

"'Pon my word, though," declared Cartwright, "this is an experience for me. First in regard—if you don't mind me saying so—to a lady's society, and whilst I am on that topic, I may as well admit that I feel as though I had known you all my life."

"I feel that I wish I had known you all my life."

"Very nicely phrased," he said, approvingly. "Second, in regard to taking plenty of time over a meal, and having it served up politely instead of being flung at you. People can say what they like," contended the Quartermaster-Sergeant, earnestly, "but comfort isn't a thing to be despised. Out there, all these months, I've dreamt over and over again, in my waking hours, of a nice little house, Forest Hill way, and a nice little garden with scarlet runners growing near the nice little wooden palings, and a nice little wife—"

"Your ambitions appear to be on a small scale."

"Don't misunderstand me," he begged. "I don't mean she's got to be a dwarf. My idea has always been someone about your own height." He helped himself, with some confusion to enough mustard to serve a regiment. "Tell me if I'm talking too much," he begged. "I get so much into the habit of laying down the law that I'm inclined to forget myself."

"That doesn't matter," I remarked, "so long as you don't forget me." I declare I said this only for the sake of keeping the conversation going: he put his large hand across the table impetuously, and gripped mine.

"Don't you ever keep awake at nights," he said, "worrying about that. I shall recollect this day that we're having together when everything else has vanished from my memory."

I think we both recognised that we were travelling faster than the rules permit; for the remainder of the lunch we were more guarded in speech. He talked about his father and mother, and I made some allusions to the Hillier family. It seemed he had the notion that I was a friend and an equal: he assured me Master John had once spoken of me in a way to support this, and one could not help feeling it was good of the lad to convey the impression. George Cartwright had a cigar, recommended by the head waiter as of a brand smoked by all the nobs, and I followed the head waiter out of the room, and settled the bill. The head waiter said, with great heartiness, "Thank you, miss; thank you very much indeed. Wish there was more like you!"

I expected—or feared—that George Cartwright would want to hurry off. Mentioning that his latest recollection of Greenwich Park was connected with a Sunday School treat—

"Lord!" he said, setting his cap at the mirror, "but I've learnt a bit since those days. And most of it wasn't worth the learning!"

He suggested that the afternoon was fine enough to excuse a stroll up the hill to the Observatory. We walked first along the narrow pavement near the river, came to the old Trafalgar Hotel, now an Aged Merchant Seamen's Institution, and Cartwright, by request, gave to the old chaps standing outside, the latest news of the war. Then we strolled towards the Park.

I may as well admit that I had never before enjoyed a stroll so much. It seems a foolish thing for a woman of my years to say, but for the time the business in London Street mattered nothing, the Hilliers at Gloucester Place mattered little. One of my customers met us near the gates of the Park, and rushed at me with an inquiry concerning a Bible box; I sent her off with a direction to call and see Millwood. At the top of the hill, and near the edge where green chairs were placed, we found the elderly couple of the ground floor in Gloucester Place; they were seated there holding each other's hands, and gazing down contentedly at children tumbling about on the slope.

"Miss Weston," said the old gentleman, rising, and saluting with a sweep of his curly brimmed hat, "it needed only your presence to make the afternoon entirely charming. Pray do me the honour to introduce me to your military friend."

I had no reason to be ashamed of the Quartermaster-Sergeant. Some men, in his position, and after a good lunch, might have felt inclined to ridicule the Wintertons; they looked as though they had emerged from past centuries or stepped from a mantelpiece, and, indeed, they ware not exempted from comments and criticism of frivolous young people who went by. But Cartwright listened to Captain Winterton's explanation of the windings of the river, drawn on the gravel with the point of a malacca cane, was deferential to the old lady when she spoke of the highly cultivated society in which she had mixed during early years. She was careful to make no errors in the various branches of any genealogical tree.

"The Admiral," she said, in her precise and leisured way, "perhaps neither of you knew; he was long before your time. But his eldest daughter whom you may have met, she, as I need scarcely say, was a most highly accomplished young woman, playing the harp divinely, and singing 'Juanita' in a manner that caused sensitive hearers to swoon away. She married a Mr. Todhunter, a most humorous gentleman who used to make really wonderful puns, and afterwards took to drink. She, as you are doubtless aware, removed to New Cross, and gave music lessons. The second daughter, whilst less gifted in music, had a passion for making woolwork slippers that you seldom encounter nowadays. Everyone said that she was going to marry a bachelor clergyman of the neighbourhood, but she ran off with her father's coachman. It chanced that I heard some of the Admiral's remarks upon this lamentable occurrence, but not all, because my dear mother intervened and—You didn't have the privilege of knowing my dear mother, Miss Weston, but it will be a delight, some fine day, to shew you her tombstone."

"My love," said Captain Winterton, solicitously.

"My sweet."

"Think of your throat," he begged.

"I was about," remarked the old lady, "to turn up the collar of your overcoat. We are not yet favoured with the balmy weather associated with spring. The Quartermaster-Sergeant," she went on, beaming at Cartwright, "will recall the lines of Mr. Browning that contain an allusion to the present month."

Cartwright jerked his head knowingly, and remarked that poetry was very stimulating if you were but careful not to take too much of it at a time.

"My love!" said the Captain, with deference, "Do you think, in all the circumstances—April afternoon, a highly intellectual audience, and the surroundings of youth—that you could manage to recite your set of verses?"

The old lady protested modestly. She had written them, it appeared, in the early sixties, and she argued that fashions in poetry changed as in everything else. We insisted, and she gave, with gesture and a rapt expression, some lines about trees and bees, and birds and words, and flowers and bowers; her husband listened eagerly with a hand at ear, and occasionally prompting her when memory failed. Cartwright and I ejaculated at the end, "Beautiful, beautiful!" and Captain Winterton said we might be interested to know that these verses were composed not many yards away, under an elm which had, most unfortunately, been blown down in the gale of '81. But he could shew us a still more interesting feature of the past in the shape of the oak that witnessed his proposal to the lady whom he now had the honour to call his wife. We had to see this, and as we left the elderly couple, we heard him say:

"My love, I never heard you give those lines with greater force and expression."

And she remarked:

"My dear, I hope we didn't bore the young people."

I took pains to assure the Quartermaster-Sergeant, in walking along the avenue, that the Wintertons were genuine in their admiration for each other, and he declared that, of this, he had no doubt. He seemed rather quiet, and I asked him what he was thinking of; he answered that it would be many days ere he managed to send the Wintertons out of his mind.

"What I mean to say is," he explained, "married all these long years, and always in each other's company, and still on friendly terms! Why, it's the greatest achievement that anyone can hope for." I remarked that the two might be looked upon as exceptions. "Granted," he said, taking my arm, "but why are they exceptions? There's no good reason why they should be exceptions. If they can do it, anybody can do it, and a happy old age ought to become the general rule."

"Perhaps hasty marriages are sometimes to blame."

"Ah!" releasing my arm. "Hadn't thought of that. I suppose it's pretty safe to assume that they are usually a mistake. Glad you reminded me."

I furnished other reasons, and spoke of the case of Miss Muriel, of my anxieties concerning the girl. It appeared to me that with her mercenary views there was, for her, but small prospect of happiness; the Quartermaster-

Sergeant agreed, but pointed out that in this world, and especially in stirring times like the present, you could never say for certain what was going to happen. He urged that I should not worry myself, overmuch, concerning other people. He said that whilst it was undoubtedly a mistake to concentrate thoughts too much on Number One, it was certainly possible to err in the opposite direction.

"Oh, but I'm a manager," I remarked. "That's my job in life."

"Doesn't follow that there isn't some one who could manage you."

"Explain yourself."

An interesting conversation might have taken place, but that a heated lad came up at this moment, cricket bat in hand, and begging Cartwright, as a man of years, and moreover possessing military authority, to come across the heath, and arbitrate on a nice point that had arisen. The Quartermaster-Sergeant complied at once. It seemed that the youth, sneaking a run, as he described it, found himself some yards from the stumps, and the ball coming to the gloved hands of the wicket-keeper; he thereupon, with great presence of mind, flung his bat, and this, it was agreed, reached the inside of the crease ere the bails were knocked off. Cartwright's decision was that the action, though ingenious, was not sufficient. In his view, the batsman and the bat had to be reckoned as inseparable.

"I s'pose, sir," remarked one of the players, "you couldn't stay on and umpire, could you? It'd mean a great saving of time."

"If I stay on," said the Quartermaster-Sergeant, loosening belt, and taking off tunic, "I take a more prominent share in the game. What about me playing for both sides?"

"Good old sort!" declared the youngsters.

"Mary," he begged, "fairest of thy sex, and more intelligent than most, look after that military property I've thrown down on the grass."

I should have preferred that we had gone on with our talk, but I knew enough about men to be aware that, with many, cricket comes ahead of everything else. Cartwright enjoyed himself. The ground was not too good, but he bowled well, and took wickets, and made catches, and when the lads found that he did not propose to take his turn with the bat, their admiration for him became frank and genuine. And I felt interested for a time to watch the boyish side of his nature, but only for a time, and I was not sorry when one of the keepers came along, and pointed out the date was not sufficiently advanced to make the playing of the game legal and permissible on open spaces. It looked as though our walk and our conversation could now be resumed, but the keeper had two sons out in Flanders and—well, people are very sarcastic at times about the way women-folk chatter, but when you get men discussing affairs, it is difficult to guess when they will stop, and not easy to find a method of arresting the debate. I strolled off, found the boys, and persuaded them to set up their wickets once more. Returning, I pointed out to the keeper that his authority was being derided. He hurried away.

"Thought you were never going to finish your cackle," I remarked to the Quartermaster-Sergeant. "What time do you want to be starting for home?"

"Tired of my company already?"

"Of course not. Only that there are your parents to be considered."

"For one day at least," he announced, "I'm going to consider myself. And you. We're going to a theatre together. A theatre up in town."

He went on first to choose a play, and arrange about seats; I called at London Street, where Millwood grumbled at my long absence, and mentioned that he had never before seen me with such a colour. "Makes you look like I don't know what!" he declared. "And mind you don't go getting yourself talked about, Mary Weston. Greenwich is a rare place for gossip."

As though I cared! As though any woman would have cared, with the prospect of going to a theatre, and sitting next to a soldier man, home on leave, after doing fine work for his country, and soon going out to do more!

I could tell you everything about the play, and could give you all the particulars of the dresses (I did furnish these details the next day, first to Peter at the shop, and afterwards to Miss Katherine at Gloucester Place). The incident worth recording here is that when my Quartermaster-Sergeant Cartwright saw me off at Charing Cross station that night by the eleven-thirty train, we shook hands through the open window of the railway carriage, and he promised to see me again before he went out. And, without saying "By your leave!" or "Hope you don't object!" or any remark of the kind, he, as the train moved out, kissed me.

CHAPTER IX

Millwood felt tremendously gratified because his example in regard to abstinence from alcohol was followed in high quarters, and he became from that moment, not only a supporter of royalty, but a man of ideas regarding the deportment of folk staying at home. He had a row one evening in a South-Eastern train with a stubborn passenger who argued that there was no sense in the order concerning the pulling down of blinds. He ordered a strict method of economy in London Street, and gave lectures on the subject to Peter who, endeavouring to pass them on to his own household at Deptford, found himself slapped by a mother who, a pronounced bungler and a most inefficient person, evidently considered she had nothing to learn in domestic management. I had to check Millwood when I found that to new customers he was in the habit of saying:

"Now, the question you've got to put yourself, is, not 'Can I afford to buy this?' but 'Can I manage to do without it?'"

He did work that met with greater approval from me, in addressing outdoor meetings during the special fortnight of recruiting. I happened to hear him speak at one of them. A military gentleman of the Colonel Edgington school stood up, and fiercely denounced the young men present who had not enlisted; they accepted his thundering attack with calm. A soldier who had been through Neuve Chapelle offered a grisly, and, no doubt, exact description of the fight; the youths shook their heads knowingly as though to indicate that they were far too wise to run any such risks. Then my brother-in-law stepped up and told an anecdote in his London accent: they began by laughing at him, and finished by laughing with him; he kept them amused—I had never before guessed that he had a sense of humour—for about eight minutes, and in the last two minutes of his speech, became forcible, strenuous, pathetic. He pointed to Greenwich Park—

"Where your mothers and fathers went sweet-hearting, my lads, years ago, and where you go sweet-hearting now, and I don't blame you!"

—And said we were at war that this might remain in our possession. He sent his arm out towards the river—

"Look at British commerce going up and down there, a-carrying food that keeps me and you from starving!"

He drew their attention to a double line of children going along under the control of an assistant mistress from one of the County Council schools—

"It's to protect dear little kiddies like them, my lads, that we ask you to become soldiers, and prevent the Germans from arriving here!"

Twenty young men walked up to the Recruiting Sergeant when Millwood ended his address: the band played "The Red, White and Blue," grown-up folk—and I was amongst them—gave signs of tears.

News of air raids did something to back up and support the arguments of my brother-in-law. The attacks came for the most part at night, and generally over the East coast, but an enemy's aeroplane appeared once, at mid-day, near Faversham in Kent. We were alarmed at Gloucester Place, because Miss Muriel—taking every advantage of any opportunity to get away from Greenwich, and from her people—had gone there to visit acquaintances and (as she told me frankly) in the hope of finding some eligible husband. A relative of the family, she added, a man who had gained a fortune in the United States, was shortly coming home for a holiday. Miss Muriel gave his name. I was curt with her, but when the news came about the attack over Faversham, I felt sorry I had been so outspoken. On discovering from the journals that no damage had been done, I wished I had been more candid and abrupt with her. But I sent her something for her birthday.

The *Lusitania* was sunk by an enemy's torpedo early in May, and it is referred to here because it had some effect upon a member of the Hillier family. In the absence of Miss Muriel, everything was going comfortably at Gloucester Place. It often happened that I was not called upon there to do any sort of work in the whole course of a day. Mrs. Hillier seemed to find a pleasure in carrying out the duties of the household during the week; on Sundays she and her husband took short trips together, either up the river, or out into the country, leaving me to look after Miss Katherine and Master Edward; an easy task.

Everybody can remember the afternoon that news of the sinking of the big liner arrived, and not many people will ever forget the manner in which the information reached them. I had been to a sale at Blackheath where the auctioneer's announcement suggested the possibility of finding bargains, and after giving a couple of hours to the big house, I found there was nothing that justified a nod of the head from me; the owner of the place had been taken in, right and left, and an agent of my acquaintance, in referring to him, and to their earlier dealings with each other, expressed regret that there were so few mugs of the kind left nowadays. I walked quickly across the heath to get rid of the annoyance created by the waste of time; the feeling had not disappeared as I went down the slope of Lewisham Hill. Outside the news-agent's shop at the foot was the staggering placard. Folk stood around gazing at it. One or two said hopefully that it was nothing but a catch-penny.

"Lot of use having a Press Bureau!" they remarked, with bitterness. "These papers are all out on the make, and, seemingly, it's no one's business to stop 'em."

The next morning, full confirmation arrived. The ship had been torpedoed off the western coast of Ireland. Many well known people were aboard, and as I glanced down the passenger list, one name struck me as being familiar, but, at the time I could not place it. Mrs. Hillier came, in great haste, to the shop, bringing a telegram from Faversham. "Is Muriel with you?" it said. I took charge of the task of sending the negative reply, and assured her there was no cause for anxiety; it probably meant some temporary confusion or misunderstanding that would be cleared up ere the day was out. But, being by no means so confident as my words, I rushed off directly that Mrs. Hillier had gone, taking my chance of trains, and finding myself lucky in this respect. I was at Faversham by two o'clock, and I caught the three-three back to Victoria. It was an express, and in view of the information I was taking home, I wished it had been a slow train.

"She left that house this morning," I informed Mrs. Hillier. "Here is the note she placed on the hall table. And you must try not to be upset about it, ma'am, because nearly everything comes right if you do but allow enough time."

"Read it, Weston," she begged, piteously. "Trouble seems to be all around us, and it has got into my bones, and into my eyes."

The slip of paper in Miss Muriel's handwriting had evidently been written in haste. It announced that she was tired of encountering disaster, and in no mood to receive condolences. "I am doing the vanishing trick. Explain to my people. Tell Weston not to make a fuss."

All the particulars gained from the girl's friends, I supplied to Mrs. Hillier. The nephew of the family, whose name and fortune had been mentioned by Miss Muriel, had taken a berth on the *Lusitania* at New York; he wrote beforehand to say that his aunt's allusion to Miss Hillier's impending visit induced him to accelerate his voyage home. American girls, he added, were too independent. Although he had become naturalised in the United States he was sufficiently English to recognise this. He held pleasant memories of Miss Hillier, and trusted she had not forgotten him. The lady at Faversham—she seemed to be one of the few remaining experts in match-making, and her disappointment at the upset of her plans was even keener than her sorrow at the loss of a nephew—assured me Miss Muriel had taken an enthusiastic share in the preparations for his arrival; had composed an affectionate and welcoming telegram to be sent by the family to Liverpool; had assured the aunt that a good marriage was the one piece of fortune she particularly desired. "A sweet, ingenuous, simple nature," the aunt remarked to me, with emotion. "The very child for a romantic episode. Really she might have stepped out of a novel." I could not help thinking that our Miss Muriel had surely worked hard and industriously in order to succeed in conveying this impression.

"Had the dear girl any money with her?" inquired Mrs. Hillier anxiously. "You didn't remember to find out."

"I found out everything there was to be discovered, ma'am. She had a postal order for ten shillings which her father had sent her for her birthday."

"And that was all?"

"And one for two pounds that I sent her on the same occasion. She changed them this morning at the local post office. At the station, they could give me no particulars; she was not known by sight to any of the officials there. The local police are going to make inquiries. On the way from Victoria just now, I put an advertisement into the newspaper she was most likely to see, asking her to communicate with me."

"I might have guessed," said Mrs. Hillier, gratefully, "that you would do all that was possible. But she is a queer child, and I wish I could tell what is likely to happen to her."

It was just because Miss Muriel had always behaved differently from anyone else that I felt anxious. All the same, I declared to Mrs. Hillier that it was impossible to share her fears; I spoke of Miss Muriel as a rather spoilt young lady who would very quickly resent the discomforts she encountered, and, the two pounds ten gone, we might expect her to ring the bell at Gloucester Place, and demand to be fussed over, and treated as though she had acted courageously and with shrewd common sense. There was no music from the pianoforte that evening. I went up to my rooms, at the top of the house, as early as convenient, leaving a thoughtful family group to discuss the matter. To detach myself from worry, I wrote a long letter to Quartermaster-Sergeant Cartwright. In his last pencilled note, he had explained that his father, taken ill on the second day of Cartwright's leave, required his attention during the rest of the time, and he seemed to hint that I might have some excuse for feeling annoyed at not seeing him again. My letter was calculated to re-assure him. I asked for the address of his people, and promised, when this came, to call and see them. It can be added that the part of Cartwright's note which gratified me the most came at the end where three crosses had been drawn, small enough to be over-looked unless one was searching for them.

My intention was to give my full time to the job of discovering Miss Muriel. The advertisement appeared, and in answer to it, I received a card from her, postmarked London, N.W., bearing nothing more than three words—

"Quite all right!"

—And I should have made an effort to search the postal district indicated—although, as I knew, it included Kentish Town, and Hampstead, and Cricklewood, and all sorts of distant places—but for the fact that I was suddenly bound, hand and foot, to London Street. Millwood left, and in the circumstances one could not blame him for leaving. His effective talk at recruiting meetings had been noticed by the authorities, and he received an offer that excited him, and gave him enormous gratification; he bustled around before leaving for the tour in the manner of a junior clerk starting for his first holiday. One speech, they told him, would be all that was needed, and this speech was to be delivered in the Midlands, up in the North, and, in fact, wherever he was instructed to go. So Millwood—when I had chosen a new suit for him, and selected a new hat, and made him look fairly respectable, without suggesting prosperity—Millwood went off, and on the top of this, Peter's mother came from Deptford, and with a preliminary announcement that she intended to behave herself in a lady-like manner, asked what the blazes I meant by paying her boy twelve adjective shillings a week, when, at the Arsenal, he could be earning untold gold, and thus save his poor father from the necessity of going out to work. She described my origin as German, and warned me to look out for an attack on the shop; I stopped the shouted tirade by handing to Peter the wages due, and advising him to follow his extraordinary parent.

"I don't want to go with her, miss," he pleaded. "I'm very comfortable where I am."

"That," said Peter's mother, to her reflection in a mirror, "that is what your modern child has come to. That's one of the consequences of them 'aving a education. That's the result of waiting on 'em, hand and foot, and struggling for 'em, tooth and nail, and stinting yourselves so as they should live on the fat of the land. A nicely managed world," she added, bitterly, "that, I must say."

"It's bad enough," argued Peter, "to have to go home there at nights, and find the old man blind to the world, and called upon to make the beds myself, because she's too lazy to attend to them."

Peter's mother called Heaven as a witness on her behalf, declaring that Heaven knew, better than neighbours or relatives, or friends, how she had laboured morning, noon, and night, working her fingers to the bone, and becoming a mere slave in her desire to bring up her boy as a credit to herself, and a model for all other youngsters.

"I shall run off on my own, mind you," Peter warned her, "jest as soon as ever I can!"

I dismissed the incident from my thoughts, but one remark offered by the Deptford woman came back when mobs began to smash windows of shops owning names which gave a foreign hint of other nationalities. They were not too particular, and, starting with confectioners and bakers where the origin was possibly Teutonic, they extended the sphere of their operations. The *Lusitania* affair had saddened some people, impressed many, and excited a few: it was the few who set out during the day, and occasionally of an evening, to enjoy revenge, and to give themselves the luxury of committing reckless damage. In High Street, Deptford, there were at least a dozen shops with not a sound piece of glass in anyone of them; from the upper floors, blinds and curtains bulged out of empty windows, and carpenters were engaged in nailing up a wooden protection. There followed stories of the rioters helping themselves to any article of domestic furniture which appealed to their fancy. There came rumours of the paying off of grievances against shopkeepers who had incurred unpopularity by requesting the settlement of accounts. The mob, it was stated, preferred to throw stones at establishments where no man was in charge.

"You can get on without me," I said to Mrs. Hillier. "For the time I must look after myself. I don't intend to leave London Street, for a moment, day or night."

"We must find some one to stay with you, Weston, and help to protect the shop."

"Mr. Hillier is too old, and Master Edward is too young. Besides, I know as well as you do that they are both scouring London, every spare minute they've got, trying to find Miss Muriel. If it wasn't for this bother I should be helping them."

"Wish one knew when the dear girl was likely to come back."

"She'll be running short of money pretty soon now," I mentioned, encouragingly.

"That is the time," said Mrs. Hillier, with a shiver, "I am fearing more than any other."

A cheery letter came in Master John's writing, dated from Darmstadt, and headed with a number and a company and a baraque, with the long German word, "Kriegsgefangenenlager," that went across the entire breadth of the sheet of note-paper. His leg was getting better, he wrote; he was receiving our parcels; he hoped we would write often; the German doctors had been good to him; he sent his love to all, and especially to Weston. "Ask Muriel to send me some books," he added, "and to write on each that it contains nothing concerning the war. 'Dieses Buch enthält nichts über den gegent wärtigen Krieg.' Muriel well knows the kind of volumes to select. And she might include a German grammar, and any of my old school books in the same language. Tell Muriel that I managed to bring her photograph through safely, although I lost many treasures, and it is now smiling at me as I write. I am glad to have her for company."

The news made us feel slightly more tolerant concerning our enemies, but the shadow remained at Gloucester Place. The earlier suspense concerning Master John had been sufficiently trying, but that was one of the events of war, and many families had been called upon to endure a like experience; the tension concerning Miss Muriel seemed an undeserved and an extravagant suffering. From Mrs. Hillier down to Master Edward, the entire group became older, graver, more subdued. Miss Katherine made an effort to brighten the atmosphere by giving an imitation of senior clerks at the bank.

"Regarded as an entertainment, Weston," she remarked, aside, "a pronounced and dismal failure."

"We're on the toughest job we've had, up to the present," I agreed. "A pity we can't all get away for a holiday."

A Continental Railway Guide had not been issued since August of '14, but a copy of this date had been brought on from Chislehurst, and I recall that one wet evening at Gloucester Place, when a desperate suggestion was made by Edward that we should all take the bull by the horns, and go to the Picture Palace (this was not seconded, and therefore fell to the ground), then Katherine recommended we might start on the trip which had been cancelled by events. It was decided, in order to avoid delay and trouble, to take the old services, and—the crossing satisfactorily accomplished on a smooth Channel, with everyone on deck, and protesting against the building of a Tunnel as unnecessary—at Calais, Mr. Hillier's counsel was adopted, and by the aid of the Guide we visited one or two places that had become conspicuous. We found that, according to the book (which we trusted) Ypres was "an interesting, clean old town," and that Zeebrugge was "a fashionable and secluded sea-side resort; restful and quiet." The Guide added to the list of attractions at Zeebrugge the word "shooting." Taking up the journey on the main line, we travelled to Paris, and stayed a night at the Continental in the rue de Rivoli, but dined out previously at a restaurant in the Avenue de l'Opera, where the meal was really admirable. Nothing could have been better. Unambitious perhaps, but adequate. The selection of dishes was left to me, and I ordered the following:

> *Tortue Claire au Marsala.*
> *Saumon bouilli.*
> *Cotelletes d'Agneau.*
> *Pointes d'Asperges.*
> *Jambon d'York.*
> *Caille rotie.*
> *Bombe glacée.*

The train for Pontarlier left at rather an early hour, but with Continental travel, one has to be prepared for some inconvenience, and we were at the P.L.M. station in good time, and Mr. Hillier (at the hearthrug in Gloucester Place, and in charge of the Guide) had managed to reserve a compartment, and despite the crowded state of the train, our comfort suffered no interference. There were places of importance to be looked out for on the way, and the Guide was disinclined to allow us to miss any of them, but we did miss some because Mrs. Hillier (from her arm-chair near the window) said the great thing was to arrive at Lausanne, and get along to Territet. Territet, said Mrs. Hillier, was a good centre for the making of excursions. It was important, declared Mrs. Hillier, that being in Switzerland, one should see all there was to be seen. I took charge of the meal at Territet. A light repast made up of

> *Poulet roti.*
> *Langue de Boeuf.*
> *Pâte de Pigeon.*
> *Gelée a l'orange.*
> *Anchois en croute.*

The first trip was to Champéry by steamer up the lake, passing by the Castle of Chillon, and at Bouveret, on the opposite side, we took the train for Monthey. From Monthey by electric railway through Trois-Torrents and Val d'Illiez. We liked Champéry. We thought highly of the rock galleries. We gave a word to the Cascade de Bonaveau. Returning to Territet, I was called upon to order dinner; pleading that invention demanded a rest, I advised that we should take the table d'hôte meal.

On the other days—each occupying not more than ten minutes—we went by the funicular up to Glion, and Caux, and the Rochers de Naye; by train to Bex and by the electric railway to Villars (4,250 feet up) and the lunch taken at the Hotel Muveran, by special and particular arrangement with the management, was as follows:

> *Tortue verte en tasse.*
> *Truite saumonée.*
> *Poussin de Hambourg.*
> *Biscuit glacé.*
> *Canapé Favorite.*

My companions regarded this as one of my lesser triumphs, and were frank enough to say so. "You've left out the meat," complained Edward (from the music-stool). I declined, on artistic grounds, to make any alteration. There followed a move to Chamonix where we at first stayed, I think, at the Hotel de Paris, but found it over-run by visitors, and we transferred ourselves instantly—no harm in being snobs in theory—to another establishment. And we visited the Glacier des Bossons and showed a proper interest in the Glacier "where the remains of Captain Arkwright were found in 1897, after being entombed in the ice for thirty-one years," and we went up La Flégère, and to the Gorge de la Diosaz, and to the Montanvert Hotel where the meal was too good to be omitted here. (The considerable advantage of these travels of the imagination was that one could always order anything, in season or out.)

> *Hors d'Oeuvres variés.*
> *Langouste Parisienne.*
> *Coeur de filet de boeuf.*
> *Poulet en casserole.*
> *Asperges vertes en branche.*
> *Dessert.*

We did Zermatt pretty thoroughly, and then Mrs. Hillier (glancing at the clock on the mantelpiece), pointed out that time was getting on. Edward and Katherine protested, Mr. Hillier offered no opinion, and I, answering a direct question, declared I was in no hurry to find myself home at Greenwich again. So we rested for a few days at Lausanne, and lunched once at a large hotel in considerable grounds at Ouchy, where we, most fortunately, met several English people whom we had always wished to encounter; Mr. Rudyard Kipling (chatty and communicative), Mr. Lloyd George (who promised to do something on Edward's behalf, later on), the editor of a London journal (knowing John Hillier well, and ready to give notices of his songs), Mr. J.R. Mason (who gave us several interesting and little known facts concerning first-class cricket). I fancy that these and others were our guests at the lunch; expense was naturally of no object. This was the meal I ordered, pleading now that on the return journey, one should be reckoned exempt from the task. Edward begged that, in these circumstances the details might be solid and satisfying, the repast one—in his phrase—that you could get your teeth into. I give a copy of the menu card:—

Petite Marmite.
Suprême de Sole.
Noisettes de pre-Salé.
Pommes.
Volaille en cocotte.
Salade de Saison.
Aubergines au gratin.
Pêches Melba.

Mrs. Hillier was definite, after this, in ordering that the trip should be considered at an end, that the game of imaginary travel should finish, and I left the room to prepare the evening meal for the family. It consisted of cold ham, cheese and lettuce.

I had put up the shutters one evening, and I was in the room at the back of the shop, when the booming came of distant voices. I ran upstairs and, without turning on the light, gazed out, and caught sight of the Deptford crowd. There was a good deal of incoherent shouting, with bass notes from the men, shrill voices of the women; one carried a flag, and boys knocked at anything that could be reckoned as a substitute for a drum. A ring came from downstairs; I assumed it to be only the lad with the evening newspaper, and if it happened to be anybody else, I was certainly not going to open the door. As the crowd came nearer, I could see Peter's deplorable mother in the front ranks; she was gesticulating wildly and screaming an instruction. They made some effort to range up near to my shop. A few constables were about and one was sent off, at full speed, to the police station. As I watched, I saw young Peter dash up and catch hold of his mother; he pushed her along, and once he had got her on the run, it was not long before the two disappeared. More names were being shouted now, and some of the excited people, to my relief, began to move; at that moment I heard a cracking of wood downstairs, and it appeared certain to me that my shop, with all the valuable articles I had selected so carefully, was about to be smashed and ruined as evidence of the patriotism of the wreckers. Footsteps came on the staircase.

"Hullo," said a husky voice. "All in the dark? War time economy?"

I kept very quiet.

"Surely," the voice went on, "you've got a kiss for me?"

I struggled fiercely as arms went around me. The lights in the road were suddenly turned on, and I found myself giving a bang, with the flat of the hand, on the head of my own dear nephew.

"A fracas in London Street," cried Herbert, amusedly, on seeing my apologetic distress. "Well known resident in assault case. How the warrior boy was welcomed home."

"Herbert," I said, "if I had only guessed it was you—"

"You ought to be out in Flanders," he declared. "Strong fighters are just what we need. But you're trembling, aunt. What's wrong?"

"I'm afraid of these rough people out in the roadway."

He lighted the gas, and throwing up the window, leaned out. The crowd, recognising a soldier, cheered, and somebody started one of the popular airs. Three mounted policemen moved their horses sideways, and the mob surged off.

"Thought you'd got more nerve, aunt," said Herbert.

"I always use to have plenty," I declared. "But, just lately, my stock seems to shew signs of giving out."

"For any special cause?"

It was not necessary to load him up with troubles directly that he arrived. To a challenge about meals, Herbert admitted that he felt peckish. To another inquiry, made as I found the grill, and started the fire, he explained that he had managed to enter the shop by the device of putting one shoulder against the door, and forcing the lock to give way.

"Corporal Millwood," I remarked at the fire-place, "of the Guards is a very different lad from Herbert Millwood who used to pore over his lessons, and get bible-backed and gain scholarships."

"Sergeant Millwood," he said, drawing himself more upright than ever. "Sergeant Millwood, if you please."

I had not observed the extra stripe. "You'll be an officer soon, my dear," I said.

"There happens to be a special reason," he confessed, colouring, "why I should like to get a commission. By-the-bye, now are all the Hilliers? And how's the dad trundling along?"

I told him of his father's new engagement. Herbert, seated at the table, so soon as the meal was ready, could not help breaking off in conversation to return to the subject.

"Fancy the old chap holding such a good hand of trumps!"

"And doing more work for his country, I'll be bound, than many a Staff Officer."

"And the last time I heard him speak in public, he was arguing that we ought to abolish the army and reduce the navy."

Presently, he asked a serious question. "How does he manage about his aitches?"

"It's my belief," I declared, "that half of his success is due to the fact that he doesn't bother in the least concerning them."

Herbert, on the way to the base, had, it appeared, met the Quartermaster-Sergeant; he said that Cartwright spoke, with enjoyment, of the first day of his leave, and insisted upon giving all the details, excepting (I was relieved to find) the last incident at Charing Cross. Herbert said that Cartwright was a good man at his job—which I could well believe—and one of the toughest and sternest N.C.Os. in the British army—which seemed to me incredible. Herbert wished to spend the days of his leave at Greenwich, and I went off to air his father's bed for him.

"Whilst I think of it," he said, when I returned. He was about to put a match to his briar pipe, but held it free of the tobacco whilst he spoke. "Did I ask you how Miss Muriel was, or did I, perhaps, only mean to do so?"

I told him all that happened, described the anxiety we were all experiencing; the match burned down to his finger, but he did not appear to observe the fact. I said Mr. Hillier went up to town each evening, after his work at the Arsenal, and walked, at a swift rate, about different quarters of London in the attempt to find his elder daughter. That Master Edward had supplied officials on his railway with a copy of Miss Muriel's photograph, and an urgent appeal that they would keep a good look-out. That Miss Katherine, in all of her spare time from the bank, made inquiries at girls' clubs, and homes, and associations. That the one card received by me was written in a confident manner, and that I was still hoping.

"Still hoping?" he echoed, rather sharply. "No use in doing that. Plenty of folk are still hoping in regard to the war, and doing precious little else." He found his cap, and put it on: looked around for his great-coat.

"Where are you going, Herbert, my dear?"

"Going to try to find her," he answered. "If she's lost, I don't care a hang what becomes of me!" Within two minutes he had gone.

The extraordinary thing, from my point of view, was that I, reckoning myself a woman who took notice of everything that went on around me, should have omitted to notice that my nephew was in love, should have had no sort of idea that he was in love with Miss Muriel. I wished I had taken the opportunity to tell him of the girl's defects; her indifference to everyone but herself, her ever-changing projects, her frank intention of marrying money, the circumstance that she alone, out of all the members of the Hillier family, had allowed the war to have no effect upon her. But when I considered this, it became clear that nothing I said would have made any alteration, so far as Herbert was concerned. If someone had called at the shop and mentioned that Cartwright had killed three wives, and was now liable to a charge of bigamy, it is probable I should have contented myself with the remark that at any rate he was a well-spoken and a good-looking man. And this in no way means that love is blind. On the contrary, love uses eye-glasses which have the ability to exaggerate all the virtues of the person looked at, and to minimise all the defects.

A postcard arrived from Herbert on the last day of his leave: it was headed Victoria Station, and it had been written with an indelible pencil.

"Have not discovered her. Good-bye. Please send me news."

I had little time to enjoy the pleasures and amenities of Greenwich, but I saw enough of the borough to assure myself that, despite an air of increasing age, it was not without its attractions. There was always the riverside with the pier and arriving and departing steamers, ships going up and down, and a walk to be taken along the narrow railed passage from King William Street to Park Row, and, at low tide, bare-legged youngsters playing on the beach, or larking with the high and dry boats. There was the market, off Nelson Street, where those of us who were economically minded made selections and effected bargains.

I recall, in particular, a Sunday afternoon of May when the Park gave me a special comfort of mind. The week had been a trying one. The *Lusitania* shock had not passed off, a question of re-arranging the Cabinet was in the air, and local politicians shook their heads, and, making groups near the Baths corner of Royal Hill, discussed the matter gravely; the London tram-strike was still on; one or two journals were making an attack on Kitchener; up in the north there had occurred the worst railway accident that ever happened in Great Britain, with two hundred of the Royal Scots killed; a two days' list of casualties from the front contained over three thousand names; the Germans were using new methods, and we had lost some ground near Ypres; there had been naval disasters, and a wooden tip-cat, driven by an energetic child with a stick, had caught me just under the eye. I went out of Gloucester Place where sun-blinds had been fixed on the balconies, and entered the Park by the Crooms' Hill gate that enabled one to avoid the at times over-crowded lower part. The pink hawthorn was in full blossom, yellow laburnum was at its best, chestnut trees were candelabraed with white, and, in the enclosure at the foot of the Observatory Hill, wild grasses stood thick and high. The inclined roadway took me to the tea-house, where, inside the tall railings, folk sat at tables in the shadow of trees, and watched the friendly sparrows that hopped about on the close-shaven lawn. There, it was possible on that Sunday afternoon to forget about the war (on week-days there came the boom of testing of guns at Woolwich to remind, and the hurrying to and fro of Red Cross vans, and the War Department motor lorries). There, one could gaze north and see nothing but the calm sky; at the end of the Avenue the Park took a sudden dip, and landscape was out of sight. Captain and Mrs. Winterton came in at the gate as I was at my second cup; folk commented on their odd appearance, and young women giggled, but to me it seemed that the surroundings fitted them appropriately.

"Miss Weston," said the old gentleman, in his courteous way, "you are enjoying solitude, and we will not permit ourselves to intrude upon your thoughts."

"I happened," I remarked, "to be thinking of nothing at all."

"A fortunate state," he declared. "I discover, in my own case, that a slight effort is needed to effect this."

"The terrible war, sir—"

"My love!" Turning to his wife. "Shall we tell her? I think she would be interested to know? We can regard Miss Weston as a friend."

"Do as you think best, dear," said the old lady.

He gave orders to the waitress, and taking me across to the railings, pointed with his malacca cane. "Under that tree," he whispered, confidentially, "in the month of May and in a year that was long, long before you, dear madam, graced the world with your presence, I proposed marriage to the lady who is now Mrs. Winterton!" He stepped back two paces, and gazed at me; I (for the second time) gave the look of surprise that was expected. Captain Winterton offered his arm, and we returned to his wife. She nodded pleasantly to indicate that I might now reckon myself amongst the privileged few, and inside the circle of friends.

In the Wilderness at the south end of the Avenue, sweet smelling azaleas welcomed one, and the imposing rhododendrons were at the summit of their pride; in a week or two they would lose colour, and come down in the world, but on this afternoon they were wealthy aristocrats. Young couples sat about, declining to disengage hands when older folk approached, and the sight made me think that I might perhaps have cultivated romance, and thus have rendered my life the happier. The gates to Blackheath, and there, after the shade of the Park was a sun-illuminated space, so extensive that, but for the distant houses on the borders, it would have been easy to imagine oneself in the country. The heath furnished a slight breeze that invigorated, and I walked along Dover Road to Shooters' Hill, turned and came down into Blackheath village, took Belmont Hill to the Obelisk, and so home by Lewisham Road and South Street. By the time I arrived, I had forgotten to worry about the absence of sentiment from my current life; a Sunday evening newspaper boy racing up Royal Hill, brought my thoughts again to the war.

I think I was not alone at Greenwich, in owing a debt to the Park. For the folk in mourning who increased in number each week, church was perhaps more consoling, and it was significant that even my brother-in-law, Millwood, no longer jibed at people who attended places of worship.

In looking back, I find it difficult to understand how it happened that folk managed to keep up an appearance of serenity and composure; I think there must have been tears on pillows, but nobody showed them to the world. For one thing, there was the example of the men out at the front. We all knew, from the start of the war, that they would fight well; few guessed they would fight so gaily. I used to take cigarettes and illustrated papers along to the hospital in Greenwich Road, and my friend, the Sister there, could always introduce some humorist who had returned grievously wounded perhaps, but rarely so much damaged as to be deprived of his diverting outlook; the exceptions were to be found amongst those who suffered from the gas poison first used by the enemy, and for these the world did seem wanting in attraction. When other subjects failed, and when the good-tempered men had exhausted jokes about water-filled trenches, and shells that sent earth into the soup, and mines that blew up unexpectedly, then there remained the visitors. These were always well meaning, but they often seemed imperfectly furnished with openings for conversation. (In my own case, I found that the carrying of a box of matches, and the offer of it to a patient who was about to smoke, proved a useful method of starting talk.)

"Where were you wounded?" was the usual inquiry, and the soldier could never tell whether the questioner wanted geographical or bodily information. "I am sure you must be dreadfully keen on getting back to the fighting line," was a remark that did not always gain an enthusiastic and affirmative answer. "How we envy you in being able to take a part in the struggle!" sometimes received a non-committal jerk of the head; the Sister and the nurses listened later to the comments on this aspiration. The sentence that remained long in the memory of the ward was one made by a wealthy woman from Blackheath. She arrived, with the obvious determination to say the correct, the tactful, the exactly appropriate word.

"And what injuries have you sustained, my man?"

"Well, lady, as you see, I've lost my left arm, and I've got rather an extensive collection of shrapnel in my right leg."

"Oh," she remarked, casually, "is that all!" And passed on to the next bed. The Sister declared that imitations of this visitor were popular for weeks.

I think women-folk showed to better advantage in the entertainments they arranged. There were large houses in the district, possessing extensive grounds, and parties of convalescent soldiers would be taken by cars, and a concert provided, and plenty of food, and if the men were not rendered shy by excessive suggestion of patronage, they enjoyed the outing, and it counted for restoration to good health. And some of them must have felt astonished to discover kindness where they had never guessed that kindness existed; I know, from what certain of them told me, that they would remember it for the rest of their lives.

"You can take my word for it, ma'am," said one, impressively. "The upper classes ain't nearly so black as what they've been painted!" He ruminated for a while. "Human beings," he went on, "that's what they are. Human beings, almost as good as the rest of us."

I felt myself drawn towards the north country-men, who had trouble in making themselves understood by Londoners, and who became puzzled by the methods of London speech. Four of these came from Northumberland, and when they were allowed to go out of an afternoon, they understood that, if the weather chanced to be erratic, and the Park gave no welcome, they could make their way to London Street, and rest in my shop, and look at newspapers, and smoke, and have high tea; the great attraction offered was freedom to talk amongst themselves with no interference. As each recovered, he went home on leave, and I treasure now, more than most things, a sheet of exercise book paper, written by a child living at South Shields:—

> "Dear lady,
> Thank you verry much for being kinde to my Daddy,
> Your loving friend,
>
> Milly."

CHAPTER X

A letter came from my Quartermaster-Sergeant.

"We have been having a busy time lately. Nothing else but marching and fighting, and the regiment was in the great attack described correctly in the London papers of the 15th under the heading of 'British Check.' But I am pleased to be able to tell you that another attack has taken place, which proved a huge success, and the advantage is being followed up at the time of writing.

"Would you like to send me two re-fills for my electric lamp; address in the Strand enclosed. It is difficult work to find one's way about at night on unfamiliar ground. Hope you are keeping well and fit, as it leaves me at present."

There was the strike on with the tramway men, and I had to go by rail to make the purchase. The train went to Cannon Street only, and in running across there from one platform to another, I nearly came into collision with Guard Richards who was also in a hurry.

"Caught sight of your Miss Muriel t'other evening," he called out.

"Where," I demanded stopping, "and how was she, and what is she doing?"

William Richards had disappeared through one of the barriers, and did not hear my question. It was something, however, to know that the adventurous girl was still alive.

At the shop in the Strand I put the usual inquiry to the attendant—"How do you find business?"—and he said he found nothing to complain about, and I mentioned that I, too, had no cause to grumble. Hedging slightly, he remarked that he felt sorry that in the old days, before the war, he had devoted so much time and money to a favourite hobby; his wife—"She's got a bitter way of talking when she likes!"—aided and encouraged by her mother, never failed, it appeared, to hold him up to ridicule of an evening when he returned home, to take supper. I had given a few vague words of sympathy, and the counsel to take no notice, and was leaving when he happened to say that anybody who once began to collect old furniture was considered by non-collectors as on the road to Colney Hatch. Within ten minutes, I had promised to wait for him near the post office, and journey northwards in order to look at his stock, and to see whether I felt inclined to make an offer, and take the whole lot off his hands. There would have been less celerity over the early part of the transaction but that, as I explained to him, it was rarely I found myself so near to his district, and, as he explained to me, he had, to appease his wife and her relatives, given the assurance that he was taking active steps to get rid of the articles which crowded the rooms. On the way, he suddenly expressed the wish that I had been a member of his own sex. He did not know what his wife would say when she found he had brought a lady, unknown to her, into the house. He expressed the view that if the Zeppelins ever dared to come over London, they would receive from her as good as they gave.

The wife quickly informed him of her attitude in regard to my visit. So soon as he opened the front door of his house with his latch key, and immediately that she heard my voice, she ordered the two maids to go upstairs. Herself conducted us into the drawing-room.

"I've been anticipating this," she said, tearfully, "and I fully recognise, David, that I'm partly responsible. I've got a jealous disposition, and I expect it will be my curse and companion to the very end of my life."

"Miss Weston has come here—" he began.

"I know!" interrupted his wife, finding her handkerchief. "I quite understand, and the fewer words we exchange on the subject, the better. Perhaps if there had been children, it might have been different. Very likely if I had been more tactful in speech, this terrible business could have been put off for a while. Think as kindly of me as you can, David."

"I always do, my dear, and—"

"No," she contradicted, with a show of truculence. "I'm not going to allow you to say that. I am ready to take my just share of the blame, but not more. You know as well as I do that I stand very low in your estimation, compared for instance with that Oliver Cromwell chair you picked up somewhere in Essex three years ago. I needn't tell you that you love that gate table in the next room with a devotion you never gave to me, even in the early days of our acquaintance. It's been a hideous blunder, David, this marriage of ours, and now that you have taken a definite proceeding by bringing another woman into the house—"

"What a foolish person you are!" I exclaimed.

"Don't you dare speak to me," she ordered. "David I am sorry for, but you I consider beneath my estimation. Heaven knows by what tricks and dodges you have succeeded in weaving your mesh around him."

"My dear," said her husband, "this lady and I have met this evening for the first time."

"That makes it worse, David. But I always suspected you were really fond of tall women, and I cannot be blind to the fact that I am short and stout. I only hope—"

I managed to induce her to cease talking after a while, and, in a few sharp words, described the reason of my visit. The strange thing was that so soon as I had forced her to comprehend this, her annoyance with her husband knew no bounds. Why had he mis-led her in this preposterous manner? Why was he never so happy as when inducing his poor wife to make herself a laughing stock? As to the furniture, she felt by no means inclined to allow it to go. Any allusions she had made in the past were given, she declared, more for the purpose of keeping up genial conversation than anything else. Certainly, she did not propose to have the house emptied of half its contents, bought mainly with her cash, in order to gratify a man who rarely thought of any plan or scheme likely to make her existence cheerful.

"Nothing can be done," I remarked to the husband. "It isn't your fault. I must see about making my way back to Greenwich."

"I'd like you just to look at my collection," he said. "You're a bit of an expert, I can tell, and it would be interesting to know what you think of the purchases I have made during the past ten years. I may have been taken in over some of them."

"I can give you fifteen minutes."

In the list of eccentric people I have met, the lady of this house well deserves a first place. During the quarter of an hour, her mind went to every point of the compass. When I said a word in praise of the half-dozen Hepplewhite chairs, she announced that she would sooner die than permit anything to be taken out of the house: when I commented strongly on a faked Sheraton sideboard, she said disconsolately that a van had better be sent for the rubbish on the following morning. Her husband was described alternately, as the wisest and shrewdest darling in the world, and, a moment later, as a drivelling idiot.

"Don't you think so yourself, ma'am?" she inquired, at one moment.

"Undoubtedly," I answered.

It appeared I had carelessly agreed with one of her condemnatory remarks, and, swirling around, she ordered me to leave the house. Who was I, she would like to know, to venture to criticise her David? What did I mean by coming there, a perfect stranger, simply in order to hold her dear one up to ridicule? The dear one conducted me to the front door, muttering apologies on the way.

"Never marry anyone who's got money," he counselled.

"There doesn't seem to be much of a catch in it."

"Sorry you have been brought all this way for nothing. You've got a fine night for your journey home, anyway. Fortunately, you're one of the sensible people who take no notice of all this wild talk about air-raids. Mind the steps," he added, counting them as I went down. "One, two, three; that's right!"

The first thunderous clamouring bang came as he had nearly closed the door. He rushed out, caught hold of my arm, and pulled me in. Another tremendous report sounded as we stumbled over the mat. The two maids rushed wildly down the staircase and, throwing themselves upon me in a hysterical manner, babbled questions, begged that I would save them, urged that I should remain in the house for their protection.

"There's no danger now," I said. "It's all over. The Zepps are a long way off by this time. Come into this room, and let us see how your mistress is taking it."

The lady of the house had fainted with great promptitude, and the discovery of some one more considerably affected by the incident than themselves, restored the girls to composure. Dogs were barking out of doors, and there was shouting by children; the explosions had awakened birds in the trees at the back of the road. A fire engine went along, clanging its bell.

"I'm all serene," announced the astonishing lady, when she was able to sit up. "Appear to have taken it much more calmly than the rest of you. It's a great mistake to let the Germans imagine they can frighten us. David, give the maids something to drink, and let them go upstairs again."

She mentioned, when the others were out of the room, that her people had always been renowned for their courage, and that it was a considerable help, in time of need, to feel one had to keep up this reputation. I remarked that the bombs had fallen near enough to excuse alarm; for myself, I had no desire for a closer acquaintance.

"Now that they have come once," she said, complacently, "they will come again. I shouldn't wonder if they arrived every night, regularly."

"Cheerful anticipation!"

"I can always look facts in the face," she remarked. "Nothing daunts me. I possess the heart of a lion. The word 'fear' has no existence where I am concerned." She went to the mirror, and beamed at her reflection. "Do you think he will mind giving up the house?"

Her husband's return saved me the trouble of guessing at the meaning of this inquiry. He was ordered to find the A.B.C. and, this done, accepted, with bowed head, all the responsibility for the circumstance that no train ever left Paddington for Wallingford after nine-fifty p.m.

"Then I go there, David," she announced, "early to-morrow, and stay at a farmhouse until the war is over." She asked me rather anxiously whether I thought the enemy's airships were likely to get so far as Berkshire, and, meeting a glance from her husband, I gave the opinion that the county referred to, might be looked upon as safe. In all likelihood, the Germans had never heard of it. "My view exactly," she said. "You will get rid of the house, David, and go into your old bachelor rooms."

"But the furniture, my dear?"

"He has no head for management," remarked the lady to me, apologetically. "You and I must settle this. Name a figure for all the old stuff, and the remainder can go to one of the auction rooms."

Her husband, in seeing me once again, to the front door, mentioned, with a chuckle, that Zeppelin raids had their drawbacks, but that they did appear to be capable of solving a domestic problem.

The circumstance that my journey had not been wasted, in a business sense, helped me to make my way home cheerfully. There was some excitement amongst the people travelling, a great deal of interest, and very little of anything resembling nervousness. One or two who had been at the moment in underground trains regretted their ill-luck in missing the sights and the sounds, declaring that this was but a sample of the misfortune which persistently dogged their footsteps through life, and the others tried to console them up by prophesying hopefully that the occurrence would undoubtedly be repeated. No one could have complained that night of the reticence of the Londoner. Everyone talked to everybody, and one woman with a basket of groundsel possessed special information that made her seem richer than any of the rest of us; she exacted a respect that had, it is certain, not hitherto been paid to her. All the values were, for a time, disturbed. At

Greenwich station I met Mr. Hillier. He was waiting for Miss Katherine and her brother, who had gone to a theatre, with orders that had been presented to Master Edward; some of the invented scraps of news had come by the down trains, and Mr. Hillier was anxious. He walked the three sides of the courtyard outside the station, and I remembered the announcement thrown to me by Richards.

"Well now," he declared, "that is really something to be grateful for. Muriel is alive, at any rate. But what I can't understand is, why she is doing it? I don't see the reason. What induced her to run off?"

"I think, sir, that she was fed up with everything. I imagine that she wanted to start afresh."

"But she might have taken you, Weston, or me, or one of us into her confidence."

"Miss Muriel never gave much thought or consideration to other people. She fixed all her regard upon herself, and for that reason, I feel pretty sure that she is not likely to come to any harm. There's plenty of work for girls to do nowadays, and she ought to be taking her share. But I admit I'd like to know more about what's going on."

"I had great theories," he remarked, "when I first married about the bringing up of children. Wonderful theories. Magnificent theories. And, in the result, the children brought themselves up. With help from you, Weston. You came along in time to save three of them; if you had arrived earlier, you might have helped the other one. Don't assume, because we rarely talk about it, that we forget."

"Only earnt my wages, sir."

"I may have taken that view at the time; I see it all more clearly now. And if you should ever meet any of the maids of the old Chislehurst establishment, I'd like them to know, Weston, that I appreciated the services they gave there. I did see one of them on a platform the other day, and I should have spoken to her, but she and her husband were travelling first and I was going third." He drew in his breath sharply.

"You've had a lot to put up with," I remarked, "and, in my opinion, you have stood it uncommonly well."

"Don't mind confessing to you, Weston, that at first it took a bit of doing. Now that I'm in the swing of it, it doesn't require so much effort. Look at my hands!" They gave evidence of hard work in the Arsenal. The palms had become hardened; lines were marked darkly; there was a cut or two, and one finger had the protection of a stall. "Honourable scars, Weston," he said, rather exultantly. "And there are some, too, on the mind, that no one can see. Discover from your friend the guard, so soon as you can, where he caught sight of Muriel. Here come the other two."

Miss Katherine and Master Edward arrived in the high state of excitement that youth can gain from a visit to the play; they were not greatly interested in my news of the raid, but insisted on telling their father and me, on the way to Gloucester Place, the plot of the musical comedy they had seen; a task which made a demand upon their combined efforts. We found Mrs. Hillier waiting up, with a post letter addressed to her husband that, as she admitted, she had refrained from opening only by an effort; I could not help recalling the times when she would have shown no such consideration. The writing was Miss Muriel's; we made an eager semi-circle to listen to the communication.

"I'm sorry," said Mr. Hillier, brokenly, "but I—I can't read it. Weston, you try."

Miss Muriel gave no address at the head of the letter, and the wording had something of the romantic and poetic touch that she always favoured. Having encountered a railway friend of Weston's who mentioned that her people were worried and perturbed about her, she was now sending a line to assure her father that she was well, and in no need of money. Miss Muriel announced that she had engaged upon the task of re-forming her character, and did not intend to return home until this process was completed. She sent love to all, "including dear fussy Weston." The note contained nothing more, and each of us, in turn, searched it carefully, and held it up to the light, examined the envelope.

"Not much," decided Mr. Hillier, "but better than no news."

"The dear child is in good health anyway," remarked his wife.

"The dear child," said Miss Katherine, "might have a little more consideration for her relatives. If I happen to meet the dear child, I shall talk to her in the manner that Dutch uncles are supposed to adopt."

"'Re-forming her character,'" quoted Master Edward, taking the note again. "'Re-forming,' with a hyphen. I haven't the slightest idea what she means. A silly phrase, I call it."

"She means improving it," I said, quickly. "And I like the tone of her letter. The handwriting is firmer than it used to be. She's in no trouble, and that's the great thing."

"But," argued the lad, frowning, "how is she getting money?"

"This parcel of mine," I said, changing the conversation, and producing the articles bought in the Strand, "ought I suppose to go in a wooden box if it is to travel safely to France."

Miss Katherine, following my lead, inquired regarding the contents, and pointed out to the others that Weston was sparing no efforts in the endeavour to trap and secure the Quartermaster-Sergeant. Going on with her chaff, she expressed the hope that she herself would never have to adopt such unworthy means in order to capture the affections of a male bird. Rather than force gifts upon a coy recipient, Miss Katherine declared she was willing to remain a spinster with nothing in the shape of love but a deep and unswerving affection for bank work. Master Edward, coming in on my side, mentioned that Katherine had lent her opera glasses that evening to an enamoured youth seated beside her in the stalls. Miss Katherine declared that the gentleman was in no way enamoured, that his age was well over seventy, and that she had offered the glasses with no other motive than that of preventing her brother from gazing through them absorbedly at a six foot lady on the stage. The two gave us some of the tunes they had heard, acted one of the scenes.

"Bed, children," ordered their mother. "You both have to be up early in the morning."

"Shan't feel much inclined to turn out."

"I'll see to that," I promised.

Whereupon the young people described me as the curse of the household, as a woman with an insane craving for breakfast at eight, one devoid of consideration for anybody under the rank of a Quartermaster-Sergeant. I put an end to the discussion by taking Miss Katherine in my arms, and carrying her upstairs as I had often done when she was a small girl; I threatened to return and perform a like service for Master Edward.

"Weston," said Miss Katherine, in her room, "joking apart, and speaking with a full knowledge of the importance of the announcement, let me tell you in strict confidence, that the hour is not far distant when I shall not have to depend, for company, upon my respected brother. Of course we can't insure against war risks, but the outlook, Weston, may be regarded as hopeful. Decidedly hopeful."

"When the time comes, miss, I can only hope you will be as happy as you deserve to be."

"I am looking forward," remarked the girl, "to being much happier than that!"

Cartwright acknowledged receipt of the package in a long letter written with such an ineffective pencil that, at first, I did not trouble to read it to the end; a van, at the moment, was arriving from the north of London, and the elderly men in charge, explaining that all the firm's young chaps had enlisted, announced there had been difficulty enough in loading the furniture; they appeared to regard the task of discharging it as impossible. Luckily, my brother-in-law, Millwood, came along: he had some engagements to speak near town, and desired to take up residence at London Street for a few days. He took off his coat at once, put on green baize apron, set to work. Sales had been good at the shop of late, and by a little shifting, and re-arrangement, space was made. Millwood talked as we engaged upon the job, and I had difficulty in understanding the trend of his remarks. After a while, I discovered that he was cultivating alliterativeness in speech, and, being challenged, he admitted that he found the trick extremely effective in speaking to audiences.

"I enjoy myself no end," he remarked, as we carried in an escritoire. "Generally I'm called upon at the finish, when everybody has just about had enough of 'igh class talk, and of well-educated chaps saying the same thing over and over again. I give it to 'em straight from the shoulder. Definite as a door-knocker. A tornado of truth. An avalanche of asseverations."

"And don't they guy you?"

"In some places, a slight tendency to do this, at the start. But I tell 'em a pathetic story about a soldier's little daughter, and after that I can do what I like. I make 'em cry, and I make 'em laugh. The tribulation of tears, and the deportment of diversion. See what I mean? And, before I sit down, I turn on the patriotic key, and they shout the blooming roof half off. Mary Weston, you ought to see the swell ladies come up afterwards and offer their congratulations."

"No doubt, a picturesque sight."

"Sometimes," my brother-in-law went on, chuckling, "sometimes they're at the railway station to bid me good-bye. Floral tributes. Illustrated papers. Shaking of hands, and come again soon. Three cheers for Mr. Millwood. And the other passengers regard me with the envy of—" he appeared, for a moment, to be floored—"the envy of enthusiasm. By-the-bye, why didn't my 'Erb come and listen to me when he was home on leave?"

"Herbert was busy," I explained. "And he felt anxious about a certain young woman."

"A mistake his father never committed," said Millwood. "With the exception of your poor sister, there's never been one of them able to exercise the slightest attraction so far as I am personally concerned."

"You'd better touch wood," I suggested.

The two elderly men were relieved to find the undertaking satisfactorily completed, and in accepting silver, they mentioned that if all lady customers were as business-like and as generous as I proved to be, the drawbacks experienced in emerging from retirement and taking up active duties would be considerably lightened. "The very female parties," they asserted, "that were always a-badgering our young chaps with 'Why aren't you in khaki?' are just the ones that complain now because some of us old 'uns are a trifle careful in our movements!" I counselled them not to place too much importance on exceptional cases, and called their notice to the fact that women-folk were doing remarkably good work in munition factories, and elsewhere. The aged carmen closed the debate with the remark that it took all sorts to make a world.

"I overheard your talk," said Millwood, when we sat at a meal, in the back room, "and it's give me an idea that I shall dove-tail into my speech at Croydon this evening. It may be that, in the past, I've taken somewhat 'arsh views in regard to members of your sex. Probably I have shown a certain aloofness so far as they are concerned. A deportment of disdain. An attitude of inattention."

"I don't suppose they minded."

"Not too late to make amends," he argued. "It'll come rather well from me to pay them a sort of a veiled compliment. I shall be careful, mind you. If they want the fulsomeness of flattery, or the slavery of serfdom, they must go to other quarters. I made a fool of myself over a woman once, by going out of my way to marry her, but—never again!" He shook his head, knowingly. "Once bit, twice shy."

"That describes your attitude fairly well," I said. "Shy is just what you are. You're always awkward, but you're more clumsy than ever when you're in the presence of women-folk."

"It's a disappointed female who's making that statement," he declared, warmly. "Oh, yes," as I protested, "I know very well what I'm talking about. I've noticed a difference in you ever since that bill was passed making it legal to marry your wife's deceased sister—" Millwood found himself in a tangle of words, and his annoyance increased. He rose and went across to the mantelpiece to find matches. "Who is this letter in the green envelope from?"

"The Quartermaster-Sergeant who was so kind when Master John was missing."

"Can I read it?"

"If your eyesight is good enough. It only came just now, and I am not sure that I finished it."

Millwood explained that he sometimes picked up useful snips of information from letters written near the trenches, and, putting on his glasses, he went through the numbered pages of the communication. Towards the end he began to frown. At the finish he threw the sheets on the table, with a gesture of irritation.

"Well," he said, curtly. "What are you going to do about it?"

"I shall write to him, I suppose, when I can find time. They like to receive correspondence out there. Makes them realise they are not forgotten."

"Yes, yes! But how are you going to answer him? What sort of a reply do you intend to give? I'm one of the family, and I have a right to know." To my surprise, he took hold of my arm, and shook me. "You women!" he shouted. "Upon my word, you do know how to exasperate. It's my belief, you find a certain delight in trying to send a man clean off his 'ead."

"An easy job, enough, in some cases. Let me glance at Cartwright's letter, and see what it is that has upset you."

"Read page four," he commanded.

It was impossible to avoid smiling, and this sent Millwood raging up and down the small room. The Quartermaster-Sergeant wrote that he wished to marry me so soon as the war was over, or, if I preferred it, at an earlier date; he begged that an answer should be despatched at once—"that the subject can be off my mind."

"Look here, Mary Weston," said Millwood, shaking a fore-finger at me, in his platform way. "You've got a mad, wild, reckless, tempestuous nature—"

"Don't be ridiculous. I'm one of the most self-possessed—"

"Where love is concerned," he insisted, "all women are alike. I know 'em well. I've studied 'em. And I ask you to put this soldier chap off. Postpone him, so to speak. Let your decision be definitely deferred. Treat his offer in a lady-like manner, but allow him to see that you are in no way eager to march immediately into the madness of matrimony."

"What I can't understand is why you are in such a state of alarm and excitement. What on earth has it to do with you?"

"Everything!" he declared. "My future is at stake. My happiness is in peril. My career——" He glanced at the clock. "Hang it," he cried, "I shall be late for my meeting if I don't fly."

I brushed his hat, and gave it to him. Reminded him of his pipe. Hurried after him with his walking stick.

"Daresay I seem somewhat peculiar in my style," he remarked, more composedly. "But the fact of it is, Mary Weston, I came home here with the full and definite intention of proposing to you, myself!"

CHAPTER XI

My mother used to say that everything in this world went by threes, and it surprised me but little to receive a prepaid telegram from William Richards; in his anxiety to economise he succeeded in being obscure, but I gained that he wished to marry me. (Subsequently I discovered he had the chance of an inspectorship at a suburban station, and entertained a fear that he might experience loneliness.) To Cartwright I sent a friendly note asking him to renew the suggestion when we were better acquainted with each other. At the back of my head, there was an apprehension that the success of the business in London Street had something to do with all this striking unanimity.

"Seeing that I've waited so long," I remarked to myself, "I may as well wait a bit longer, and make sure I'm acting wisely."

I wrote to William, giving a fuller explanation than a telegram permitted, and asked for detailed information regarding his encounter with Miss Muriel. He may have been huffed at my reply; in any case, he did not send the particulars.

The shop just then engaged me so much that not until Miss Katherine called my attention to the fact did I notice a change in her mother's appearance. July happened to be a warm month; there was a Sunday in it when the heat proved trying, and Mrs. Hillier, going out to the Park with old Captain Winterton and his wife, returned with the confession that she felt inclined for rest. I arranged a holiday for her without delay. The bank was, very generously, giving Miss Katherine a fortnight, although she had not completed a year of work, and Master Edward found himself able to get away; able too, by virtue of his position, to obtain passes. Mr. Hillier said it would be useless for him to make any application for leave at the Arsenal. So I packed the three off to a town on the Suffolk coast, and it occurred to us, as they were leaving, that nearly twelve months had elapsed since a holiday trip was stopped; we agreed that the time—closely packed as it had been with incident—seemed more like ten years than one.

"You ought to be coming with us," they said.

"Expect me at the first week end. I'm single-handed, you must remember."

"One hand of yours, Weston dear," remarked Miss Katherine, "is worth four belonging to anybody else." She took me aside. "What made you select this particular sea coast town for us, you wonderful person?"

"Seeing that letters arrive for you every other day with that post mark——"

"Weston," she said, "I do believe you are growing young. I detect a strain of romance that you have not hitherto exhibited. It shows how much influence is possessed by a Quartermaster-Sergeant in the Guards."

I closed the shop early on the Saturday. The Wintertons promised to look after Mr. Hillier at Gloucester Place. My train on the Great Eastern was crowded, although excursion fares had long since been cancelled, and a guard put me in a first-class compartment where the passenger immediately opposite was Colonel Edgington, formerly of Chislehurst, and for some time absent from my memory. Apparently I too was but vaguely in his recollection, for he grasped me warmly by the hand, assured me he was delighted to see me again, offered congratulations on my appearance of good health. I was about to speak of the Hilliers, when he started the topic of himself and his own work, and the subject occupied the whole of the journey. It appeared he was engaged at the War Office, that he had not a single moment to call his own, that he was working as he had never worked before, that he was now on the way to a point in the Eastern Counties which he could not mention (but I guessed it by the ticket that was visible in the palm of his glove) there to engage upon a task that he was not at liberty to disclose (he told me all about it ere we reached Chelmsford). The others in the compartment looked at me with respect as we chatted.

"And tell me, dear lady," he said, towards the end of the journey. "I'd like to know something about yourself. Busily engaged, I'll wager, at this period of stress and turmoil. Eh, what! Funds, and societies, and associations, and so forth. I've seen your name in the papers, over and over again."

"How was it spelt?"

"In the way you always spell it," he answered, promptly.

"But how do you spell my name?"

"To tell you the truth," he confessed, "I've a most remarkable gift for identifying faces, but I can't always find the right label. Give me a clue, in your own case."

"Chislehurst," I answered. "The Hillier family. A fire, and your kindness when it happened."

He occupied the rest of the time by blessing his soul, and reprimanding his memory, and explaining that his thoughts were occupied with important affairs. He was incredulous regarding my news concerning his old friend—

"Not working in the Arsenal? Good Lord! Whatever will happen next in these times?"

—He assured me that, in making a large number of new acquaintances, he found no one so companionable as Mr. Hillier, nobody with whom he could argue on a perfectly amicable note. Sending my mind back to the disputes that used to take place, I could not help estimating the degree of warmth that existed in present-day debates between Colonel Edgington and his friends. He asked for the address of the private hotel where Mrs. Hillier and the two young people were staying, and promised to call on the Sunday.

"I find life perplexing, Weston," he admitted confidentially, before leaving at Saxmundham. "Everything seems to be undergoing an alteration. As for instance; in talking to you I've somehow felt as though I was conversing with one almost my own equal in intelligence." It was a great temptation to retort that I had never shared this, in talking to him. But there were people in the world more deserving of being snapped at than Colonel Edgington.

Aldeburgh gave reminders of the war that I had not hitherto encountered. At Greenwich, one saw troops marching about, but there was no suggestion that any possibility of invasion existed. Here, Miss Katherine and Master Edward pointed out to me excitedly the barbed wire protections on the beach, the trenches with the usual names—Paradise Terrace, Fairy Glen, A Home from Home—mine sweepers were coming in, and we watched the ships taking up position, and the crews disembarking. Up and down the coast, sea traffic appeared to be going on as usual; Master Edward gave us a lecture on the useful work done by the British navy. In the absence of his father, the lad was taking charge of the women-folk, planning the day for them, and surprising me by his grown-up manner: it seemed that but a week or ten days since he was a school-boy with no greater anxiety in his mind than that his county should win cricket matches. At the private hotel where Mrs. Hillier welcomed me, Edward talked gravely of war affairs, and recited scraps of information he had picked up during the afternoon, gave views about the Russian retreat, saw that the thick blinds were carefully drawn so soon as the lights had been turned on. In this last regard, there was nothing casual in the military control. When a match was struck near an unprotected window, a soldier's voice from below shouted imperiously.

"Put that light out there!"

And later, came the challenging that was new to me; the circumstance of it being given with a strong London accent made me think of it, at first, as a joke. "'Alt, who gaows there? Advaunce friend, and give the cahntersign. Paws friend; all's well!" Master Edward gave me a brief abstract of the rules to be observed in the case of attack from the sea; the general impression I secured was that you would do well to make the way inland by the main roads, and that as these would be required for military purposes, no civilians could be allowed to use them. That night, the Germans did make an invasion on the Suffolk coast, and I found myself, insufficiently clad for the journey, and with shoes that came off at every other step, carrying Mrs. Hillier, and Miss Katherine, and Master Edward; the progress, not unnaturally, was slow, and I felt so gratified at encountering Quartermaster-Sergeant Cartwright that I awoke suddenly in my room. (Other people's dreams are rarely interesting, but I have never failed to take great account of my own, and I sometimes wish that, during all the long years of suspense and perturbation, I had set down details of them for my own reading. It is not easy now to calculate the number of times between ten o'clock p.m. and six o'clock a.m. that I led a British regiment to victory, and made, with my own hands, a prisoner of the Emperor William.) In the morning I had a definite reminder of the war in being called upon to fill in a Registration Form for New Residents and Visitors, with present address in the area, date of arrival in the area. A refined lady boarder complained that the Government seemed to be treating us all as though we were kitchen maids.

It was strange to be in a house where the early hours brought no domestic tasks for me, and to find myself able to dress leisurely, and completely for the early meal. Master Edward ejaculated "My Aunt!" as I entered the coffee room, and Miss Katherine—observing that other residents nodded privately to each other as though the remark confirmed their estimate of relationship—at once adopted the idea.

"We shall be proud, madam," she declared, across the table, "to include such a considerable swell as yourself amongst the family. You will do us credit. Your presence raises us in the general estimation. You are, dear Aunt Weston, as my poor brother here endeavoured to convey, nothing more nor less than a fashion plate. You are the last word from Hanover Square. I am not using the language of exaggeration, but merely the speech of candid compliment, when I describe you as absolutely It."

"You are learning how to dress yourself," said Mrs. Hillier.

"Miss Katherine gave me the first lessons."

"Aunts," said the girl, decisively, "do not, in the best society, call their nieces by the title of Miss. Aunt Weston, I'll trouble you to hike over the toast."

It took me some time to become used to the new regulation, but the young people insisted it was to be observed. The proprietress spoke to me in the hall, and, in regretting the brevity of my visit, suggested that the holiday had already done my sister and her children a vast amount of good; the remark showed how quickly inaccurate news is able to circulate. The proprietress wanted information in regard to my niece's marriage prospects, but on this point I could give no particulars, and she said it was only fair to tell me that a young lieutenant named Langford had been offering attentions to Miss Hillier, that she and several other ladies at the hotel feared Miss Hillier's mother knew nothing about it; a sense of duty, together with a feeling of responsibility made it difficult for them to keep silent. There were, in the general opinion of the hotel, too many hasty marriages nowadays, and attractive girls, from some idea of patriotism, or a notion of acute sentiment—

"It certainly isn't love," declared the proprietress, earnestly. "At any rate, not love as I've always been brought up to understand it."

The girls, she declared, found themselves whirled off to the altar, or dashing away to a registrar's office, before they had taken time to give the subject due, solemn and appropriate consideration. I assured the lady that, in calling my notice to the incident, she had done everything that could be expected from any right-minded woman. She seemed greatly comforted, and went off, I am sure, to report to the authorities.

Lieutenant Langford was so tremendously and perhaps extravagantly astonished at meeting us near the Moat House, which Katherine had urged me to inspect, that he was at the start almost deprived of speech. The other strange detail was that he happened to have leave for the day, that he had invited a group of friends to join him in a yachting trip up the river, and every one of them had sent an excuse. Young Langford begged us to realise the situation in which he was placed, and to suggest a way out. The yacht was waiting with an efficient sailorman in charge; baskets of provisions aboard, and just enough wind for a pleasant trip.

"Deuced awkward, you must admit," he argued.

"Why not take these two young people?" I asked. Langford struck himself on the chest for not having thought of this. "I'll stay here with their mother, and you bring them back in time for tea."

"It's a brain wave," declared Katherine. "Aunt Weston, how bright you are! I'll run back to the hotel, and change my hat for a veil."

I had persuaded Mrs. Hillier the trip was a safe one to be undertaken, and we were waiting for Katherine's return, when Colonel Edgington came along. One could tell from the glint in his eyes that he was about to exercise authority.

"Well-known poet man," he announced, speaking the manner of drum taps. "Lived not many miles from here. We'll make up a party." Langford was presented; the Colonel eyed him sternly, until the young fellow blushed. "Ever heard of Mark Higham?"

Langford seemed puzzled.

"A Persian writer," I said, interposing. And gave the correct pronunciation of the name. "Fitzgerald translated his verses."

"Any good?" demanded the Colonel.

"Generally considered to be readable."

"Very well then. We'll go and see his grave. Appropriate occupation for a Sunday. Nothing sacrilegious about it." He turned sharply to Langford. "You'll come with us."

"Delighted, sir," said the young officer, endeavouring to appear gratified.

"And you, Weston."

"I am going on the river," I answered, "with Miss Katherine, and Master Edward. We particularly want Lieutenant Langford to look after the yacht."

"Mrs. Hillier," he said, frowning, "I ask you to give me your support. Nothing annoys me more than to see plans upset."

"The original plans were ours," I said, "and it is you who are trying to upset them."

He tried the effect of a glare upon me. The others stood around, watching anxiously.

"I've often crossed swords with you, Weston," he said, relaxing, "and I can't remember a single occasion when I came off anything but second best. Have your own way. Consider me at your disposal." He took Langford aside, and mentioned confidentially to him and to Miss Katherine, who had now come up, that in dealing with an exceptional woman, it was necessary to act in an exceptional manner. The young people, agreeing cordially, ventured to hint that he had shown tact and diplomacy of a high order.

Mrs. Hillier and the Colonel went off in an open carriage, and we walked along the sea front to something like a quay, where we descended wooden steps, receiving assistance from a sailor who was waiting with a dinghy. "You're a tidyish bit late," he grumbled. I record this speech because they were the only articulate words we heard from him in the course of the trip. On the yacht that was lying out, he made vocal sounds in lifting the anchor, but these, I fancy, were intended to represent melody; when Langford or Edward made an attempt later to help with the ropes, he grunted ejaculations, and the tone in which these were uttered gave the impression that they conveyed blame rather than praise. For the rest, a capable man, gifted in the management of sails, and acquainted with all the tricks of the wind; as a consequence we out-distanced other craft going in the same direction, and arrived at a village before the hour for lunch. By nods of the head, he ordered us to get into the dinghy that had followed the yacht with an air of being dragged against its will, and to pull to the shore; a fore-finger uplifted indicated that we were to return at one o'clock.

Miss Katherine and her sweetheart had been slightly awed by his presence, and with myself and Edward seated opposite, they engaged on no more reckless adventure than the exchange of affectionate glances. Once on land, they gave to folk coming out of church the sight of a young officer of His Majesty's Army running hand in hand with a girl, equally fleet in movement; the two raced towards the old Castle, and went up the slope with as much ease as though the ground were flat. Edward showed a discretion beyond his years by remaining at my side, and adopting the gait of maturity. Looking at the couple as they waved to us from afar I could not help thinking that youth was the only time for love, and that when it came at middle age, whether with Quartermaster-Sergeants, or railway men, or public speakers, it brought an element of sobriety that constituted a drawback. Another point of view was given by my companion.

"They make themselves rather ridiculous," complained Edward. "I've no objection to high spirits but the line ought to be drawn. People are watching them, you know, and making comments."

"And the beauty of it all is, they don't care in the least."

"Girls are so foolish," declared the wise lad. "There seems to be no limit to their idiocy. Why in the world a sensible fellow like Langford should permit himself to take a share in such absurdities, I can't imagine."

A motor car stood in the roadway, occupied by two extremely tall ladies who had apparently decided to allow the rest of their party to make the ascent to the Castle. One said, before we were out of hearing, "Bright, smart-looking lad!" and Edward held his head erect, and said no more on the subject of the eccentricities of folk who are in love. He was impressed, too, by finding just inside the door of the ruins, a portly gentleman who said, "Ah, my boy, enjoying your holidays? That's right, that's right, that's right!" Edward whispered to me that this was a very high official in railway life; so exalted, indeed, that to be spoken to by him in this familiar way might be reckoned as a special compliment, and one that would not easily go from the memory. We went up narrow stone staircases of the Castle to upper floors, and discovered Langford and Katherine with their heads close together; Edward's excitement over the recent encounter prevented him from offering criticism. From an opening in the walls he begged us to share the joy of watching the important man, seated on the grass below—

"You'd never guess he was anyone particular, would you?"

Filling a pipe and seemingly in no hurry to rejoin the very tall ladies who were beckoning to him from the car, Langford said casually, "Oh, I know him!" and turned again to Katherine. Compared with her, even a great personage seemed of no account. The pipe was not finished when we descended and came out again into the open; Edward gave an ejaculation of warning as Langford strolled across to the smoker.

"Hullo, uncle," he said. "What on earth are you doing in this neighbourhood?"

The other raised himself with Langford's assistance, and shook hands. Langford made the introductions. Sir Charles Barrett.

"This youngster I know," said Sir Charles, breezily. "We meet, don't we, my boy, in different surroundings." Edward was so much affected by the generosity of the remark that he could not answer. "Your aunt"—to Langford—"is along there with her sister in the car. Go and keep them good tempered until I have emptied my pipe. One can't enjoy tobacco when one's driving."

"Care to have food with us out on the river?"

"Settle it with your aunt, my lad. Let her arrange. Leave the decision to her. As a matter of fact, we were on our way to discover you."

There seemed at first a possibility that the new additions to the group would mar enjoyment of the day. Lunch on the yacht was to be a crowded business, and ladies of uncertain temper are rarely at their best in these surroundings. But Lady Barrett was delighted to see her nephew, and beamed graciously upon Miss Katherine and upon me: her sister repeated the comment on Edward's appearance, and chatted to him, inviting his views in regard to cricket in the past, and in the future. The capable sailorman had everything prepared on board, and Langford and Katherine went into the cabin to serve the meal; the rest of us sat outside with Sir Charles and Edward on the cabin roof, all ready to catch food as it was thrown, and to pull corks, mix salads, cut bread, pass the salt.

It was some time ere the lad managed to get over his astonishment at seeing a respected and distinguished colleague behaving as an ordinary person: I think Edward would not have succeeded in emerging from silence during the lunch but for the occasional words of encouragement sent up from Lady Barrett's sister. The sailor took his own well-filled plate and retired to the cubby-hole; the yacht was well away from both shores, and there was nothing to prevent us from taking up the attitude of comfort. The meal over, and plates washed in the river, and tidiness restored, Sir Charles, with no sort of warning, stood up and in a baritone voice slightly out of practice, aided by a memory that could not be described as perfect, gave a song appropriate to the times, about "A soldier who never knows fear, But battles for those he holds dear, And fa la la lah, and fa la la lah, Oh, as he goes by, how we cheer." Young Langford and Katherine sang a duet from one of the musical comedies with words which hinted at a light-hearted, almost derisive view regarding the element of constancy in love, and on this Lady Barrett's sister shook her head, and gave signs of tears, and Lady Barrett patted her hand sympathetically, saying, "I know who you are thinking of, dearest, but believe me he is not worthy of it!" and the sister, recovering, smiled bravely, thus providing Edward with an excuse for giving up a scowling determination to murder some person of the male sex, name unknown. Lady Barrett's sister, after much persuasion, agreed to recite. She mentioned, however, that it was necessary for an exhibition of her art that she should face her audience, and we had to gather together and sit closely, whilst she took up a position at the cabin door and gave a long scene in dramatic form, to which we were compelled to give earnest attention for a space of eighteen minutes by the wrist watch; all the gentlemen in the tragedy spoke huskily as though suffering from colds or drink, and all the ladies possessed gentle, almost childish voices; it might have filled the half hour but that the sailorman appeared and jerked a thumb in the direction of home. The visitors prepared to leave.

"Perfectly beautiful," declared Edward, rapturously. "Never heard anything like it. Superb! May I ask the name of the author?" Lady Barrett's sister pointed in a modest, and also an exhausted, way at herself, and the lad gazed dreamily as one recognising that powers of compliment were, in the circumstances, of no avail. Lady Barrett's sister remarked to me that elocutionary efforts constituted an enormous strain upon the mind and the body; in her own case it often meant compulsory rest in a darkened room for the whole of the following day. Lady Barrett, when her six-foot relative had, with the assistance of the whole strength of the company, stepped from the yacht to the dinghy, told us, in confidence, that London managers had often and often gone on their knees to the lady, begging and imploring her to play in Macbeth, but terms had never been arranged, because one of the parties insisted that it was impossible for her to perform Scene One, Act Five, on account of the language set down, and the managers—slaves to convention—were unable to meet her views by deleting the sanguinary incident. Langford took his people off to find their car in the garage, and we exchanged signals of farewell when they reached the small quay. I imagine the four of us left on the yacht were perfectly content. The sailor had the prospect of returning home, and later, of an hour or two at the Turk's Head; Katherine, meeting her sweetheart's relatives, had been favourably received by them; Edward had fallen in love with someone about three times his own age; I had been treated with no sign of patronage.

It was indeed the sort of day which, coming in those strenuous and exacting times, helped one to cheer up, and to live on, and to preserve hope. Without being in any way indifferent to the war, folk discovered it useful now and again to become detached from it, and to escape grim fears, and needless multiplication. (So far as multiplication was concerned, dwellers in town were the great sufferers. Occasionally when I had to run up to London from Greenwich, and the news of some disaster at sea happened to be announced on the countless placards, then, in finishing the journey, the vague notion in my mind was not that we had lost one cruiser, but that the entire British navy had gone down.) On the voyage back, Katherine and her young Lieutenant held hands, and forgot, for a space, the troubles of our banking system, and the complications of military strategy. The climax to a happy period came when Mrs. Hillier met us on the sea front near to the lifeboat shed.

"Aunt Weston must be told something at once," she declared, when the young people began to give an account of their experiences. "Something Colonel Edgington ascertained this afternoon. Her nephew has obtained a commission in a regiment stationed not far from here. He is coming home to do work at musketry practice."

"Ladies and gentlemen," said Katherine, "I ask you to give three cheers for Lieutenant Millwood."

It is possible the Aldeburgh people thought we were slightly off our heads. If so, the Aldeburgh people were correct.

I travelled to town that evening in a crowded compartment of the class named on my ticket, and whilst my fellow passengers slept, I kept awake and enjoyed my dreams. Young Langford, in seeing me off at the station, had explained to me that although his aunt and her husband had regarded himself and Katherine with approval, he felt by no means certain that this view would be shared by his father; to avoid a row and to escape anything like a dispute with a parent whom he had always obeyed, he proposed, in the case of being ordered out, to come up to London and take Katherine to a registrar's office. Langford hoped he might count upon me, both for help and for discretion.

"You know she is only a clerk in a bank?" I suggested. "Not sure whether you have been told. We don't want misunderstandings."

"The dear girl has told me everything," he declared, earnestly. "And it will be a most tremendous comfort to me when I'm out there, to know that her days are occupied, and that she has a rare, good friend in you!"

My open-eyed dreams regarded my nephew Herbert. The war had, so far as he was concerned, shuffled the cards afresh, and by the hour the train reached Liverpool Street, I had settled comfortably in my mind how the new hand was to be played.

"Miss Muriel shan't have him!" I promised myself.

CHAPTER XII

I assured Katherine, more than once, that whatever the need for secrecy so far as Lieutenant Langford was concerned, no necessity of the kind existed in her case. She pleaded to be allowed to have her own way, reminded me that Harry particularly desired that the fewest folk possible should know, and eventually settled the question by informing me, on the best authority, that her bank did not favour the assistance of married girls.

"I make no promise," I said, "but I shall do what I think best."

"That will be quite good enough, aunt dear," she agreed. "And may Providence reward you suitably by giving you a husband of your own."

"One might look upon that more as a punishment."

"Foolish scoffer!" she remarked.

Colonel Edgington came to Gloucester Place, and Mr. Hillier was glad to see him, but the evening could not be reckoned a success, because the caller harped upon an idea of obtaining for Mr. Hillier a soft job of some kind in Whitehall, and Mr. Hillier declared himself well contented with his present occupation. He gave details of this with great relish to the visitor, and Colonel Edgington commented with disparaging comments, such as,

"Bah!"

"Pooh!"

"Gah!"

"Brrrh!"

It seemed likely that friendship would diminish if meetings were to be conducted on these lines, and in seeing the Colonel out, at the end, I urged him not to call again for a week. Within that period I found a three-quarter size billiard table in good condition, late the property of a local club now, owing to the absence of youthful members, in need of money. Katherine and I cleared out the half room, half conservatory at the back of the rooms occupied by the Wintertons, and used by the old couple as a lumber room for odd articles accumulated during a lifetime, and of no use, as we managed to persuade them, of no use to anybody. Apart, the Captain assured me he had been for years anxious to destroy the rubbish, but feared this might pain his wife, and she declared to me in private that her impression had always been that he valued the collection dearly. We set up thick curtains over the glass, arranged for the electric light to be fixed over the table, placed a high long seat against the wall for the use of spectators, and when Colonel Edgington paid his next visit, he and Mr. Hillier were taken down to the newly furnished room, and the old sea captain, with great importance, took up the position of marker. The game not only checked conversation on a debatable subject, but brought the two chums into something like their former terms of intimacy; each discovered an excuse for the other when any failure occurred, and said,

"If you had been playing on a full-size table, that stroke of yours would have come off!"

Captain Winterton was well intentioned at the scoring board, but seldom remembered who was spot and who was plain, and his wife, with many apologies for intruding upon the company of gentlemen, entered to assist him in the perplexing task, with the result that one of the two opponents, at the close of the game, was able to declare, upstairs, that he would not have been the first to reach the two hundred if the score had been correctly kept. The time came when Edward offered to give lessons to the old captain, and this was self-denying on the part of the lad, for no plan, however ingeniously devised—giving eighty-five in a hundred, or three strokes to one—ever assisted Captain Winterton to get near to a close finish. We encouraged him with judicious flattery, and although he usually took about two minutes to decide how to play a ball, he invariably declared that his one fault was recklessness; this defect amended, he felt sure he would be numbered amongst the experts. Meanwhile, he quickly adopted one method of the billiard room by giving copious and truculent advice to Edward, using for this a booming fog-horn voice, altogether different from his normal tones.

"Play it off the cushion, my lad!" And "For Heaven's sake, don't pot the red; the white's in baulk!" And "Chalk your cue, sir; damme, chalk your cue!" The game over, and the result announced, he went back to the usual manner of courtesy. One advantage gained from the presence of the old gentleman was that as he still declined to argue about the war, or to recognise that it existed, all of us, including Colonel Edgington, decided to imitate this peculiarity.

Which did not mean that our minds were permitted, for long, to escape the subject. From a customer, I heard that some exchanged men had arrived at the Third London General Hospital at Wandsworth, and I went over there on a Wednesday afternoon that Millwood was able to give to the shop, to ascertain whether any of them had been in the camp from which Master John's letters and post cards, with now and again an alteration in number, or company, or barracks, were now dated. There was some trouble at the gates because I had no permit, but I mentioned I had come from Greenwich, and the sentry, remarking with pride that his birthplace was Maze Hill, found a solution of the difficulty. "I'll turn my back," he said, "and pretend to have a sudden fit of a cough: you take advantage of my infirmity, and slip through."

Maimed soldiers in blue uniforms were about on the sloping lawn that went to the railway; some had groups of friends around them, and a few were alone. I went past the main building, and entered a corridor that took me past a number of wards, well ventilated, cheerful and with the faint scent of anæsthetics, and to nurses I put an inquiry; for the most part they could give no information, but one or two suggested C5. Outside C5 I found two men who had no visitors, and they replied to my question alertly and re-assuringly. They had said good-bye to Corporal Hillier but five days previously. He had gone up for examination with the others selected, but was sent back. They felt certain he would come along in the next group. They said Corporal Hillier was bright and well; his knowledge of French and German proved helpful. Being amongst the wounded, he was not called upon to perform arduous tasks. Both said the treatment was as good as one could hope for, excepting in regard to food. "The food, miss, is absolutely— well, there's no word for it! At any rate, not one that could be repeated to you." They agreed that no British prisoner could keep alive unless he received parcels from home, and assured me Corporal Hillier was more fortunate than many in this respect. "He gets two a week, he does, regular, besides them from his own family. Two a week, sent by a particular donah of his called Weston. We've noticed her name on the labels." I was about to make further inquiries, but a child's voice at the doorway of C5 called "Daddie—Daddie. Don't you know me?" and one hobbled off to greet the little girl; the other man was summoned by a Yorkshireman who, engaged in writing a letter, needed some counsel in regard to spelling. On my return I noticed in the wards of the corridor, one or two men in their beds who looked dejected and tired of everything; a Sister was explaining to some callers that these suffered from gas poison. For the rest, they were so cheery, and good-spirited that you might have thought—to look at their features, and to disregard their injured bodies—that they had been taking a share in nothing more serious than a rather exhilarating football match.

The times were all the more interesting because the age of miracles re-appeared. In a local hospital which I visited, with Katherine, on Sunday afternoons, there was a young soldier afflicted with loss of speech, following upon shell-shock. He proved a ready student, and we were gratified by the way in which, under our tuition, he picked up the deaf and dumb alphabet. We might have saved ourselves the trouble. One afternoon we called, and went directly to his corner, prepared to give advanced lessons.

"Begun to think," he remarked, in a natural voice, "that you two were going to give me the slip. What's delayed you?"

It appeared that on the Saturday, a group of amateurs had come to give a harlequinade entertainment. One dressed as a clown, in going through the ward, advanced playfully towards our soldier, holding out the red painted poker that was to take a share in the acting. The youth started back affrighted, and speaking for the first time for months, told the clown to be careful, adding that he had no desire to find himself burnt. From that moment, onwards, he made up by vivacious conversation for the period of enforced silence.

Hospitals could scarcely be evaded by anybody, and you never knew whom you might meet there. For instance, a customer of mine, after declaring that she would add nothing to her collection of old furniture on the grounds that money should be saved and lent to the Government, discovered in a friend's house a Queen Anne tallboy chest, and a craving for possession took hold of her. The friend resolutely declined to sell; my customer came to me with an urgent appeal. I saw an advertisement of one from a London square, and although I begrudged the trouble of the journey, and the giving up of time, I went to town; spent a brisk three-quarters of an hour in haggling with a gentleman who knew more of the subject than I had ever attempted to learn; made a feint of coming away and was re-called by him, to listen to a frank statement of eagerness to sell. On this, I fixed upon an Adam elbow chair, affecting to have lost all interest in the tallboy chest. I eventually obtained the chest at less than the figure I had first offered. On the best of terms now, he made me promise that before returning to Greenwich I would inspect the glass windows, not far off, which had been broken in an air raid of a few nights before.

On the way I noticed that a hospital where wounded soldiers were sunning themselves outside, announced a Pound Day and a grand entertainment for the current date. Remembering the profit I was to make out of the chest bargain, I went up the steps, put my sovereign on the matron's table. I think it was the rare sight of gold that caused the official lady to exhibit particular gratitude—there were several notes there signed by Mr. Bradbury—and anyway I found myself taken by her to the out-patient's department where a show was being given by a first class set of good-natured theatrical folk. (There seemed to be no limits to the kindness of their profession).

The matron caught sight of me as I was leaving, and dropped everything in order to intercept. I had not signed her Visitor's Book. I must undoubtedly sign her Visitor's Book. Her Visitor's Book would be valueless without my signature. On the same page, and but a couple of entries above, appeared the name of Herbert Millwood. It seemed my nephew was upstairs visiting one of the men, and feeling myself well repaid now for a burst of generosity, I waited outside for him.

"No, aunt," he said, when I made a suggestion concerning the raid as we walked in the crowded main road. "Smashed glass belonging to other people makes no call to me. Broken hopes belonging to myself are much more important."

It appeared he was going back to duty that night, and had to catch a train from Liverpool Street; I soon discovered that he had spent the day in making one more effort to discover Muriel Hillier.

"I've no patience with her," I declared. "There can't be a good reason for keeping her relatives in suspense. If I came across her now, I should have a word or two to say to her."

"And I too," remarked Herbert. "Likely enough, though our words would not be identical."

We turned into Red Lion Square to escape the crush.

"I know how difficult it is to give advice, my boy," I said, "in matters of the kind, and I'm aware that it's next door to impossible to get it accepted. But I wish you'd recognise that the situation has very much changed since the time when you fell in love with her. You're a lieutenant now. You're an officer in His Majesty's army. You've made a good record. Whilst she—"

"I don't want to hear anything for her, aunt, or against her. I only want to hear something of her."

"She may have found somebody—"

"'May,'" he echoed, impatiently, "'May' conveys nothing to me. The truth is what I'm going to find out."

"How?"

"By all the means in my power. By all the means in other folk's power that I can command with influence or money." He turned appealingly to me. "You are clever at most things, aunt."

"If I lose a needle, my boy, I don't go searching for it in a bundle of hay. I get a new one. And listen to me. You know how much I care for you." For answer, he pressed my arm affectionately. "If I've been able to do something for you since your dear mother went, why it has been done, not only because it was my duty, but because I reckoned it a pleasure. And to be quite plain and candid, I've no desire to see you, when the war is over, going back to your ordinary career, hampered, and crippled, and bothered by a selfish wife who, all the years I've known her—"

"This," he interrupted, "is an admission that you haven't put your head into the work. Be a good soul now, aunt, and do me a great favour. I promise I'll never ask for another, so long as I live."

"That's a promise I hope you'll break."

"Find her!" he persisted. "Let me know she's safe and well, and you'll place me so much in your debt that, whatever I do, I shall never be able to repay you. Give me a kiss to seal the bargain."

There was no refusing when he put the case in this way. I guaranteed that I would increase my efforts, assured him I would strain every nerve to find her. We walked through the narrow passage to Red Lion Street, and in Holborn, before taking a motor omnibus, he declared, cheerfully, that he knew I would be sending him news ere the month was out.

Young Langford received a hint that his regiment was to be ordered abroad at an early date, and news of the engagement had to be announced at Gloucester Place; this done, I took Katherine off to the registrar's office, and made the necessary inquiries. It appeared that the official there was used at the time to hastened ceremonies; he seemed to expect that I, too, had an intention of getting married without delay. We decided it was to be done by licence, and Katherine was able to state that she had lived in the district for fifteen days; she felt justified in declaring that there existed no legal impediment. It was fortunate that we acted promptly. At home we discovered a telegram of reckless extent from young Langford announcing that he was coming to town on the morrow, and leaving England on the day which followed.

"I had intended," said Mrs. Hillier, smiling, "to read my little girl a lecture, but there's no time for that now."

"It will be all hurry-scurry," I mentioned.

Hurry-scurry it was, but Mrs. Hillier and I agreed that the day was not to be exempt of formality, and we all resolved that the dear girl should not go without wedding presents. So there was shopping to be done, food to be ordered, and Captain Winterton was directed to be ready to stand by in case Mr. Hillier proved unable to obtain leave from his work at the Arsenal. I had given assistance to a next door neighbour of mine in London Street at a period when he was experiencing domestic anxiety, and, after the baby came, and all was well at home, he mentioned to me that if I wanted anyone, at any time, to look after my shop for a few hours, he would be offended unless the choice fell upon him. Katherine wrote to the bank to say a slight attack of neuralgia made it advisable that she should remain indoors for twenty-four hours; she added a dutiful apology. Edward declared that the question of his leave of absence was an easy matter: if necessary, he proposed to seek audience of Sir Charles Barrett himself and explain the reason. He found the idea received with screams of protest.

"Thoughtless infant!" cried Katherine.

"Foolish lad," I ejaculated.

Edward, reminded of the demands of secrecy, admitted he had come near to putting his foot deep into disaster, and took some credit for having enabled us to give a warning.

It is certain that no one took such a keen relish of anticipation in the ceremony as Captain Winterton. His habit was to walk the pavement of Gloucester Place on fine mornings as though he were pacing a deck; the residents knew that when he crossed and made the tour of The Circus, exercise was nearing its finish. Generally for this promenade he was apparelled in a blue serge reefer suit and a peaked cap: on the great day, the old sea captain wore a silk hat with a crescent-shaped brim that, despite good condition, marked its age; he had lavender trousers, yellow waistcoat, a frock coat of the style of the eighties, a malacca cane. Always courteous in acknowledging salutations, he now stopped to chat with tradesmen and neighbours, feeling perhaps that an explanation of his splendour was due to them. We had to thank the Captain for the fact that a small crowd of ladies began to assemble near the house, very hardly tried in the endeavour to pretend that each was there by accident; from the balcony I could hear those who had come in pairs bewailing the circumstance that the wedding was not to take place at a church.

"Seems such a skimpy way of getting married," they declared.

Young Langford arrived in good time, and shewed exuberant spirits when he found that the arrangements were complete and satisfactory. "Ought to have known I could rely upon you, Miss Weston. And I've been in a most frightful agony of mind in the train; you've no idea. Eleven o'clock? Right-o. This is absolutely topping!" Mr. Hillier did not return from the Arsenal, and he had told us to avoid waiting for him. The four of us went down the stairs, found Captain Winterton in the hall.

"I know, my love," said his wife to Katherine, coming out of her room, "that it doesn't go with your costume, but, just to please me, wear this piece of lace. It brought me happiness, and I've got the notion into my foolish old head that it may bring good luck to you. It's valuable," she added, nodding her head, "in more senses than one."

"I'll take every care of it," promised Katherine, "and you shall have it back in less than an hour."

"You're to keep it all your life, dearie. And I've some other bits for you, later on, to go with it."

It was but a short walk from Gloucester Place to Trafalgar Road, but we gained enough attention to satisfy any craving in that respect. The sight of old Captain Winterton, arm-in-arm with Miss Katherine in itself attracted notice; I wanted the party to stroll along informally, but he begged me to allow him to superintend this detail, and his joy in thus leading the procession was something it would have been a pity to hurt. Arrived, he marshalled us two deep, and went into the office to make inquiries. Returning, he appeared to have bethought himself of the fact that this was to be a quiet wedding, for he beckoned in a mysterious way, spoke in a whisper assuring us all was in order. Within, his deportment was that of a devout person in church; the discreet manner in which he gave half-sovereigns to everyone about the place willing to accept tips, suggested an anxiety to make the ceremony as legal and binding as possible. The two young people made a good-looking couple as they stood at the table, and they were extraordinarily composed; for myself, I can restrain tears, with no difficulty, at a funeral, but at a wedding—well, the one incident comes, as it were, at the end of the story, and there is nothing more to be found out concerning it: in the second, you cannot help speculating, and wondering, and sometimes fearing in regard to the coming chapters.

The registrar—I knew him by sight as well as anything, and had always guessed, incorrectly, he had to do with a picture palace—the registrar shook hands, gave over the certificate, and told the bridegroom (first inquiring anxiously whether he had seen this week's *Punch*) an anecdote concerning a drill-sergeant. I think old Captain Winterton was rather pained at this secular demeanour, for he escorted us out, sorted us into couples, and gave orders. "The wife," he whispered to me, "will be desirous of knowing that everything has gone off well." In Gloucester Place, some of our neighbours did an act that I shall always remember to their credit; from the balconies they threw down flowers as the young soldier and his bride came near. I recollect that Katherine picked all of them up, and smiled at the givers, and blew a kiss to an infant, who, held by his nurse, was clapping his chubby hands.

The meal was, for Edward's sake, taken early; the lad seemed concerned at the possibility of disastrous happenings at the head offices during his absence, and assured his new brother-in-law that railway life exacted, in these days, and under Government control, a strain that military men with their comparatively simple duties could scarcely estimate. Langford appeared to be in no humour to dispute or argue with anybody.

"People say I look worried," remarked Edward. "What do you think?"

Langford had not observed this, but if it existed, felt sure there was every reason.

"You wouldn't imagine I was not much more than fifteen, would you?"

Langford had, it appeared, estimated the other's age as higher than this; Edward showed gratification.

"By-the-bye, there was something I meant to ask when I saw you—I have such a lot to think about that—I know what it was. Your unmarried aunt whom we met at Aldeburgh. Keeping well, I hope?"

Langford was able to give re-assuring information.

Mrs. Winterton came up to the meal, bringing her present of more lace, and the rest of us exhibited our purchases. The gifts were all of a simple nature, but the young couple showed rapture over each article; Katherine reproached me with forgetting that the baby grand in the corner had always been looked upon as a wedding gift, in advance. Everything would have proceeded smoothly but that Edward, coming out of a fit of abstraction remarked suddenly:

"Wish Muriel had been here!"

Captain Winterton broke the silence which followed, by adjusting the plates and glasses before him, pulling at collar, clearing voice, running fingers through his white head of hair. Standing up, he bowed to Mrs. Hillier. He rose, he said, on this happy occasion—this festive, domestic and matrimonial occasion, he might say—to propose a toast, one which, he felt sure, we should all join heart and hand in drinking. It was a happy toast, and this was a happy occasion. He loved a wedding, and during his somewhat lengthened progress through life—and he had had his fair share of bunions: yes, we might laugh, but he was speaking the truth—as he said, he loved a wedding; he had been to many, and hoped to go to many more. Captain Winterton spoke for five minutes, and closed with these lines,

> "*The toast, the toast, the toast's the thing*
> *To make hands tingle, and glasses ring.*"

The old chap seemed greatly relieved to get the speech over: it occurred to me the style of it was somewhat away from his usual manner. Lieutenant Langford said, "Thanks, ever so much!" and we were chatting freely when the bell rang at the front door. I ran down. Colonel Edgington. He had brought a square parcel for Katherine, and was about to leave it, with his compliments, when I told him the wedding had just taken place. He bustled up the stairs, upbraided Mrs. Hillier for not informing him of the date, kissed the bride, took a chair, and declining other food, ate an orange with considerable fierceness. Katherine filled his glass, and he stood up, and frowned at us.

"I rise," he said, in a loud, determined voice, "on this happy, and I might say, festive, domestic and matrimonial occasion, to propose a toast which, I feel sure, you will all join heart and hand in drinking. It is a happy toast, and this is a happy occasion. I love a wedding, and during my somewhat lengthened progress through life, and I have had my fair share of bunions— oh yes, you may laugh, but I am speaking the truth—" The Colonel finished with,

> "*The toast, the toast, the toast's the thing*
> *To make hands tingle, and glasses ring.*"

The solution of the duplicated address came, days later, when we had discussed fully the question of coincidences. A middle-aged clerk in Edward's office, invited to a wedding breakfast, had been cautioned that he would be expected to propose the health of the bride and bridegroom. Edward was called upon to listen to his colleague's recital of the same piece of eloquence from a shilling book called, "Speeches for Every Occasion."

CHAPTER XIII

Lieutenant and Mrs. Langford went off to town, and by nine o'clock the following morning Katherine was at the bank, her wedding ring in hiding and attached to a thin gold chain that hung around her neck; I am sure she found a keener delight in the secrecy than she would have discovered in the most elaborate publicity. Young Langford's battalion left Southampton with three rumoured destinations—France, The Dardanelles, Mesopotamia—and all we could say of these was that at least two were surely inaccurate; the dear girl came to London Street that evening and in the back room, and on my shoulder had a long cry, and, this over, gave no signs of depression or tears. We had good news one Sunday night of an advance by British troops south of La Bassée, and a victory by the French in the Champagne district; to hear folk talking of this near the railway station you would have guessed that the war was almost at an end. A few days later the casualty lists of our officers came in, and we knew then some of the expense of the small victory, and could guess at the total. The newspapers were in disagreement concerning the proposed landing of troops at Salonica. A quotation from a Paris journal was headed, "Help Mother First." My customers, at times, brought me their definite and resolute views on the conduct of the war, and seemed disappointed that I was prepared to go no further than admit relief in the thought that I had not to take a share in the direction.

"Women," they argued, "couldn't make a bigger muddle of it than men are doing."

"Nothing ever happened yet," I said, "that might not possibly have been worse. Let's keep cheerful. Peace will come along some day."

"And then," grumbled a woman from Plumstead, "there won't be near so much money to be earnt as what there is now."

Certainly there was no lack of critics at that period. A blind man who sold matches and boot-laces said to me one evening that he would very much like to occupy Kitchener's position for twenty-four hours. Four-and-twenty hours; no more, no less. He refused to disclose his scheme to me in full, but hinted that it included the dropping of a bomb full tilt on the helmet of the German Emperor. "The Government hasn't got gumption," he complained. "What it wants is the help of us business men. We'd soon stop these Zepps!"

There came another and a serious air-raid, and hearing a certain town spoken of in this connection, I hurried there to ascertain whether some small houses belonging to me had been damaged. There was a considerable amount of destruction there, but my little property was safe, and I managed to get away from the excited tenants, and escape some of the vivid details of the attack. Intending to alight at New Cross station on the Brighton line, I, absorbed in the evening newspaper, found myself carried on towards London Bridge. I wanted to reach home swiftly, because the private inquiry folk, whose services I had engaged immediately after my officer nephew's urgent appeal, had hinted that they expected to be able to send me a communication by an early post. There seemed few grounds for hoping that this would be satisfactory, and bewailing my stupidity in missing New Cross, and regretting the delay, I changed thoughts from self-reproach by composing a letter which would convey my regrets at the failure of the inquiry, sarcasm at the want of intelligence exhibited. To be candid, it was only for the sake of Herbert that I wanted to gain news of Muriel Hillier. We were a comfortable group now at Gloucester Place, and the return there of an authoritative and selfish-minded girl was not an alluring prospect.

"How much is the excess fare?" I asked, at the barrier.

"One moment, madam. Stand aside, please, and let the other passengers go through."

For some reason, I had not before encountered girl ticket collectors, and the politeness of manner surprised me. Obeying the instructions, I waited in the shadow; the peak-capped young woman collected tickets, disregarded a florid gentleman's offer of a rose, gave brisk information concerning return trains. Then she turned to me, and the light of the lamp shewed her features.

"Miss Muriel!" I exclaimed.

"Excess from New Cross," she said, filling in a slip from a book. "Threepence." Taking the coin and the ticket from me, and handing over the change. "Ninepence, thank you." I went through the barrier, expecting her to follow, but she closed it and remained on the platform.

The inspector said he would certainly give me all the assistance in his power, so soon as he was free from the task of despatching a main line train. Ten minutes later, he and I searched the ticket collectors' office. Two of the uniformed girls were emptying tickets from pouches, and sorting them.

"That is the young lady I wish to speak to," I said, pointing.

She turned and faced me.

"You've made a bloomer," remarked the inspector, frankly. "You want a party with the cognomen so to speak of Hillier, I understand. This one is Miss Dumbrill."

"That is my name," she said, composedly.

"I don't care what she calls herself," I declared. "I know very well who she is." I appealed to her. "You recognise me, don't you, dear?"

"Oh, yes," she said.

"There!" to the inspector. "What did I tell you?"

"Remember you quite well," she went on, eyeing me steadily. "You had a ticket as far as New Cross, and I excessed it. You gave me a shilling, and I handed you the right change. What is your grievance?"

The other girl stood by, watching interestedly.

"I am Weston," I said. "Mary Weston."

"If that is the only complaint you have to make," she said, "it is not very serious."

"I was housekeeper for many years at your people's place at Chislehurst. I moved with them to Greenwich. Your brother John enlisted, with my nephew Herbert Millwood. Herbert is more anxious than anyone else to have news of you. He has a commission now."

"And the Victoria Cross?"

"No."

"Strange," she mentioned. "In romantic stories of this kind, they invariably gain the Victoria Cross." She spoke to the inspector. "Find out where this lady wishes to go, and put her on her way, will you? If she hasn't any money, I'll provide all that's needed."

"Miss Muriel, Miss Muriel!" I cried. "For Heaven's sake, don't go on playing this silly game. If you want to keep your independence, you can do it, without all this. You don't know how much worry your folk have gone through on your account!"

The inspector was called away by a porter. I left the collectors' room, and stood at the doorway, endeavouring to think of some plan.

"Shut the door, please," she said, attending once again to her work of sorting. She found that the order was not obeyed, and came forward.

"Miss Muriel," I whispered, urgently. "Your mother. She is seriously ill. Not expected to live. And wants to see you."

Her features became pale. With a nervous movement she tipped back her peaked cap, and she hesitated.

"Wait for me," she said in a low voice, "near the bookstall at the other station."

I did not mind any delay, and objected the less because I found at the stall my young friend Peter serving newspapers and magazines alertly; ready to chat with me, in the intervals, on what he called, with an air of enormous age, the good old times at Greenwich. He endeavoured, I am sure, to keep the suggestion of patronage out of his inquiries, but it seemed impossible for him to disguise the fear that Greenwich, since his departure, had been on the down grade, and that nothing could be done for it unless Providence thought fit to return him to the neighbourhood. Peter was still engaged with the Scouts: he had attained a notable position of authority, and was persuading all his younger colleagues to join. Peter said his firm had sent thousands of men to the war; if it lasted long enough he himself hoped to have a chance of taking a part in it. "I'd like to account for a few odd Germans," he said. "By-the-bye, how's that poor nephew of yours getting on? And his poor old father. And poor old Mr. Hillier? And poor old Mrs. Hillier?" In assuring Peter these were well, I recollected that trouble would be encountered later when an explanation had to be given of the statement used to persuade Muriel to accompany me. Always a difficult young lady, it was not easy to guess how much reason had been brought into her disposition by the change of surroundings and the new manner of life. She came up when I was considering the best moment for an admission.

"Is my mother really very ill, Weston?" she demanded.

"It's doubtful," I answered promptly, "whether she will ever be able to leave the house again."

We went up the slope to the platform; it happened that a train arrived immediately. The carriages were crowded, and as we both had to stand up, conversation—fortunately for me—was impossible. The great point was to get her to Gloucester Place, and meet her folk; I felt ready to take any amount of blame and criticism so long as this result was effected. As intervening passengers swayed to and fro, I observed, now and again, the alteration in her appearance. Muriel had lost the petulant, fractious air; in its place was a manner of determination, and self-reliance. A middle-aged man, after thinking the subject over so far as Deptford, rose and asked her to take his place; she answered that he was not to incommode himself. At Greenwich, and on the platform, she took my arm.

"Don't let us talk," she begged. "I want to get there as quickly as possible. She may be asking for me."

A small car was standing outside the door, and, recognising it, I thought perhaps the doctor had called to see the old couple on the ground floor. In the hall stood Captain Winterton and his wife: they were holding hands, and their features shewed acute anxiety. The house was very silent.

"At last," he whispered, relievedly. "She wants you, Miss Weston."

"Who?"

"That," said Muriel, "is surely an unnecessary question." She led the way briskly upstairs.

"We heard a bumping sound overhead," explained Mrs. Winterton to me. "We ran up at once, and found Mrs. Hillier in a faint on the floor. The Captain rushed at once for a medical man."

The doctor was on the landing as I ascended the staircase. He looked grave, but on that I put no great account: it is one of the tricks of some members of the profession to hint at acute difficulties and thus emphasise the credit for overcoming them. He said Mrs. Hillier had probably been attacked by sudden giddiness, and that the fall had stunned her; he was perturbed by the fact that she had not yet regained consciousness.

"She has had worries, doctor."

"Of course, of course," he said, impatiently. "Everyone has them in these days."

"Her's have been rather extra special. But the presence of her elder daughter will have a wonderful effect when she comes to."

"If she comes to," he corrected.

Katherine was home from the bank, but Mr. Hillier and Edward had not arrived. The doctor and the Wintertons had carried my mistress into the bedroom, and there I found the two girls watching their mother intently and apprehensively. I loosened a part of Mrs. Hillier's dress and took her hand; there came a slight twitch of the face, nothing more. The doctor was called from below. Returning, he said that he had been summoned to a case of a young wife in Croom's Hill; it was imperative he should attend, for no nurse was in attendance. He gave me instructions, promised to come back. I could not help agreeing that his services were more valuable in a case where an addition was being made to the world than in one, at the other end of life, where he could do little.

"By-the-bye," he said, at the front door, whilst his man was re-starting the car, "I know all about you, Miss Weston. A friend of mine, once a doctor of the neighbourhood, has a house, so well furnished that his wife is envied by the wives of all other medical men. He confided to me that the credit was really due to you. Now, I wonder whether you would mind, some day, looking in at my place, and just giving a word of advice—"

"My dear sir," I declared, "this is no time to be talking shop. At any rate, not my shop. All I can think of now is whether the dear soul upstairs is going to recover."

Edward came home full of a compliment that had been paid to his railway by a notable statesman; he hushed down at once, and begged I would give him tasks to perform. I could think of nothing else but the job of meeting his father at the station, and giving a hint of the news that waited in Gloucester Place. To the lad's satisfaction, this proved worth doing, for Mr. Hillier had intended to give up an evening to one more search in town for his elder daughter. Edward was able, from the platform, to beckon to him.

We all stood about in the rooms, talking quietly. No commotion was made over the return of Muriel, and few explanations were asked, but Edward declared himself puzzled and slightly aggrieved on hearing that his sister, for nearly all the time that we were looking for her, had been so close to the offices in which he himself was engaged.

"She's altered," he remarked. "Less disposed to make every one wait upon her, hand and foot."

I hurried from him to the side of the bed.

"Muriel," Mrs. Hillier was saying. "My Muriel!"

The girl, at a signal from me, came across, and kneeling down, took her mother's hand, placing it against her own cheek. The hand moved slowly upwards and smoothed the hair.

"Ah!" ejaculated the dear woman, contentedly. And her head drooped on the pillow. I adjusted the clothes and bent down to listen.

"Wonder how long the doctor will be," whispered Mr. Hillier anxiously, "before he comes back."

"There is nothing for him to do now, sir," I replied.

I sat up all that night—I could not tell you why—and the others rested. The two girls went off tearfully to Katherine's room; and I could hear them whispering confidences to each other until the early hours of the morning. Breakfast was ready when they all came into the sitting room; I might have spared myself the trouble of preparing anything but the coffee. The blinds remained down; the cheerful sounds of a waking day in the gardens had a jarring note.

"The funeral on Sunday," I suggested to Mr. Hillier. "Will that be convenient?" I tried to speak in business-like tones.

"Please take charge of it, Weston," he begged. "I feel rather—rather knocked over."

"You ought to stay away from the Arsenal for a week, sir."

"No, no! Work is the best thing for all of us. Especially just now." He went around the table and kissed the three, and hesitated after embracing Muriel. "My big girl," he said, nervously, "is not going to leave us again?"

"I meant to, father," she replied, quietly, "but this makes a difference. This brings us together."

"Wish John were at home," he said.

"We've been saying that," I remarked, in a brisk way, "ever since he was taken at La Bassée. We shall have to be patient until the war is over. No use expecting wonders to happen, just to oblige us."

I wrote that morning to my nephew Herbert.

Herbert's father was entitled, by his alertness, to put in a claim for a smart piece of work. He happened to be at a military hospital, Westminster way; an entertainment was being given to some of the wounded, and he had been asked to give one of his rousing, patriotic speeches. The commandant, in shewing him around, mentioned that some exchanged men had arrived that day.

Millwood said, "I want some fresh stuff to talk about. Let's have a glance at 'em, and a bit of a chat with 'em." The first one he spoke to was introduced as Corporal Hillier.

CHAPTER XIV

John was allowed by the hospital authorities to come to Greenwich for the ceremony, and his return to Gloucester Place—which we had often decided, in conversation, was to be a great incident, with flags out at the balcony, and, indoors, food and much rejoicing—found itself tempered by the circumstances. We reckoned to find him changed; it never occurred to us that his wounds and his hard experiences would have aged and altered him so much. But for his voice—and that, too, was not quite the same that one remembered—it might have been difficult for those who knew him but casually to identify him. We came back from the cemetery at Lewisham, leaving there the two simple wreaths (one from her Ever loving Husband and Children, and the other from Mary Weston, with Respectful Sympathy) to find Colonel Edgington waiting outside the house in Gloucester Place, and swelling with annoyance because he had been unable to obtain an answer to his summons with the knocker, or his appeal with the bell. The Wintertons, desirous of not intruding upon us, were out for the day, and their maid had gone to see the boys performing their exercises on the corvette that rests on a calm sea of asphalt near the Royal Hospital School; she was doubtless giving a special interest to a scholar in Boreman's Foundation, who chanced to be her brother. Although the blinds were down, and we, with the exception of John Hillier, wore black, the Colonel did not make a guess at the loss which had taken place; he explained that he had written out a telegram to Mr. Hillier on the previous evening announcing that he intended to call and provide an afternoon's enjoyment but, by oversight, had given no orders for this to be taken to the Post Office. He seemed to reckon this a trifling omission on his part, and was sketching out the programme when I took him aside.

"Bless my soul!" he ejaculated. "Good gracious me! Heart failure, you say, Weston? I never heard the poor lady suffered in that way. Why wasn't I told? People," he fumed, "seem to take a positive delight in keeping me ignorant."

"Perhaps because it's so difficult to make you understand."

"Not at all," he declared, heatedly. "Always most willing to listen. Exceedingly eager to gain information! I ought not to be treated in this fashion. Dam shame, Weston, dam shame. And I can't help thinking that you are responsible."

"We'll say that it's my fault, sir."

"No, no," he protested. "Not so much your fault as your misfortune. You ought to get married." He pulled at his uniform and, having delivered the reprimand, went across to Mr. Hillier. "My dear old friend," he said, with genuine sympathy. "What can I say to you excepting that I'm awfully sorry. Command me, please, if you want help. I'm not much use in that way, but all that I can do—" To my surprise, he broke down. At the grave-side Muriel had been the only one to give way.

Colonel Edgington, always at his best in the presence of disaster, recovered, and followed us upstairs, sat with us at the meal, and contrived to induce John to talk of his experiences. A war map had been pinned on the wall, as in most households, and John, once started, gave an animated description of the fighting at La Bassée, described the journey, taken whilst he was in a seriously wounded condition, to Lille, furnished an account of his various transfers from lager to lager, the treatment he received, the folk he encountered. We listened attentively, rather glad to have our thoughts switched away from immediate trouble, and John sent off all of his detached manner, becoming really eloquent towards the end. At the finish his young brother started the applause, and the rest of us joined in.

"But I say," cried Edward enthusiastically, "all that, you know, is absolutely ripping."

"You'll write some articles in one of the magazines, John," suggested his father.

"Any of the daily papers," remarked Katherine, "would be jolly glad to have the stuff."

"Much more dignified," said Colonel Edgington, "to put it in a book. A big book. A large book. A well-bound book."

"What about a lecturing tour?" I asked.

It appeared that none of them had acquaintance with this procedure, and all I knew had been gained from my brother-in-law, Millwood. I told them of his successes, and the fees he occasionally made; John admitted that, so soon as he found himself discharged from the hospital, nothing would suit him better than to travel about the country, and speak to audiences; he said it was likely to distract his mind, and prevent it from brooding over the misfortunes that had happened to him; by talking of them, he reckoned it possible that he might consider them less acutely. I promised to make inquiries regarding the agency of which Millwood had spoken: mentioned that, according to him, the business arrangements were taken over, and all the lecturer had to do was to make a note of the places and the dates. Ten per cent. deducted for commission.

"Occurs to me," interposed Colonel Edgington, "that there'll be a large number of returned men willing to take on a job of this nature."

"Willing, perhaps," I said, "but not qualified. Master John," I declared, "will get ten or twelve guineas for each lecture."

"I have said my say," remarked the Colonel brusquely.

"If Aunt Weston is determined John is to go on a tour," mentioned Katherine, "nothing that any of us argues, Colonel Edgington, will have the slightest value."

"Obstinacy in a woman," he announced, "is a quality that—that—"

"A quality," she said, "that in men is called firm resolution. John, you ought to have some pictures."

Here Muriel proved helpful. She remembered that her friend, once of Chislehurst, now in one of His Majesty's prisons, had given her a set of photographs that illustrated towns in Germany, and some concerned the places where John had been detained; she had also in her trunk, which was now on the way from Camberwell, German illustrated magazines which would furnish, by their war pictures, useful material. We sat around the table, discussing the matter eagerly, and presently Colonel Edgington took part in the debate, and made a very good recommendation to the effect that the agency should be persuaded to take a hall in the West End for John's first appearance; the Colonel promised to secure for chairman some one high up, either in the military or the political world. "Great thing is," he barked, "no delay. Let us be the first in the field. Every moment is of value. Prompt action absolutely necessary." I pointed out that the hospital authorities would most likely insist upon supervising John's health for two or three weeks. "During which period," ordered the Colonel, "he can prepare the lecture, and you, Weston, can complete the arrangements."

I offered to run around to London Street, and obtain from Millwood a letter of introduction to the agent. Colonel Edgington approved of this, followed me to the landing.

"This is a great idea," he declared, rubbing his hands. "Gives the chap something to do."

"Quite a brain wave, sir, on your part."

"That is so!" he admitted.

On my return with the note, I found that Mr. Hillier was walking inside the railings, hands behind back, head bent; my memory flew to the time when I saw him, in a like attitude on the occasion of his financial reverse. I entered the gate, and asked whether he required his hat. He said I was not to give myself so much trouble, but begged for my company, and in going up and down the gravelled path, confessed he had escaped from the others because their absorption in the new plan had slightly hurt him. "We have but just placed the dear woman in her grave," he contended, "and we ought to let no one else occupy our minds." I argued that there was something to be said for our methods. No advantage ever came from grieving and sorrowing over those who had gone. The world did not stop, because one person, however beloved, went away. The wise deportment in the circumstances was to select the happiest memories and preserve them. "I am doing that," he said. "There is an interval at Chislehurst, and just after Chislehurst which is already a blank. Earlier than that, and later, I have no recollections of her that are not good and sweet." We took another turn the length of the square.

"She had a great affection for you, Weston," he remarked.

"Mrs. Hillier showed it, now and then. Neither of us was the kind that liked to gush."

"I want you to have something of her's, as a memento of all the years you were together. And that reminds me. She made her will years ago. We might try to find it."

The document was in Mrs. Hillier's writing desk, together with letters from the children, written when they were at boarding school (they were all chattering now in the next room, Colonel Edgington's voice intervening, and it seemed queer to connect them with the round text hand notes that had been kept so affectionately). There was a well-bound diary, too, that started, as diaries will, in a profuse literary style, as though for publication, and dwindled to short notes, and brief figures, reviving when Muriel disappeared and the news came of John's disaster. One line caught my eye as I turned the leaves. "I have never thanked M.W. sufficiently, and I never shall be able to do so."

The will itself had been drawn up in the days of prosperity, and there were legacies that could not now be paid to one or two charitable affairs, bequests to servants who had long since gone their different ways. No mention of my name; the document had probably been filled in at a time when, for some reason or other, I happened to be out of favour; the remark in the diary fully compensated for the omission.

"You might have a piece of her jewellery," said Mr. Hillier.

"It all had to go, with the exception of her wedding ring."

"Wasn't aware of that."

"I told her you wouldn't notice, and she wanted to get rid of it, when money was short."

"Can you suggest anything?"

"Yes," I answered. "Let me stay on upstairs on my floor, and manage the family just as I've always done. I couldn't help overhearing you telling the young ladies that there was now no excuse for taking advantage of my services. As a matter of fact, you will all need me more than ever. It's true I shan't be wanted as a companion to her, but the rest have got to be looked after. And," with a burst of frankness, "I don't particularly wish to see anyone else doing it."

"You'll work yourself to death, Weston, if you are not careful."

"There are many less interesting ways of reaching there," I said. "You know that as well as I do."

"I shall be glad," he admitted, "to find myself back in the Arsenal again. Taking a day off makes me feel that I'm neglecting my share in the war." He returned the papers to the desk, and locked it. "The scoundrels," he exclaimed, with sudden anger, "killed her. They killed her, just as they have killed other innocent people." He raised his arms. "May God never forgive them!" he cried.

John Hillier's first delivery of his lecture was a great evening for us. I think it can be said, although I took some part in the arranging, that it was well managed. On my suggestion, the profits were set aside for the Red Cross Society, and any entertainment, at the period, which had an air of benevolence was supported by generous folk; John's name was known only in connection with his songs, but the newspapers were kind in giving preliminary paragraphs; Colonel Edgington secured, as chairman, one of the members of the Government whose popularity had not been chipped and damaged by the conduct of the war. When, on placards outside the hall at the upper end of Regent Street, the notice was fixed "All Tickets Sold," then the demand at the box office became urgent and appealing. Folk who had relatives detained in Germany urged that their special interests justified presence at the lecture; they were referred to coming dates and to places near London where Mr. John Hillier could shortly be heard. John had been given his discharge from the army. He worked hard at the preparation of the lecture whilst he was in the hospital, forwarding to me the sheets, a dozen at a time, and I had these type-written at an office in Greenwich Road. Edward and I went through them carefully of an evening, and found, to our satisfaction, that John had contrived to treat the subject, not too seriously, not too aggrievedly. When the last instalment came, Edward, at a raised table, delivered the lecture, in platform style to all of us, and timing by the watch I discovered it lasted for near upon two hours. From Millwood came the valuable hint that this was far too long. An hour and ten minutes, said Millwood, yes; an hour and twenty minutes, perhaps, but two hours, no. Most decidedly, no. "What you want to do," argued my brother-in-law, "is to go off, and leave the audience wishing to goodness you'd gone on cackling for another quarter of a hower. That's the 'ole secret of it." So John's task, once free of the hospital, was to cut down the lecture, and although we bewailed the loss of precious words, it was obvious the address became improved by the operation.

"Do you feel nervous?" I asked.

"I think the rest cure at Darmstadt got rid of my nerves," he said. "But there's no use in disguising the fact, Aunt Weston, that I am anxious."

"We shall all be there."

"My own people are the critics I fear."

We arrived at the hall in good time, and our party was amongst the earliest to go in. I do not know how the others felt, but the place—with folk whispering to each other, and stewards on tip-toe escorting new comers to seats—the place struck me as having a singular resemblance to a place of worship; the coughing that went from stalls to balcony, and balcony to gallery increased the impression of solemnity. Moreover, the hall was slow in filling up; there were huge gaps on the ground floor; a woman behind us was complaining to her husband of his mad carelessness in purchasing tickets when the money could have been better laid out on a musical comedy at the Lyric. It came to ten minutes to the hour, and some one near said, in an undertone, that society people often bought tickets for entertainments connected with a charity, and destroyed them. The stewards made a group near the doors, chatting to each other. I thought of John's dismay when he came on the platform, and saw the vacant rows of seats.

"Why on earth don't the people come in?" cried Muriel, agitatedly.

As though reminded of duties by this question, they arrived in crowds at every doorway, brandishing tickets, and insisting upon being shewn at once to their places: the stewards performed their duties at a rush: the empty places filled; the noise of spring seats being pulled down went like pistol shots; animation began to shew itself, everyone talked in natural tones. The chairs on the platform at either side of the white screen no longer had the aspect of desolation. Captain Winterton and his wife went along a gangway, arm in arm; their old-fashioned appearance caused a titter, and we forgave this in consideration of the circumstances. Colonel Edgington bustled on to the platform, and examined the height of the reading desk, slightly altered the position of the high-backed chair.

"I expect," said young Edward, across to me, "he's jolly glad you aren't down there to interfere."

The Cabinet Minister came, accompanied by John, who was able to walk now, for short distances, with the aid of a stout stick; the audience stood up and applauded, and Colonel Edgington bowed profoundly. I think he would have remained on the platform, but the chairman, with a jerk of the head, intimated that his presence was no longer necessary, and the Colonel withdrew reluctantly to engage at the side upon a brief altercation with a strong-minded lady who declined to comply with his order to remove her hat, on the grounds that she was not, as it happened, wearing one. People called out "Order, order!" and the Colonel disappeared.

The chairman introduced John in a dozen words, thereby confuting the apprehensions we had expressed in the train, coming up; we had felt bound to agree with Mr. Hillier's suggestion that political folk when they faced an audience, rarely knew where to stop. The chairman said he proposed to keep any remarks he had to offer until the end.

The hall was defensive in its attitude at the start, and John had a little trouble in getting his voice to the right pitch. He remedied this, and there was no more coughing, no signs of inattention. He gave accounts of small incidents connected with the engagement, with imitations of some of his comrades and their wonderful light heartedness; he told one or two anecdotes that went well, and suddenly, ere people had finished their laugh, switched off to a dramatic and exciting description of the struggle. Master John had got them well in hand by this time. When the lights were lowered, and it was seen that his pictures were not of the type called 'moving,' there came a slight ejaculation of surprise; a moment's thought and folk seemed to realise that British prisoners of war were not, perhaps, furnished with a cinematograph machine. John was particularly fair to the enemy. He had a good word for the German doctors, a severe one for a commandant who had not apparently set out to achieve popularity. He re-constituted the lager, and took us through a day there; it was not prejudice on my side in favour of a young man whom I had known and liked for years that made me feel that this was more vivid and more illustrative than the printed word. John finished with a couple of sentences full of hope and enthusiasm, and declaring that all who had suffered for their country enjoyed a pride they were not disposed to change or to forget.

Our party, flushed and warm with content, had the idea that the afternoon might well end here: the rest of the audience evidently wanted a speech from the chairman. A speech he gave, and it was interesting for us to compare the two styles; John's endeavour to use only the indispensable words, and the Cabinet Minister's large and luxurious manner of the practised orator. The hall, I admit, liked the great man's method. The hall indicated its approval of the chairman's compliments to the lecturer: it became uproarious with excitement when he quoted the Crispian speech from *Henry the Fifth*. Edward assured me the quotation was not really correct (and proved later, by production of his Shakespeare, that his criticism was right), but the people, I think, liked the recital all the better for the touch of undesigned originality, and when he closed by asking us to sing "God save the King" and we all stood up, and sang our best, and ladies in the front rows of the stalls took the bunches of flowers they wore and flung them on the platform, and Colonel Edgington—the fusser!—came on to guide the chairman, and our John, to the exit, as though the perfectly obvious way had to be made through a scarcely penetrable forest—why then we knew, and everyone knew, that Mr. John Hillier had received what is called a good send-off.

"Who," asked Katherine as we reached the vestibule, "who, pray, is the eccentric but seemingly perfectly happy gentleman dancing all by himself in a corner over there?"

"He," I was able to answer, "is the lecture agent!"

CHAPTER XV

One ought to have been made apprehensive and cautious by the fact that everything seemed to be going so well. In congratulating myself on the smoothness with which the machinery was running, I should have adopted one of the precautionary measures of a superstitious nature, handed down to me and impressed on me by my mother. But it was satisfactory to observe the chastened deportment and comfortable peace in the Hillier household—the loss endured seemed to have brought all the members closer in affection—it was cheering to find that John's tour could be reckoned a success; it was so pleasant to discover in the notes from Herbert Millwood a new tone of cheeriness, that there seemed no grounds for anticipating disaster. Herbert was unable for the present to obtain leave; he wrote that he intended to come up to town and see Muriel at the earliest possible moment; I gave her the message in a way that deprived it of any special meaning, and she said, casually,

"It will be interesting to see your nephew again."

The war had passed the first anniversary of its birthday and still went on, and the news that arrived was occasionally of a cheerful nature; no justification, however, occurred for putting out the Union Jack I was keeping in reserve. We had a flag day of another kind in Greenwich, and I provided tea in the shop for some of the white-gowned young ladies who sold the decorations; as they left a middle-aged man came to the doorway and thanked me in an elaborate way for the hospitality shown; I took it that he had something to do with the organisation, and answered civilly, nothing more. He made a sympathetic allusion to poor little Serbia, mentioned the attacks that were being made on Lord Kitchener and said he did not approve of them. He thought the single young men ought to join, before the married men were called up. He did not feel inclined to trust Winston Churchill. He offered to bet sixpence that Greece meant mischief. He doubted whether the Government was acting wisely in announcing a further restriction of licensing hours, and argued that the people ought to be consulted in these matters. His conversation seemed to me to be lacking in originality, and I was getting tired of it when a police-sergeant came along, known to me by an occasional exchange of nods, and a friendly remark concerning changes in the weather. Looking around, I discovered that my talkative visitor had vanished hurriedly.

"How's business, ma'am?" inquired the sergeant.

"Mustn't complain," I answered. "Thanks to Woolwich, I'm able to muddle along. How do you find matters?"

"Slack," he said, regretfully. "Nothing doing at all. 'Pears to me, crime is becoming a lost art. I shall soon be like Othello."

"Not jealous of your wife, are you?"

"I mean my occupation will be gone. I'm suffering from monotony; that's what's the matter with me. Fortunately for you, you're not troubled with it. And I'm told you're uncommon keen on a bargain."

"My work is to buy cheap, and sell dear."

"It's a job," remarked the sergeant, "where you have to keep your wits about you. By-the-bye, I heard something in your favour the other day, but," he tapped at his forehead, "it's gone. I shall think of it when I'm trying to remember something else."

The middle-aged man called again the next afternoon, but I was busy with a customer who had bought a pianoforte and was explaining to me that her neighbours, hitherto friendly, were declaring that the music produced from the instrument by her two little girls was in no way pleasing to the ear. She happened to be one of the newly affluent, and my suggestion that a pianola arrangement should be fixed, received her consideration. The other caller, seeing that I was not prepared to break off the discussion in order to attend to him, placed a card on a dresser, and said he would pay a visit at a more convenient moment. The card bore the name of Professor Basil Chailey; in the corner, the title of a West End club. I noticed that on the back was pencilled what seemed to be a day's expenses. Newspaper, lunch (ninepence for lunch), tea, railway ticket, pair of boot-laces. Evidently the professor was obeying the suggestions regarding war-time economies.

He came in that evening, as I was about to put up the shutters, and go to Gloucester Place. The shop closed early at that time, because with the regulations concerning the lighting of windows, it was impossible to shew off my goods, after dusk, to any advantage; besides which, folk were not going out at night as they had done, and the anxiety concerning air-raids still existed. My visitor carried a small box from which one or two wires had escaped; he wore, on this occasion, a tweed cap.

"I am in rather a hurry," he announced, speaking carefully, "and I shall not detain you long. I happen to be one of the many suffering from a diminished income on account of the war. There is no need to disguise the fact that the sudden loss of a berth of about six hundred a year is no joke."

"It certainly wouldn't make me laugh."

"All of my students," he went on, "have joined the Army. My classes have been shut down, and I find myself, to use a vulgarism, stranded. On the rocks. In other words, suffering from an acute financial embarrassment."

"I never lend."

"There," he said, approvingly, "I think you are wise. My own resolve is not to get into the hands of those who are willing to make monetary advances at an exorbitant rate of interest. My knowledge of the world is not great, because all my life I have been devoted to science, but I do know that once a man is involved in the coils of these people—"

"Hurry on with what you have to tell me."

"Finding myself in this awkward position," he said, "I look around with a view of ascertaining how I can dispose of some of my property. I have for years made a hobby of collecting silver. That silver I wish to dispose of, quietly, and at a fair price. I don't expect to get the money I paid for it, but I have no desire to be swindled."

"Give me your address, and I'll call and look at the articles."

"Pardon me," he said. "My two sisters with whom I reside; they must know nothing of the transaction. It would be the death of them."

"But they will notice that the silver has gone."

"I have a device," he remarked, holding up a fore-finger, in a shrewd way, "for accounting for that. A midnight burglary. A window left open. Do you follow me?"

"Go back now," I suggested, "and bring the goods along as quickly as you can, and I'll stay here, and wait for you."

He seemed doubtful concerning this plan, and I spoke rather abruptly; on this, he agreed that there was much to be said for my recommendation. I inquired where he lived, and he answered promptly, "St. John's Park, Blackheath." I mentioned that this was some distance away, and he could scarcely return within less than an hour. He assured me that he would use celerity, and, with great politeness, declared his regret at causing inconvenience.

I went over to Gloucester Place after closing, took supper with the Hilliers, mentioned to them that I had some dealings with a strange customer, and hoped to make a profit out of the transaction that would compensate me for the trouble I was incurring. At the shop, there were no signs of the professor, and as I sat there in the dim light on a saddle-bagged chair, and time went on, I determined he should suffer for the delay. My hours were too valuable to be wasted. An appointment was an appointment, and should be kept even by middle-aged gentlemen connected with scientific occupations. A policeman went by trying doors, and when mine opened, he glanced in and apologised.

"Working overtime, eh, ma'am?" he remarked.

"Expecting a caller," I said.

"Not afraid of being alone?"

"Prefer it, sometimes. Good-night, constable."

"I can take a hint," he said, glumly.

My new customer arrived in a taxi-cab as I was on the point of making up my mind to go; he dragged across the pavement a large bag of green baize.

"Sorry I'm behindhand," he remarked, exhaustedly.

"I, too, am inclined to regret it."

"Had to wait," he explained, "until my sisters went upstairs. We needn't lose any time now. I will pay the driver whilst you look over the articles."

Everything seemed in good condition, and it was clear that the silver had been treasured and polished carefully. I set each piece on a sideboard and estimated the value roughly, adding up the amounts in my head. The professor had returned, and he stood watching me with some impatience, as my lips moved in the effort of reckoning.

"How much?" he asked.

"I shall have to weigh—"

"No, no," he interrupted urgently. "Give me a fair sum, and let me have the money now. I'm not used to adventures of this nature, and I want to get the matter over."

"You will take a cheque?"

"I would rather have had cash," he said, "but, in these days, that is too much to expect. Make it payable to bearer, and not crossed." I mentioned that I had about thirty pounds, as it happened, in Treasury notes, and part payment could be made with these; he shook his head and said that, on consideration, he preferred to take the cheque. I suggested an amount: he agreed to it so swiftly that I blamed myself for not quoting a lesser sum. He gazed over my shoulder as I filled in the slip. Snatching at it, he, without another word, hurried from the shop.

I was placing the smaller articles in the safe, and congratulating myself on an easy bargain, when the door opened. Turning, I saw two quietly dressed men, of severe countenance. One advanced, pulling hard at a note-book that fitted too exactly the inside pocket of his overcoat.

"Got my pencil, sergeant?" he asked of his companion.

"You had it last, inspector," replied the other.

"I distinctly remember lending it you," said the first with warmth, "as we were coming out of the Police station. You said you wanted to make a note of something concerning the robbery, and I handed you my pencil case, and you never gave it back. 'Tisn't the first time that has happened. If it occurs again I shall report the matter to the superintendent." I asked what they wanted with me. "Your name is Miss Weston," he said.

"That's right."

"We are two plain clothes detectives," he went on, "and we have a rather painful duty to perform."

"I suppose your tasks are never very pleasant."

"True for you, ma'am. Sergeant, close the door, and tell our men outside to be prepared in case any attempt is made to escape. Now then!" Addressing himself to me. "You have just purchased a quantity of silver. Tell me what you gave for it."

I mentioned the sum.

"Not much more than the full value," he suggested, ironically.

"People in my line of business rarely pay more than they are obliged to do."

"Generally a good deal less. And that is where they sometimes find themselves in trouble. Now, I don't wish to frighten you, ma'am, or make a scene of any description, but that silver represents stolen property, and we shall have to take charge of it, and you'll have to stand in the dock, and answer—"

I screamed.

"Keep calm, keep calm!" he directed. "As a matter of fact, we are not going to take you away now, providing you give us your word of honour to attend at the Police Court to-morrow morning. I'll tell you what'll happen. You'll be there, with your accomplice, facing the magistrate. If you're wise, you'll get a solicitor to take charge of your case. Not sure whether you've had much experience—"

"I was never," I wailed, distressedly, "mixed up with anything of the kind before. Please give me all the advice you can."

"And he'll probably reserve your defence. He may, as you have hitherto been a respectable shopkeeper, manage to have you let out on bail. Anyway, you'll be committed for trial, and when you appear at the Old Bailey with a jury on the right hand side of you, and the Recorder just opposite to you, and a couple of warders, one on either side of the dock—"

I put the impetuous question that is likely enough offered in most cases. He scowled, and I feared the inquiry had annoyed him. He beckoned to his companion.

"Sergeant," he said, "you're a man of discretion and tact, and although I am your superior officer, I should like to have your advice. This good lady wishes to know whether there is any means of squaring the case, so far as she is concerned."

"I'm opposed to it, sir. Much too risky."

"But if it could be managed, I should be inclined to consider the project. She has undoubtedly been taken in by a plausible scoundrel."

"People who are foolish enough to do that," declared the other, stolidly, "must submit to the consequences."

"I grant you that, as a general proposition. I'm with you there, heart and soul. I can't, for a single moment, argue that you're wrong. But supposing—I only say supposing, mark you!—supposing this poor woman had a certain sum, either in cash or notes, ready at hand—"

"I've got nearly thirty pounds," I announced.

They conferred apart, and I, gripping my hands, waited anxiously for the decision. The two talked in bass undertones, with one for, one against. "There can be no hard and fast rule in these affairs; each case has to be decided on its own merits." And the answer was, "I've no wish to appear obstinate, but if it ever came out, you know as well as I do, that we should be ruined." Gradually the opposition seemed to weaken.

"Ma'am," announced the visitor who was on the side of clemency, "we have decided to accept your offer."

"Thank God!" I exclaimed.

"Your gratitude should be expressed to us. Fortunately for you, you are dealing with two of perhaps the most kind-hearted men in the whole force. Sergeant, pack up all this silver ready to take away, whilst I count the notes. And tell the chaps outside that they needn't wait."

It was indeed a relief to me to see the two prepare to go. They found the green baize bag heavy, and I suggested they should allow me to fetch a cab; they declined, and before going, gave me a lecture on the necessity, in dealing with strangers, of exercising care and even suspicion. I remarked that I could give the bank a warning not to pay the cheque when tendered, and they hinted, in duet, that I might consider myself a favourite of fortune.

It has often been said that women suffer from their defect of garrulity; something happened which proved that, in the other sex, consequences ensue. For, as they were impressing upon me the great good luck which had come my way, there came a sharp knock at the door. They tried to stop me, but I had opened it before either could get at my wrist. My friend the sergeant stood there.

"Seeing a light," he remarked cheerfully, "I thought I'd call to tell you that the something I heard about you wasn't really about you at all, but about a party with a different name altogether. Hullo, Albert!" he said to one of the men.

"Evening, sergeant." Respectfully. "Coldish for the time of the year."

"You know these two gentlemen, I expect," I remarked.

"Ought to," answered the sergeant. "What's in your bag, Albert? Anything special?"

"It isn't our bag, sergeant. It belongs to this lady here. It's her property."

The other man, apparently, dissented from this procedure, for taking the bag in both hands, he swirled it around, just missing me, and hitting the sergeant. The two rushed out. I snatched a police whistle from a hook, and blew it. The sergeant, recovering in a few moments from the blow that had dazed him, hurried through the doorway, and with a speed amazing in a man of his proportions, ran after a tram-car that was turning opposite the Church; the green bag, hauled up the stairs, was on the point of disappearing from sight.

There is no use in pretending that I came out well from the incident, or that my respect for my own business-like capacity did not suffer. The professor had to give evidence, and his two sisters remarked audibly, at the Police Court hearing, "We can never trust Basil again." In the corridor

I found him endeavouring to persuade them that a crime had undoubtedly been committed, and whether it took place at St. John's Park or at London Street was a point of small moment. The Treasury notes found on the prisoners were, after the sentence at the Old Bailey, returned to me. One of the men, not represented by counsel, cross-examined me in a cheeky way, and a newspaper headed the account of this with the title "Dignity and Impudence." The Judge made some remarks intended to be humorous, and dutifully smiled at by the jury, in which he recommended Miss Weston to obtain the aid of a husband who would help her in looking after the establishment.

There was reason to feel indebted to my friends in the trying period of waiting for the case to come on. William Richards took a day's holiday, and, looking quite smart in his new railway uniform, became my faithful attendant; Millwood paced up and down the large hall with us; Edward hastened to the court in his dinner hour and took me out and gave me a meal. Glancing back, it seems ridiculous that a self-possessed woman like myself, with no excuse for nervousness on the grounds of youth, should have felt so much terrified at being called upon to act a small part in a court of law; I suppose the experience is always trying to folk who lead quiet lives, and suddenly find themselves in the limelight. At any rate, I am speaking the truth when I say that I had no desire to go through a similar ordeal again, and I determined to use every care in avoiding another collision with the law. And this, perhaps, was the result the law, by use of pomp and elaboration, and of imposing and terrifying methods, intended to effect.

At Greenwich, the Judge's facetious suggestion was taken up by young Edward, and commented upon by him with considerable relish. Mr. Hillier, and the two girls, observing that I was not amused, gave him a private warning to make no further allusions to the Quartermaster-Sergeant.

I was careful to send out no newspapers to France that gave a report of the case, but Cartwright, in one of his pencilled letters mentioned that he had heard of it. "If ever you are in any legal trouble, go to my brother at the enclosed address." It was the first time he had spoken of this relative. The old people at Lewisham had not referred to this son; conversation when I called there was restricted to the soldier. Particulars of greater importance in the letter had a place on the last sheet. "I have been feeling out of sorts, and they tell me I need a change and a rest. But I do not want to come home until the job is ended. Fritz has got to be downed." Whilst I was receiving correspondence and sending it with scarcely a single mishap, my dear Katherine found that her communications and parcels to Mesopotamia were subjected to erratic treatment; now and again a steamer taking the mails was torpedoed in the Mediterranean, and this accounted for some of them, but not for all. Lieutenant Langford, on one occasion, cabled to her: "Are you writing?" and it cost about two pounds to reply, stating that she had been sending to him each week since he left. To me, in a moment of confidence induced by her anxiety, Katherine communicated a secret.

"And aren't you as pleased, my love, as ever you can be?"

"In a way, yes," she answered perplexedly. "But it means I shall have to leave the bank."

"Only for a time."

"They'll say I ought to have been straightforward with them. They'll be annoyed. They can be very stern when they like."

"Important folk, no doubt," I remarked, "but it isn't for them to give permission for dear, beautiful babies to come into the world. And don't forget when the time comes, that although your poor mother is gone, I shall be here."

"Shouldn't like to be facing it, Aunt Weston, without you."

My Quartermaster-Sergeant walked into the shop at London Street one wet day when Greenwich was looking something short of its brightest, and neighbouring tradesmen had called to give me their private and business anxieties. He said, "Hullo, Mary, my girl!" and kissed me, and, at once, other people's troubles vanished from my thoughts and for all I knew sunshine might have taken the place of rain. He was slightly thinner, and he had one or two lines on his forehead that I had not before noticed; it struck me there was a touch of grey about his moustache. Also his manner seemed quieter.

"No," he said, when I had sketched out plans for the evening. "Rather not, if it's all the same to you, go to a theatre, and, unless you're keen on it, we won't go up to town and have dinner. I'd prefer to just sit here on this sofa, and gaze at Miss Weston."

"That won't be very amusing for you."

"Seem to have got out of the habit of laughing. Takes a bit of an effort, in these days, for me to smile. But I don't want anything better than to hear you talk, and chat to you, and find you contradicting me. And," as I placed a cushion under his head, "how's the nephew, and how are the people in Gloucester Place, and how's everybody?"

He admitted, later, that he paid but a small compliment to me by falling asleep as I was chatting to him. "Where's my manners?" he asked self-reproachfully. Before this, I had put a screen near the sofa, and if anyone came in the shop, warned them to speak quietly. I set the kettle on the fire in the back room, induced a passing lad to buy for me a two-ounce packet of the Quartermaster-Sergeant's favourite tobacco. His pipe rolled out of his pocket as he turned in his sleep, and I filled it, placed it ready for him, with matches at hand.

I proposed to tell him of my fears regarding Muriel Hillier and my nephew, and to mention that Herbert was shortly coming up on the retarded leave. I thought of explaining that Muriel had changed but that it was not clear the change was permanent. My Quartermaster-Sergeant had just awoke, and was once more blaming himself for inattention to the rules of etiquette, when William Richards appeared at the doorway.

"Bit of a railway accident, Mary Weston," he announced, shortly. "Your nephew, the officer chap, is I am sorry to say in it!"

CHAPTER XVI

It was the way of things in the long months of the war that in addition to news from abroad, one was called upon to receive information concerning events at home, and when it happened that both were of a serious and alarming nature, one was almost knocked down by the double blow. One generally managed to get up again before ten was counted, but for the moment, the effect was staggering. I could have wished for no better companions than Cartwright and William Richards, and they proved the more useful when my brother-in-law Millwood arrived, a broken and a tearful man, unable to offer any suggestion or to join in the conference which, once I had recovered, took place; he went into the back room, and gripping the top of his head with both hands moaned and wailed. All the cheeriness which he was able, at public meetings, to communicate to his audience, had gone. I opened the door with the idea of giving a word of sympathy.

"Go away, Mary," he said. "Please go away. I want to be alone."

The accident, it seemed, had occurred near to London, and injured passengers were brought on to the terminus and conveyed to hospitals; William Richards was able to give me the name of the institution to which Herbert had been taken and the title of the ward. "I asked the question you are now putting to me," said William, in his stolid way, "and the answer was 'Both mental and physical.'" Richards had to leave in order to resume his duties, but he urged me to count upon him for any assistance required, and advised the Quartermaster-Sergeant to go back to France at the earliest possible moment. "No offence meant," he added, at the doorway, "but I've knowed her," with a jerk of the head in my direction, "a sight longer than what you have. And if I could only get appointed to a nice station down in the country—". He decided not to complete the sentence, or to describe, in full, his plans.

Cartwright, aroused from contemplation of his own state of health by some one else's disaster, offered to carry out any orders I had to give. I felt unable, at the moment, to go to town and endure the risks of ascertaining worse news, and did not care to leave Millwood; Cartwright put on his thick overcoat, and set out with no delay. In the back room, I found my brother-in-law searching the contents of the bookshelf.

"Want a prayer book," he said, in a muffled voice, "or a bible. Or a 'ymn book. Anything of the sort'd do."

I ran in next door, where the proprietor was a chapel man; his wife would not permit me to take a copy of ordinary size, but forced upon me a family bible, under the impression, I fancy, that size and weight would increase helpfulness. The considerable volume I took to Millwood; he asked me to guide him to comforting passages, and this, after some effort of memory, I was able to do. Called back to the shop, I could hear—as a visitor begged me, on the grounds that she was dead nuts on crime, to give a full and particular account of the silver incident—could hear him reciting verses aloud in tones that became strong and determined.

"Funny thing," he remarked, later. "Such a lot of us don't give a thought to religion unless something 'appens that we've got no control over. Then we begin to take notice of a 'igher power. You remember the story of the sailor in the Liverpool docks?" The fact that Millwood was telling an anecdote proved that he was regaining composure. "Chap falls from top of mast, and cries out, 'Oh, Lord, pray 'elp me!' 'Alf way down he catches 'old of a rope, and swings into safety. 'Don't trouble, Lord,' he says, 'I've done it meself!'"

We talked quietly after this of Herbert's accident, and of the steps to be taken. I suggested that the lad, so soon as he was free of the hospital, should be brought to my rooms at Gloucester Place; replying to Millwood I had to admit that, with the calls of the business on my time, it would not be possible for me to nurse him, but I felt sure the services of a capable woman could be obtained. To make certain of this, I went along to the Post Office and rang up the doctor who had become a recent customer, and had proved friendly and helpful. His answer was definite. "No chance of securing a nurse for a long job. Everyone busy, and overworked. The patient had better remain in the hospital. Extremely sorry unable to assist. Brighter luck next time. Good-bye!"

At Gloucester Place that evening, the news was received with concern. Mr. Hillier said that no one would hear of the accident with more regret than John. John had been looking forward to a meeting with Herbert so soon as the tour was over; he had some idea of taking Herbert away to Cornwall, where the pair could enjoy a holiday together. Muriel came in as the others were guessing at the extent and nature of the injuries; Edward spoke of concussion of the brain, and, as an authority on railway procedure, suggested that if any immediate compensation were offered, it should not be accepted, but the matter instead placed in the hands of a solicitor. Legal folk, he said, managed to get more out of a company than an ordinary individual obtained.

"Has something happened?" asked Muriel. I explained. "If you want any one to look after him," she said quickly, "when he comes here, let me do it."

"But, my dear," I protested. "Means such a sacrifice for you to make."

"It is time," she said, "that I did a little in that way. I shouldn't be so good as a qualified nurse, but I'd do everything I was told to do. We'll consider it settled. Unless," she added, "unless he objects."

"You are the one person in the world that he would like to have for company." She contracted her forehead slightly, and I could see that my impetuous remark had not included the quality of tactfulness. "I should have said you are one of the few persons." Muriel accepted the correction with a nod.

The particulars brought by Cartwright suggested that the hospital would be ready to give Herbert permission to leave so soon as he could be removed with safety, and I heard from Miss Katherine that her sister had given notice to headquarters of an intention to resign. Katherine thought it a risky procedure, but admitted that the demand for women's work existed and was likely to continue; the talk of compulsory service by men seemed likely to result in definite action. Katherine, in speaking of the war and the call for more recruits, mentioned that she could not decide whether she wished her little one to be a boy, or a girl, and I pointed out to her that, in these matters, wishing was of small avail.

Cartwright gave up his hours to attendance at the hospital; he had always, he said, felt a partiality for the lad, since Birdcage Walk days, and although at times Herbert could not speak to him, the Quartermaster-Sergeant sat by his bed and waited to see whether conversation, in small doses, was required. It was Cartwright who, when the day for transfer came, took charge of all the arrangements; for once in my life I was willing to abstain from exercising control. When the ambulance drew up in Gloucester Place, and the invalid chair was brought out with my dear nephew upon it, he glanced wearily at me, without sign of recognition, and I knew his convalescence was going to be no short job. Captain Winterton and his wife looked on sympathetically; the old lady whispered to her husband and, coming forward, he begged, in his courteous way, that I would consider the ground floor at my disposal. Cartwright and the driver of the ambulance said the stairs were not difficult and could be managed. I thanked the Wintertons and assured them the top floor had been chosen by the doctor; no other invention would have arrested their hospitality. At the last landing stood Muriel in a neat print costume and blue over-all; her features had become tanned by out-door work and I felt that Herbert might well be excused for failing to identify her. He opened his eyes as the chair stopped.

"Yes," he said, gratefully trying to put out his hand to her. "You! You!"

I have never been able to make up my mind whether, if Herbert had arrived safely and without the intervention of the railway accident, Muriel would have shewn any extraordinary regard for him; there is, at the back of my mind, an impression that with her thoughts concentrated on work, and with the memory of disastrous experiences in earlier days, she had decided to contemplate the other sex with aloofness. (Afterwards she told us one or two incidents connected with impressionable season-ticket holders that seemed to confirm this view.) The clear and certain thing was that she entered upon her new duties with a serenity that would have been impossible for her in Chislehurst times, that she shewed also a touch of authority, accepting suggestions from nobody but the doctor, and allowing none of us to enter the room and chat with Herbert unless we first obtained permission from her. Cartwright was inclined to rebel. Cartwright said he had met nurses out in France who, at the start, had to be argued with firmly, and this over, proved sweet enough and reasonable; I warned him that a procedure effective with some might fail where Muriel was concerned, and advised that he should imitate my example, and abstain from interference.

"That isn't usual with me," he declared, "and I'll swear it's a bit exceptional with you. I often find myself wondering what sort of discussions and arguments and family words you and me will have when we're married."

"Don't you bother your head about that," I counselled. "It takes two to make a wedding, and I haven't by any means come to a decision yet."

"But why then do you let me kiss you?"

"Because I like it," I said. "Take a book, and go out and sit down in the Park, and get yourself fit and well as soon as ever you can. We shan't have this war finished if many of you hang around here at home. Besides, the neighbours in London Street are beginning to talk."

"I don't suppose they ever belonged to the deafs and dumbs, and I'll guarantee there's few people in Greenwich who care less what's chattered about them than you do. As a matter of fact, I'm going to run up to town to see my brother. I want to get him to draw up a will for me."

"You ought to have done that long ago."

"Possibly," he said. "But long ago I hadn't anything to leave, and long ago I didn't know anyone special I wanted to leave it to. I'll trouble you, Mary Weston, for a fond embrace."

The Quartermaster-Sergeant, soon after this, was detailed for duty at Seaford, where he had to look after the convalescent men who were preparing to return to the front. I did not tell him, and did not inform anybody, how greatly I missed him.

Herbert's progress was slow, but there came a time when he was able, with Muriel's assistance, to walk about the gardens of Gloucester Place, and I noticed that their conversation was often animated, that they called each other by Christian names. Then there came news of cruel treatment of (amongst others) a chum of Herbert's, now in a German lager not so well managed as the one in which John had been detained, and Herbert worked himself up to a state of excitement over the methods that had been practised, and his own inability to help in taking revenge. The doctor summoned a specialist from Wimpole Street, and Muriel told me privately of her fears that she might find herself replaced by someone owning greater qualifications. The specialist gave orders regarding treatment, asked no questions concerning Muriel, approved her careful manner of taking notes. Herbert was not to be left alone at night, and I offered my services.

"Are you his sister?" inquired the man from Wimpole Street. I explained the relationship. "Heavens!" he cried. "Incredible! Bless my soul! How difficult it is, in these days, to guess a woman's age."

"Thanks for the compliment, sir."

"It isn't a compliment," he retorted. "I'm hinting at the facts. If anybody asked me, I should say you were in love."

"Nobody is likely to ask you," I remarked, "and you needn't pledge your word to a statement of that kind."

Millwood came back from some platform engagements, and Muriel described to me the scene of his meeting with Herbert; she mentioned that she would have felt more touched by it, but for the common and ordinary accent used by Herbert's father. It occurred to me there was still a trace of haughtiness to be found in the girl, and that this needed to be erased before she could be reckoned good enough for my nephew. Millwood bought and presented to her, as acknowledgment of her attention, a brooch the like of which I had never seen before, and, with luck, will not see again; she was on the point of declining it, but a glance from me induced her to change the intention.

"You can either wear it," said Millwood, impressively, "on 'igh days, and Bank 'olidays, or you can put it by, and keep it in stock, so to speak, as family heirloom, to be 'anded down to your children, and their children's children after them." Muriel said she would take the second alternative, and that she was ever so much obliged. "Tell you what I did," he went on, emphasising the importance of the occasion, "I didn't consult me own taste; I tried to imagine what your selection would be, and d'rectly moment I set eyes on this, I knew I wasn't going far wrong!"

It was, I suppose, the sleeping upright in a chair at night that made my dreams more than ever twisted and perturbed; it may have been Cartwright's talk about his will that accounted for his presence in these imaginings. The number of times the Quartermaster-Sergeant was blown up by mines, or sniped by the enemy was past counting; it often proved an intense relief when Herbert awoke, and his call aroused me. Occasionally, when sleep was tardy in coming to him, Herbert spoke of his mother and his own early days, and the money I had spent on his education, and a dozen other subjects; he rarely alluded to Muriel, and when he did so, only in an incidental way. From which, I assumed that they had made terms with each other, and that peace was near. It seemed to me now that this was perhaps the best thing that could happen.

I should have done well to keep in mind the nursing instinct. In my own case, with the maids at Chislehurst, it had often happened that a particularly tiresome girl fell ill, and, at once, all my annoyance with her ceased, and I tended her as though she were my dearest friend. I have known mistresses who got rid of servants because they were so healthy as to prove wholly uninteresting. It is a virtue or a defect with women. And certainly it proved, in case of Muriel, that so soon as my nephew gave signs of recovery—I was glad for his sake, and not regretful for my own, for the want of proper rest was beginning to tell upon me, and I had no desire to escape the kind of flattery that the Wimpole Street gentleman had offered—so soon as this occurred, Muriel went up to the City, obtained employment in a forwarding office in Gracechurch Street at twenty-five shillings a week (the head clerk had been a season-ticket holder who shewed deference in her ticket-collector days), came back and reported the circumstance. This readiness for work in war time was no help to sentimental match-makers like myself. I took Herbert to task.

"I'm sorry, aunt," he said.

"You have oceans of pluck in other ways."

"Possibly, possibly. But it requires a special sort of courage to speak in that way to any one who is so far above—" He made an upward gesture with his hand.

"On any well regulated set of scales," I declared, warmly, "your qualities would considerably outbalance hers. As a fact, she is even now not nearly good enough for you."

"You expect life to resemble a *Family Herald* story," he said, smiling.

"Life might often do worse."

"With every male patient marrying every nurse, and living happily ever afterwards. There wouldn't be enough nurses, my dear aunt, to go around. And because Muriel has been so good as to attend to me during my illness is a reason why my admiration should increase, but it gives no excuse for assuming that she is bound to become my wife."

"Then, I suppose, we must hunt about for someone else likely to suit your lordship."

"A waste of time," he assured me. "I shall never think of caring for anyone else. And to have been in her company all these weeks is a privilege I did not deserve, and shall never forget."

"Boy," I cried, "you're talking like a blessed Crusader."

An army medical officer came to see him one day, and announced that Herbert was not yet fit to return to duty. Herbert took him down to the riverside, by the Naval College, and argued with him for an hour by the clock, and they came back to Gloucester Place, where the medical officer said that Lieutenant Millwood's health had so much improved that he would rejoin his company the following morning. I knew quite well that Herbert would have been less eager to go away from Greenwich if his lady had not now been catching the eight-twenty train every morning to Cannon Street. It had always interested me to watch folk who are in love, and this, perhaps, was due to the circumstance that until the Quartermaster-Sergeant came on the scene, I had few experiences of my own to engage attention. And being accustomed to pull wires and see the figures obey, I was a trifle moody in bidding the lad farewell.

"No more railway accidents, please," I directed. "I did think this one might have been of some use, but I was mistaken. And I'm disappointed."

"Had a letter from the railway company this morning," he said. "They seem to make a very fair offer."

"Give it to me. You mustn't accept the proposal until I have considered it."

"If you were in command of the British army, aunt—"

"I like everything to be done right."

At the earliest opportunity, when Millwood was able to look after the shop for a couple of hours—he had a bible of his own now, and read it with all the interest of one to whom its contents were new, declaiming passages aloud and committing them to memory—I ran up to town and saw Cartwright's brother. He was an abridged edition of the Quartermaster-Sergeant, only about five feet five high, and small featured; in the way of short men he took an assertive manner, and there was scarcely any opinion I offered during the early part of the interview that did not receive immediate contradiction. Perhaps he accentuated this attitude because, at the start, he said, "Oh yes, Miss Weston. The lady to whom my soldier brother wants to leave his money!" It was a time, you will remember, when we all bragged of relatives in the army; the little solicitor was not exempt, and one could see that he blamed himself for disclosing information concerning the will. I said promptly that I had no need of the Quartermaster-Sergeant's money, that I had enough of my own, that he would have done better to look after his parents. "They," remarked Cartwright's brother, "are under my charge." We came to the subject of the railway company's offer.

"Oh, no," he said, promptly, "your nephew is not going to agree to that. These folk never expect their first offer to be taken. This is a matter which will require correspondence and discussion, and consultations, and so forth, and so on."

"We don't want to run into too much expense for your so forth and so on."

"You will be troubled with no bill of costs in this matter," he said. "Any friend of my brother's has a special claim upon me."

I apologised, and we became more friendly. He told me his parents had made great sacrifices in regard to his preparation for the law, and that George had willingly agreed to this. He admitted there had been a period when one did not take much trouble to speak of a brother who had enlisted in the army; he remembered arguing the matter with George very seriously, and for some years they were not on speaking or writing terms; the war had promptly brought them together. I spoke of other conjuring tricks performed by the same medium. Of my nephew Herbert, stopped in his educational career. Of the Hilliers, and in particular of Muriel.

"But that ought not to be a difficult task," said the little man, across the table. "To bring those two together, I mean."

"It ought not to be difficult," I agreed, "but I can give you my word that it is."

"He is very much in love with her?"

"That's right."

"And she cares for no one else?"

"So far as I know."

"Have you," he asked, "considered the usefulness of exciting jealousy?"

It is fair to say that he did, in the result, persuade the railway people to increase the compensation by about fifty per cent., that he declined to take a penny for his work, and that his suggestion concerning Muriel appeared, when I had given full time to consideration, one which deserved a fair trial. The chance came when a stout widow of Maze Hill, a lady customer who collected articles of brass, spoke to me of her intense sympathy for lonely men in the army; she had four on her list with whom she was in frequent postal communication, and wanted more. "My heart goes out to them," she declared, emotionally. She was grateful for the full address of Lieutenant Millwood, of whom I spoke as from hearsay, and she subsequently shewed me a brief but very courteous note received from that young officer. "They're always shy at first," remarked the Maze Hill widow, acutely. "But I know just how to write to them. The great thing is to cheer them up, make them realise that someone cares for them, and send them plenty of cigarettes." In one of his notes to me, Herbert alluded to the kindness he was receiving from a Mrs. Kenningham. I spoke of this incident at Gloucester Place, and Muriel said she considered that some women with nothing else to do were making themselves foolish and intolerably fussy in pressing their attentions upon army men.

Katherine left the bank, and stayed at home for a few weeks. The post from Mesopotamia was still imperfect, and it was all I could do to keep her hopeful and happy. Her baby came one morning at twenty-five past six, and I sent a cable to Lieutenant Langford that seemed to puzzle the attendant in the Post Office. It said,

"Beautiful boy!"

CHAPTER XVII

The arrival of the baby boy at Gloucester Place made an extraordinary difference in many ways. Katherine might well have protested against being deprived of some of her rights; instead she looked on good-temperedly and with an obvious pride in the interest created by her son; her own talk was mainly of the bank, and the possibility that the authorities might allow her to return so soon as she was sufficiently restored to health. It depended, she told me, on the quality of girls newly engaged there since her departure; a highly placed official named Cummings would have a voice in the matter.

"Cummings is a bachelor," she went on, "and he won't be very amiably disposed in my case. When a bachelor reaches the age of fifty he is inclined to take what he calls the common sense view. And common sense will be all against me."

"What is his first name?" I asked casually.

"Timothy," she replied, "but the scandalous circumstance is not generally known. He hopes that people assume it is Thomas."

Mr. Hillier, advanced in position at Woolwich, and able, at times, to return home at an early hour, came now at a trot from the station, and his first inquiry as he ascended the staircase always concerned the infant; Edward gave up his occasional evenings at the theatre to return home, chat to Katherine, and, by permission of nurse, find himself allowed to hold the baby for a few minutes; old Mrs. Winterton discovered amongst her treasures, mid Victorian toys such as ivory rings, china dolls with black painted hair, and a wooden horse of barrel shape with circular stripes, The greatest change to be noticed was in Muriel. Muriel, in the presence of Master Langford, threw off all the masks that she wore at various times—aloofness, indifference, studied composure, sedateness—and, as Edward said, gave herself away completely when the baby was in sight. She talked to him in the mysterious language that the very young are supposed to understand, she was deferential towards nurse in order that she might be allowed to share nurse's duties; to be permitted to glance at him, the last thing, as he slept, was counted by her a remarkable privilege. Muriel assured me that the slightest whimper from his cot during the night, aroused her instantly.

"At office," she mentioned, with good humour, "I seem to have been making him the one topic of my conversation. At any rate, a round robin was presented to me to-day signed by all the girls in my room, and pointing out that I am not the only aunt in the world. I suppose it is true, but I wrote in reply that few aunts had such a brilliant and exceptional nephew."

"I felt just the same," I commented, "when Herbert arrived. For a time people used to say that it cost half a crown to speak to me."

Muriel was silent for a few moments. "I must write to Herbert," she said.

When nurse left, we formed a syndicate, and my earliest grievance against the shop was caused by the discovery that some one would have to be engaged to look after the baby; I was free only in the early hours and the late hours, and those were periods when the other members happened to be ready to give their services. Katherine herself could have remained at home, and she had a desire to do so, but she admitted to me that loneliness meant grim imaginings of disaster near the Persian Gulf, and I recognised that work, and nothing else but work, was necessary to her. So I had to look around for some responsible woman—not a slip of a girl, and not so advanced in age as Mrs. Winterton, who had offered to help—and the task of finding one proved difficult; there were occupations so well paid at the time that few wanted to engage in domestic tasks. (I declined Mrs. Winterton's suggestion with a gentleness not, I fear, usual to me; I had an idea that the old Captain was beginning to shew signs of breaking up, and if this happened, I knew her hands would be full.) I did, at last, find a nurse who produced a guardedly-worded testimonial from her latest employer.

"I'm all right," she said, candidly, "so long as no one gets in my way. Once that happens, I fly straight off into a rare old fit of temper."

The engagement was made subject to the decision of the bank people. Katherine wrote, and the reply directed her to call the following Monday morning; she rehearsed the interview more than once, and declared her belief that Cummings would prove the one barrier. On the Sunday, I took the trouble to write to Mr. Cummings a letter, beginning My dearest Tim, and expressing the fear that he no longer remembered me, but saying that the note was intended to assure him that, in spite of the long lapse of time, he was never absent from my thoughts, and that I remained, now and always, his ever affectionate Daisy. It is not clear whether my action could be defended on moral grounds, but I did ascertain from Katherine that she found the recipient of the letter in a dreamy, slightly absent-minded and quite reasonable state, and that he handsomely granted her appeal.

"But," he said, gazing hard at the inkstand, "any repetition of the error will, of course—er—Good morning!"

It was enough to make a woman feel important to note how swiftly members of her sex filled the vacancies caused by the departure of men. Mr. Hillier spoke of munition factories at Erith and other places, where thousands of girls were employed. At Woolwich, the canteens were run by women. It had long since given no astonishment to see a lady driving a motor-car; they seemed to do it more easily, less fussily than did their predecessors. I heard of waitresses in West End clubs, and of girl letter-sorters in the district Post Offices; I saw, when business took me to London, high booted, short skirted alert young women taking 'bus fares; from the kerbs came soprano voices calling the evening newspapers; lifts in the big shops were managed by smartly uniformed girls, and one observed them doing outside establishments the work hitherto performed by commissionaires. Some of my lady customers were deeply perturbed and shocked.

"It don't do to think what poor old Queen Victoria would have said," declared one, mournfully. "Thank Heaven, she wasn't spared to see this day. If she had been, it would have been the death of her. She'd never have survived it, dear soul. It's a mercy she was taken off when she was. Providence knows best."

The great argument with these good folk was that the occupations were unwomanly; they did not trouble to consider who else there was to do the work, and I always discovered they were the first to complain of any slight inconvenience to them created by the war, and full of indignation against some individuals whom they called the authorities. The authorities ought to have done this, the authorities should have done that; it was especially charged against the authorities that they were lacking in fore-sight, and deficient in the valuable quality of common sense. The most strenuous critics happened, by a coincidence, to be those who never contrived to remember whether my early closing day was Wednesday or Thursday.

I allowed conversation to go on in the shop, partly because one had all the natural curiosity to pick up any bits of news that were flying about, mainly because it was worth while that the place should offer an appearance of traffic. I have often seen people stop, attracted by the window, crease their features over some of the contents with a look of perplexity, and then, if the shop were empty, decide upon postponement and move away;

if customers were inside, and there seemed a likelihood of an article of furniture being on the point of changing hands, then the shop was entered without delay. I hit upon the notion—it is improbable that I was the first to think of it—of placing some desirable arm-chair or attractive cabinet well in the foreground, and on it a ticket with the word "SOLD." The dodge rarely failed. Grapes that are out of reach invariably look the sweetest.

"Now could you manage, Miss Weston," it would be said, coaxingly, "to just write a nice little note to your customer, and say you're extremely sorry to find a mistake has been made? And send this round to my house on a hand-cart at once, and it will be there in time to be a surprise for my husband when he comes home!"

These were, of course, the exceptions. Plenty of my ladies were shrewd women doing good work with the various societies and associations that had been started in the borough, and I was rarely tired of hearing about their experiences, and always ready, I hope, to put my name down on their subscription lists. London grows kinder year by year, but there never was a period when amiability was so generally shown; perhaps there had never been a time when it was so much required. The need did not consist in money, but in friendliness. There were some who stood in urgent want of this.

A woman with her two children waited near to my door one day, gazing at the tram-cars in a bewildered manner. I went out, and asked if I could be of any assistance.

"I do feel such a looney," she admitted, cheerfully. "To tell you the truth, ma'am, I've never been out of Greenwich before, and now I've got to find my way to a railway station up in London. My man's coming home on leave, and he expects me and the kids to meet him. And we want to meet him, because if we don't he may come across other friends, and—Well, you know what soldier chaps are, don't you?"

I read the pencilled note she held in her hand. Millwood was upstairs, resting his voice. I put on my hat and coat in the back room, and called out a direction to him.

"I'll pilot you up there," I said, "and look after you until your husband arrives!"

The children were excited on the journey, wondering what Dad would look like, and what Dad would bring for them, and how long Dad would be able to remain at home, and how many Germans Dad had accounted for, and whether—the great question—whether he would take them to a picture palace. The woman herself was almost off her head with delight at the prospect of seeing her husband again. I remember she carried a small hand-bag with an unreliable catch; it contained all his letters and post cards, and I should think I rescued it from the floor twenty times.

"Without your help, ma'am," she declared gratefully at the London station, "I sh'd no more had been able to get here than nothing at all."

The boat train was due in ten minutes; we waited in the crowd near the barrier, the youngsters dancing about expectantly, and too much engaged to test the automatic machines. The tallest of us in the crowd presently saw the engine approaching, and we made the announcement; the crowd surged to and fro, chuckling and delighted.

"I shall scarcely know him, I expect," said my agitated companion, "after all these months."

Mud-covered soldiers began to alight from the train ere it stopped; cries of identification went up from people near to us.

"That's my Jim," she exclaimed. And, contradicting herself, "No, it ain't. Same height though. This must be him, coming along now. No," disappointedly. "That ain't him, neither!"

The men and their friends went off, chattering; the crowd diminished and the features of those who remained shewed anxiety.

"Anyone here called Mrs. Barford?" inquired a deep voice.

"That's me," whispered my companion. "You go and see what he wants, miss. I'm too nervous. I'm all of a tremble." I went forward.

"If you are Mrs. Barford," said the Corporal, speaking to me formally and deliberately, "I regret to have to inform you that your husband fell down, and died he did, just as we was about to get in the train at Bailleul. Heart attack probably. I need not say how sorry I am to be the bearer of bad news." He went off with his wife and son.

I had to take the sad group home to Greenwich, and to give all the comfort and sympathy I could provide. And wished, with all my heart and soul, that I had been better fitted for the task.

It was not long ere the new nurse and myself stepped inside the ring. If she had been an angel from Heaven (which she was not) I should probably have found some excuse for challenging her; she admitted, when it was all over, that she found Gloucester Place too quiet for a person of her disposition, and that she was, when the first discussion occurred, spoiling for a fight. I had received a visit from William Richards that afternoon, and a letter from my nephew contained an enclosure, to which I had been looking forward, from Mrs. Kenningham. William called to tell me he was married —

"And this I very well know, Mary Weston, means a rumpus so far as me and you are concerned!"

— Married to a lady hitherto engaged at a railway refreshment counter, and, as I remarked when he shewed me her photograph on the back of a postcard, looking it to the life. I assured him there was no objection so far as I knew, and that I trusted he would be happy; William could not get rid of the idea that an apology and a full explanation were due to me, and with some notion of tempering the blow, made an offer for a bookcase that stood in the shop. Guessing at the motive, I gave many reasons for declining this. The bookcase was not for sale. I myself had taken a fancy to it. Two or three customers were making a bid. The owner had gone abroad, and might return any day. Eventually, William became so piteous that I insisted on making him a gift of the article.

"Wish you hadn't taken it to heart like this, Mary," he mentioned in going. "But I suppose gels are more sensitive than what we men are. They brood over affairs of the kind, and make a grievance of 'em. Only, don't forget this. You had your chance, and it's no one's fault but your own that you didn't take advantage of it. I'll send for the bookcase in a day or two, and thank you kindly."

There was really nothing in this to worry about, but as I went, after closing the shop, I did feel William might have made a better selection, and I argued that the chances of his happiness were not great. At the exit from Gloucester Place to Crooms' Hill I caught sight of baby's nurse talking to the milkman. I waited until he began to pull at one of her white cuffs, and then, wondering how grown-up people could be so stupid, hurried on to the house. Baby was alone, and crying; he stopped on seeing me and was as right as ninepence in less than a minute. My lady arrived, and demanded to be told what I was doing with her child. I gave an answer pretty quickly. One word led to another, and when Muriel arrived the two of us were having a rare brisk discussion, hammer and tongs, give and take, such as I had not had a share in for some time past. Muriel stayed the argument, begged me to go to my rooms, and settled down for her usual talk with the baby. When she came up later, I was feeling penitent.

"You are working too hard," she said, firmly, "and unless you go slowly you'll be ill, Aunt Weston. It's beginning to get on your nerves. We must see what can be done."

"You don't imagine, my dear, that I'm the kind of woman who will put up with any interference from other people?"

"Sure it wouldn't be an easy task," she agreed, smiling. "What happened to-day to put you out?"

She listened to the William Richards incident without great concern. But when I shewed her the letter that Mrs. Kenningham had written to Herbert, and the note from him which requested me to call on the lady, and tell her frankly that he was in no need of affectionate communications, then Muriel exhibited an energy and a vehemence of which I had not reckoned her capable. She was willing to accompany me to Maze Hill, and to go without delay. This style of woman, she said, forcibly, had to understand once for all that kindness must stop short of ridiculous infatuation.

We found in the drawing-room of Mrs. Kenningham's house a cabinet photograph of my nephew; it was set in an expensive silver frame, and I wondered how many applications the lady had made before obtaining it. It was gratifying to me, as a wire puller, to notice that Muriel had not yet managed to suppress her annoyance; she went across to the pianoforte and, despite my warnings, extracted the photograph. Underneath were two portraits of other soldiers whose loneliness had apparently, at an earlier stage, obtained the lady's attention.

"How do you do," said Mrs. Kenningham, entering breathlessly, "and I hope you are not going to detain me, because one has so much to see to, and such a quantity of letters to write, for at a period like this it is everyone's duty—"

"My name is Hillier," said Muriel, calmly. "I am engaged to Lieutenant Millwood. He has received this preposterous communication from you."

"Oh dear, oh dear," cried the lady, alarmedly, "I am so sorry. I've put my foot in it this time, and that's a fact. Do hope you'll believe that my intentions were good."

"Possibly. But your procedure was intensely foolish. Don't let it happen again."

When we were out of the house—our departure watched by the penitent Mrs. Kenningham—I asked the girl whether she had spoken the exact and precise truth.

"Aunt Weston," she answered, "I may have anticipated events slightly; whatever crime there is in that can be charged against me. But I'm not going to stand by and see any other woman snatch at him. Let me reply to his letter."

"Your news, my dear, will make him very happy."

"Been trying all my life to find happiness for myself," she said, "and I haven't succeeded. Maybe I shall be more fortunate in endeavouring to give it to somebody else."

We had a great meeting of friends, shortly after this, at Gloucester Place; so extensive that Mr. Hillier spoke of the drawbacks attendant on living in a flat, and compared the advantages of a house away from London. Singing was, by consent, barred. A gentleman belonging to the music-hall profession had come to live next door, and his habit of giving a birthday party every Sunday night was not without its inconveniences; it is only fair to say that when I called on him at the request of old Mrs. Winterton, he proved as amiable as anyone could be.

"Had no idea," he declared, self reproachfully, "there was anything like illness about, or else it wouldn't have happened. Say so, won't you, ma'am, with my compliments. Assure them that, until they give the word, hospitality is off. The old Captain's honestly ill, is he? Well, I'm sorry, and I can't say more. I expect the war has been too much for him. It affects a lot of people who try not to shew it. Here!" He took me aside. "Between ourselves, I'd give anything for that suit he wears, if ever he wants to get rid of it. I can assure you it would get me a roar the very moment I went on."

So that at our gathering we had no music, but there was plenty to talk about, and my nephew Herbert and Muriel were, to my great delight, on excellent terms—they had agreed, she told me, to wait until the war was over—and John was home from his tour, giving imitations of chairmen he had encountered, and obtaining the aid of Edward in reckoning the profits; the total when announced by the lad was received with applause. John's leg still gave trouble: he spoke of the old and less exacting task of writing songs. Colonel Edgington was there to play billiards with Mr. Hillier; I took coffee down to the room and found the two disputing in a manner that reminded me of Chislehurst days. The Colonel, I gathered, was arguing not for the first time that he either possessed influence or knew someone who owned it, and he desired it should be used on behalf of Mr. Hillier; the contention of Mr. Hillier was that he had every reason to be thankful for the position he now occupied.

And there was Katherine and her jolly baby. I wish I could describe to you how fond we all were of the little chap; how relieved I was to find that his nurse had asked for the day off; what a joy it was to me to watch him and to help his young mother in looking after him. Katherine and nurse appeared to get along well enough with each other, but my antagonism to the girl had in no sense diminished, and as I sat near the window, looking across the gardens at The Circus, I tried to fix the details of a plan for getting rid of her, and securing for myself a greater control over the dear mite. (You will perhaps think that I was always scheming to get my own way, and you are probably not far wrong.)

"The work at the shop in London Street," I overheard Katherine say to John, "is telling on her. Do wish she'd give it up."

"Something must be done," said her brother.

"Millwood ought to be able to help," she remarked. "He seems to be a man of intelligence."

The great wonder to me was that my brother-in-law remained modest, continued to take the same size in hats. Before the war, he had been nothing more, so far as the public was concerned, than a minor local politician, reckoning himself lucky if the *Mercury* gave his name amongst a number of others; occasionally it appeared on small bills that were posted furtively, by enthusiasts in the cause, who knew how to run a meeting on economical lines. Now and again, when the borough elections came on, he was in the sunlight for a space, and anyone who wanted to deal at that time in second-hand furniture, had no chance of doing business. At a parliamentary election, he was what is called an organiser.

Now, it appeared that he was necessary to the success of recruiting meetings, indispensable at all sorts of public occurrences that had connection with the war. I found a card for a drawing-room reception to meet Her Royal Highness the Princess Somebody of Something at a house near Pall Mall; the card announced three speakers, and one of these was H. Millwood, Esq. The date of the affair happened to be an early closing afternoon, and I made up my mind to go to town and ascertain how my brother-in-law comported himself in the presence of the higher aristocracy. I had seen him amongst the Greenwich people, had heard of his success with larger audiences elsewhere, but it appeared tolerably certain that Millwood would make grievous blunders in Carlton House Terrace.

There was time to spare when I stepped out of the tram-car on the far side of Westminster Bridge, and in St James's Park I found the lake still empty;

on Horse Guards Parade a band was playing, and recruiting sergeants conducted sets of newly enlisted to the railway station; near The Mall and just inside the railings, a row of buildings had been set up for Admiralty work, and cars with staff officers, and navy men, hurried to and fro. There was no forgetting here that a war was going on. At the house mentioned on the invitation card, I hesitated. The ladies going in appeared distinguished (I recognised some from their portraits in the illustrated dailies), they were handsomely dressed, and I feared I might be stopped in the hall and called upon to answer searching questions. A dowdily-garbed woman came in at the carriage way, and I followed her. The footman inside the doorway bowed as he took her card.

"Has the meeting started yet?"

"Not yet, Your Grace," answered the footman.

I was sufficiently flustered to put, in a parrot-like way, the same question, and the man was well trained enough to give me the same kind of answer. At the foot of the broad staircase, another polite attendant asked us to ascend, and on the landing everyone was being announced to and received by the lady of the house.

"Miss Weston!" called the man. The lady of the house shook hands, pleasantly, said it was exceedingly good of me to find time to come, urged me to take a seat without delay.

"There will be a crowd," she remarked, contentedly. In a side room, I could see Millwood in his blue reefer suit chatting with a young woman who seemed about twice his height.

The ball room was, on one side, of irregular shape, and I managed to discover a corner, where, from a gilded chair I could watch without being seen. A small raised platform had been fixed; the windows looked out on the Park and Government offices. About me, as the room filled and the rows of chairs became occupied, the talk was of the war and its progress, or the need for its progress. One could not help observing, once more, that the appetite for rumours, fresh and seasonable and tasty, was as keen in the west as in the south-east of London.

The Chairman entered escorting H.R.H. (she was the tall young woman with whom I had seen Millwood chatting). We stood up. H.R.H. placed her bouquet of flowers on the table where there stood a silver tray, and a glass jug (that I should have liked to buy) and tumblers. A well-known actor-manager, a notable Judge, and Millwood followed. The audience sat down, made itself comfortable, and assumed the look of calm resignation that is appropriate when a flood of talk has to be expected. The Chairman opened with compliments to H.R.H. and, declaring that the speakers of the afternoon would save him the trouble of explaining the proposals of the new Association, went on to describe these in full detail. At the end of twenty minutes, he called upon the Judge. The Judge said the Chairman had given all the information that was necessary, and his own talk would therefore be simple and brief; he took twenty-five minutes to repeat, in slightly varied words, the speech of the Chairman. When the actor-manager advanced to the edge of the small platform, we all bent forward eagerly and hopefully; it seemed likely that here would be something to break the steady and persistent dulness. The actor-manager, with fine declamation and admirable gesture, started with an epigram that missed fire; my own view was that, by an oversight, he offered it upside down, and thus robbed it of pungency. Discouraged by this (and by the circumstance that he could not make out his notes excepting by the aid of spectacles, which he had decided not to wear) the actor-manager contented himself by echoing the statements and arguments already made.

"As you, my lord, have so truly remarked, and as my learned friend, if I may so call him, has so admirably suggested—"

I glanced about to discover a chance of getting away; an elderly lady of great proportions in the next chair, was now well asleep, and to arouse her would have produced a commotion.

"Your Royal Highness," announced the Chairman. "I call upon Mr. Millwood."

My brother-in-law came forward, one hand in the pocket of his jacket. He gave a rather awkward bow to H.R.H., nodded to the Chairman.

"This is a deuce and all of a rummy affair!" he said. The sentence seemed to box the ears of the jaded audience; everybody became alert; the stout old lady next to me woke up. "When you come to think it over, I mean. Before August, nineteen fourteen, you ladies and gentlemen knew nothing about me and cared less, and what I thought of you isn't worth mentioning. And here we are to-day, all friends. All chums. All brothers and sisters. All regarding one another with a real and vurry sincere affection. And why is it? Why, because we've been attacked, without any warning, by a bully that wants to murder our men, women and children, and whose aim it is to wipe us off the face of the earth." Millwood jerked around suddenly, and spoke with deliberation. "He ain't a-going to be allowed to do it!" The cheering came for the first time; loud cheering, and long. "Out there, just now, on the 'Orse Guards Parade, I spoke to a young chap who was going forward to the tent where they're jotting down the names of recruits. He appeared not much more than a boy, and I took the liberty of speaking to him. I says, 'My lad, what induces you to leave your good mother, and go and join the army?' And he says, 'It's just because I've got a good mother, that I'm going to fight on her behalf,' he says."

It is impossible for me to describe the way in which Millwood gripped and held those people. Set down in writing, there would appear to be little in his homely anecdotes, his ordinary illustrations, his touches of domestic pathos. What I do assure you is that at one moment the folk were laughing, and at the next they were in tears; the great virtue of the speech seemed to me that it finished within ten minutes, and I joined with the rest in making the ineffectual appeal of "Go on!" Once or twice he had made adventures into the alliterative manner, and these were his only errors. In the room downstairs where the visitors took tea and coffee, and I had the opportunity of inspecting furniture, everyone was asking for Mr. Millwood. The lady of the house regretted he had somehow taken his departure, unobserved by her.

That evening, when Millwood returned to London Street, I asked how he had got on at the afternoon meeting.

"Moderately fairly well," he replied. "Can't say more than that!"

Millwood and I came into collision, and each showed an irritability over the incident not usual with either of us. My own idea is that my brother-in-law's manner was responsible. He bounced into the shop one morning when the rain was pelting down, and spattering up from the pavement; he was in the habit of taking great credit to himself for never carrying an umbrella, and on this occasion he was without an overcoat. His first act, the swinging to and fro of his wet bowler hat, caused me to speak sharply.

"You needn't worry," he said. "I'm coming back here. I'm going to take charge again. They tell me I've nearly wore out my welcome, so far as the public is concerned—getting too refined in my manner, or something—and my name will once more appear above the shop windows."

"Have you been breaking the pledge?" I asked.

"Unfortunately, no," he replied. "Otherwise I sh'd be in a better temper than what I find myself. I've come 'ere, to have a straight talk with you, I have, Mary Weston."

"You'll probably get a straight talk in return. What do you mean by this nonsense about coming back?"

"When you took the shop over," he said, deliberately, "it was understood I was free to return and take possession whenever I felt disposed so to do."

"Have you any proof of that?"

"Got it in my inside pocket now. A letter, or note, or communication in your own handwriting. Contents of the place to be valued by some independent authority unless the figure could be agreed on between us."

"I'd forgotten about that," I admitted. "But, in any case, it isn't worth the paper it's written on."

"How do you make that out?"

"Go and consult a solicitor," I retorted, bluffing. "He'll tell you, in half a jiffy, that you've no legal claim. Now be off, and don't bother me with your nonsense any longer."

"If there's going to be any consulting of solicitors," he declared, "it's you that had best do it."

When one is dealing with an obstinate, pig-headed man, serious argument is of no use. I tried a more appealing way, but Millwood shook his head, and said I was wasting my breath. I remarked that I knew a well qualified and highly reasonable legal gentleman up in London who could give wise advice on the subject, and Millwood, after some discussion, went so far as to agree that he would accept Mr. Cartwright's decision. Millwood wrote out a copy of the letter I had been foolish enough to give to him some eighteen months or more earlier.

"Be a sport," he warned me. "Shew him this, and tell him everything in a truthful manner, and come back here, and tell me what he says. I'll look after the shop until you return."

My Quartermaster-Sergeant's brother was busy, and, in his office could give me no more than five minutes: he placed a watch on the table to make sure that this period was not exceeded. Before I had time to state the case fully or to produce the copy of the note, he stopped me.

"You must give up possession," he said, definitely, "at the end of the current week. Good-bye! Thorough April weather, isn't it?"

I could not help suspecting that my friends—little Mr. Cartwright included—were just now associated in a design to control and guide my career.

Something that looked like an opportunity for dealing with the conspiracy against me came when young Pinnock, of a shop over the way in

London Street, went before the Tribunal. There were always establishments to let in the thoroughfare, but I had fixed an eye on Pinnock's because of its special build and expansive windows; I could see there a business under my control that would be in opposition to Millwood, in more senses than one. (I fancy there was some idea, at the back of my head, that I was a piece of machinery which could not risk the danger of stopping lest it should be reckoned of no use, and find itself thrown upon the scrap heap.)

Young Pinnock was of the very few who declared openly a resolve to take no part in the war; he had a thousand and more arguments, and the important one, which he repeated at his doorway, and occasionally shouted across the street, was that the trouble on the continent of Europe was not of his making. This we had guessed, but it did not prevent us from saying that young Pinnock ought to take his share as the rest were doing; that he constituted an undesirable example to youths who were growing up, that the drill would make a man of him, and perhaps induce some girl to offer her admiration. Pinnock found a new contention, each day, to support his attitude, and when he caught sight of my brother-in-law, rushed out to present it; Millwood was always able to knock the suggestion over with no trouble, and the youth returned to his shop to ponder, and to build up a fresh one. He exhibited an air of great confidence one evening on producing the statement that his mother had begged and prayed of him not to enlist, declaring that his departure was likely to be followed immediately by retirement to a bed which she would never leave.

"Give me her address," said Millwood, curtly, "and I'll give the old gel a look in."

"I don't profess that I'm giving you her exact and actual words, Mr. Millwood."

"My lad," remarked my brother-in-law, "what reelly keeps you back is not your mother, or any other relative. It's yourself. When the war is over, you ought to have the Humane Society Medal."

"What for, Mr. Millwood?"

"For saving your own life. And don't worry me with the subject again. If there had been many like you, we should have had the Germans here by now. I've got no patience with your sort."

"Wish somebody had," complained young Pinnock. "My difficulty is to get people to listen to common sense."

It proved that his mother was, in fact, anxious that he should go; it happened that she was the only parent in her road at Charlton who had not made some contribution to the services, and she declared that her position was not to be envied. Pinnock tried, later, the plea that if he joined up, the shop would close (Millwood said the world was not likely to come to an end on account of this), that there were texts in the Bible supporting his attitude (Millwood, as a new and careful reader, was able to produce some war-like quotations from the Old Testament), also that his principles would not allow him to take life, (Millwood remarked that the possession of a rifle, and the sight of a Prussian aiming a bomb, would modify these views.) Finally, and before appearing at the Tribunal, young Pinnock announced his intention of arguing that he had no right to set his own existence in danger. That, he said, was the point. Life was entrusted to us as a high and sacred charge, and any man who, wilfully and with his eyes open, exposed it to peril was to all intents and purposes committing suicide and deserving of the blame the law could give. Nothing but an unsound mind, argued young Pinnock, and this he in no way claimed, excused the act. Indeed, he described himself as a thinker; one who refrained from borrowing views from other people, preferring to make his own.

"And I'd like you to come along, Mr. Millwood, and hear me argue the question in front of these gentlemen, because I've got the notion that I shall be more successful with them than what I've been with you."

"No special treat to me," said Millwood, "to see a chap make a fool of hisself."

"But I owe you something," urged the young man, "for inducing me to give up arguments that wouldn't hold water. Thanks to you, I've got one now that's absolutely without a flaw. Shouldn't wonder if my case gets reported in the evening papers. I feel absolutely confident it'll make a sensation."

Millwood and I were not on too friendly terms at the moment, but he told me, on his return from the court, all that had happened, and told it in the dramatic way that a man of his type can adopt in describing an incident which has affected the imagination deeply. Of young Pinnock entering the room with a determined air—"He would have stuck his chin out," said Millwood, "only that he hadn't got one!"—of being directed to take a seat, and finding himself disconcerted by this; the rehearsals apparently had always been taken in an upright position. Of Pinnock recovering gradually powers of speech and gesture, and proceeding to declaim his views on the sanctity of human life, and more especially the duty of every man to preserve his own life, in a way that made the members of the court—exhausted as they were by attending to appeals on a variety of grounds, and sometimes on no grounds at all—listen with care. Of the Chairman presently stopping the applicant with the remark that the case had been put forward with conspicuous ability; the Court would give its decision later in the day, and announce then whether any exemption could be granted.

Of young Pinnock leaving the room, and going out of the building in a great state of exaltation, talking to folk he met, and—on the edge of the pavement, still propounding his views—being run into by a small boy on a scooter. Of poor Pinnock staggering under the unexpected collision, and trying to recover himself, and not succeeding, and falling into the roadway as a motor-car dashed along.

The shop was closed on the day of the inquest, and remained closed, but some feeling of superstition prevented me from making any effort to secure it. The incident, small in comparison with the large events which were happening, touched me. And I could understand and sympathise with the remark that the mother made.

"I should have felt a lot happier," she said, wistfully, "if my boy had been killed on the field of battle!"

CHAPTER XVIII

I assumed at the moment that it was annoyance with the contrariness of events which made me feel out of sorts. It happened that no one at Gloucester Place advised me to see a doctor, and if this counsel had been given I should have rejected it at once; on my own account I discovered my earliest customer, who occupied the first half-hour by shewing me the contents of the house added since his original purchase through me. This over, he gave attention to my case.

"You have come nearly to the end of your resources," he said.

"Nonsense!" I ejaculated.

"Another month or two of the work you have been engaged upon, and you would have proved outside and beyond any treatment from me."

"Ridiculous!"

"Your mind, for a considerable period, has had nothing resembling a holiday or rest. You have gone from one task to another, without an interval. You are not sleeping well, are you?"

"I can do with less than most people."

"In future, you will have to take more sleep than most people get. I don't want to give you anything to make you sleep, but—"

"Shouldn't take it, if you did!"

"I understand you to say that you are now clear of the shop in London Street."

"By pure dodgery and sharp practise, I've been turned out of it. It's a scandal that the law—"

"Now, now!" he interrupted. "Don't let us become excited unless there is good need for it. Has your brother-in-law paid you a fair sum?"

"I'm not grumbling about that. As a matter of fact, he gave me what I asked, without any haggling."

He nodded approvingly. "If it had all been arranged by wise friends," he said, "it could scarcely have happened better."

"And do you too think, sir, that my people have been scheming and planning—"

"You mustn't get so flushed and emotional, Miss Weston," he ordered. "I know nothing whatever about your people, or what they are doing. Just you take matters quietly, and be thankful you can afford to do so. I'll send some medicine along this evening. Call again, if you find you are no better."

I challenged Millwood later with being one of the members of a conspiracy, and he smiled and said nothing. The suspicion would not have galled me so much, I suppose, but for the circumstance that I had always reckoned myself a stage manager directing other people, and the positions were now reversed. I decided to say nothing of it at Gloucester Place, where it seemed likely the chief movers in the plot might be found, and this was the easier because Katherine's baby occupied my attention; we went into the park together, and rested near the trees, and I picked flowers that delighted the small person and were treasured to be presented later to mamma. Also, at home, old Mrs. Winterton was glad of my help and my advice.

"The Captain talks of nothing now but the war, my dear," she explained, "and I can't help wishing he had done so earlier, like most folk, instead of bottling it up. But I am hoping we shall get peace almost directly, and then he'll be comforted, and he will begin to mend, you see."

"Do you really imagine the war is nearly at an end?"

"It can't last for ever," she argued.

"But I see no signs of a finish. The Germans occupied Easter bank holiday in trying to bombard Lowestoft; the Turks are holding us out where Lieutenant Langford is; there's trouble in Dublin, and the Zeppelins seem to come over when they like."

"Yes, yes," said the old lady, "I know, I know. But I've always been able to get anything I earnestly prayed for."

"Perhaps you haven't made such a large request before."

The Captain had aged greatly during the last month; without the help of his elaborate collar and tie, and his frogged overcoat, he appeared to have become limp, and if a cushion in his easy chair moved, he slipped with it. His courteous manner towards his wife in no way changed; he was grateful for any aid I could give, but it was clear that he favoured her company, her assistance. The content they found in each other's society made me think of my Quartermaster-Sergeant, and I began to write often to Seaford, on the excuse that I now had time to spare. Cartwright replied with a new spirit, declaring my letters were as welcome as flowers in May, and admitting that some chaps were more greatly favoured in the way of correspondence than himself; he always looked out for the *Punch* I sent weekly, but preferred the briefest note to the most amusing journal. For myself, I can confess that, at this time—when I had to be careful of my health, and to watch my temper, and to keep cool, and not allow small incidents to disturb me—I had reason to be grateful for his notes. If one arrived by the first post, there was competition between Muriel, Katherine, and Edward for the privilege of bringing it to me. Sometimes, Mr. Hillier was the messenger.

"Better than all the doctor's bottles, Aunt Weston," he said.

Mr. Hillier was in exceptionally good spirits. It seemed there was a prospect that he might be leaving the Arsenal, where the work, I am sure, had become monotonous; the rest of us had often expressed the hope that he would, some day, be induced to give it up. But this was not resignation, but a chance of transfer, and I could not help a slight feeling of jealousy on discovering that the credit was due to Colonel Edgington, once a fidget of the highest standard, but now, by reason of circumstances, a person of some authority and influence. The appointment had to do with a munition factory to be opened shortly; a well qualified person was required at the head. I confessed I itched to be taking part in the affair: it appeared to me that the plan could scarcely reach success without my help. This view was hinted to the Colonel.

"Don't you dare!" he cried, threateningly. "Let me catch you interfering in any way whatsoever, and upon my soul, woman, I'll have you shot. Or put away in an asylum. Or gagged. This is my fishing, and I won't allow you, Weston, or any one else to poach. Understand that!"

I happened to find some recompense in a kind of flying interview with an auctioneer from Chislehurst. Him I encountered near to the park gates that lead to Blackheath; he was entering and in jerking to me a scrap of news concerning The Croft, he sprinted along the avenue towards the river. I turned the perambulator, and to the astonishment of Katherine's baby and of nurses, raced along after the hurried auctioneer, putting eager questions, and obtaining fragmentary replies thrown over the shoulder. At the Observatory I was forced to give up the chase. When the baby had been induced to start on his morning's sleep, I sat down and enjoyed a dream that, like most dreams, seemed too good to come true. Finding a pencil and a sheet of note-paper, I made some calculations. My friend, the police-sergeant, went by, in ordinary clothes, and accompanied by his little girl.

"Give him my love as well," he shouted, chaffingly.

My existence, since I had been turned out of the shop, seemed to be wanting in ingenious plans. The one now before me was so magnificent that my pencil shook as it wrote the figures.

At Gloucester Place, of an evening, we all pretended an indifference to the prospects of Colonel Edgington's idea; sometimes we went so far as to deride it, and I, in particular, referred to incidents of the past which he had handled clumsily, pointed out that as a man grew old, so confidence in himself increased, and his mental abilities diminished. I think I suggested that the war would have been successfully terminated, long ere now, if Headquarters had been served by younger and more intelligent people. Secretly, we were hopeful that Mr. Hillier would obtain the berth. I found his silk hats, that had long been enjoying a rest cure, and polished them with a handkerchief.

Because I had given a small donation to the fund—it was difficult in those days for even a thrifty woman to say "No" to the applications that came—a ticket reached me inviting my presence to the dedication, by a Lord Bishop, of war ambulances, one to be given to the British Red Cross Society, one to the French Red Cross. The circumstance that a speech of thanks was to be made by Colonel Edgington would have discouraged me, but the affair was to take place on a Saturday afternoon, a period when Katherine, home from the bank, expected to be allowed to take exclusive charge of her son; I had to stand back and to look forward to resuming control of the little person on the Monday morning. Muriel advised me to go, and to bring back an account of the proceedings: she declared that my imitation of Colonel Edgington was always amongst my triumphs.

Some one directed me wrongly, and I happened to be late in arriving at the school playground where the ceremony was to take place, but my old lad Peter, there in a position of authority with Boy Scouts, caught sight of me and, leaving everything, conducted me to the raised platform as the Russian National Anthem was being sung by the children. Folk, noting the deferential manner adopted by Peter, assumed I was a guest of importance; a steward discovered a vacant chair in the second row and would take no notice of my signals indicating a preference for a more retired place. I found myself immediately behind the Mayor who, anxious I suppose, to shew that he identified everyone in his borough, turned and shook hands warmly, introduced me by an unintelligible name to the Bishop, who declared he had often heard of me, and was charmed now to make my acquaintance. I listened to the youngsters giving the last verse.

> "God the all-wise! By the fire of their chastening,
> Earth shall to freedom and truth be restored.

> *Through the thick darkness Thy kingdom is hastening,*
> *Thou wilt give peace in Thy time, O Lord!"*

As somebody offered a prayer, I thought of these words, looked back in my mind, and realised—almost for the first time—how gentle the war had been to me, in comparison with the treatment it had served out to other people.

The Mayor followed with a statement, and the Bishop rose. Colonel Edgington, seated near, turned, and in turning glanced at me; the old chap was too much absorbed in the importance of the affair and his own share to recognise me, and from this moment, throughout the dedication and the address, he occupied himself with his notes. I admit I was touched by the fervour and patriotism of the Bishop's words. Maybe I had not been fortunate in some of the clergymen encountered during my life: here was one out of the ordinary. I joined in "Oh God our help in ages past," feeling more earnest and impressed than I had ever done in church.

"You're not going," protested the Mayor.

"I have an engagement," I answered readily. It struck me as I spoke that it did not take one long to escape from religious influence, and to slip back to ordinary habits.

"But there's tea to come," he argued. "And I'm just going to call on the next speaker."

It was impossible to move ere Colonel Edgington rose, and I resigned myself to the ordeal of hearing the voice of my opponent. The Mayor whispered around that the speech was to last but five minutes, and this was accepted as an encouraging piece of news.

"—Pleasure and honour to accept," said the Colonel, with more than his usual pomposity of manner, and barking the words so that some were extraordinarily audible, and others indistinct. "Doing fine and glorious humanitarian work—succour the wounded—taken a great part myself in this work—industry not restricted to this—may mention that near neighbour of yours, and dear friend of mine, name Hillier, been this day appointed to—— working for the last year and more, whole heartedly—now gained his reward—happiness shortly in informing him——"

Colonel Edgington read with care from his notes a quotation, and the Mayor said in an undertone, "Time, Colonel, time!" Everybody stood up, and I surprised and pained some of the guests by moving to the back of the stand as they sang,

"—And ever give us cause,
To say with heart and voice,
God save the King!"

I arrived at Gloucester Place, breathless and panting; my hat at not quite the correct angle, and my features crowded with excitement. The girls came out to the landing and received me apprehensively.

"You're bringing bad news, Aunt Weston."

"I'm bringing," I declared, "the best news you could possibly imagine!"

The baby was instructed in the art of clapping hands, and Edward, on arriving, threw off his air of maturity until he was reminded that old Captain Winterton, below, might be disturbed. We went to the balcony, and watched for Mr. Hillier. He generally came by the Royal Hill entrance, but now and again he walked through the Park and across Croom's Hill.

"We'll draw lots," I suggested, "and see who is to be the one to tell him."

"But," said Muriel, "didn't you say that Colonel Edgington was coming on to do that?"

"He ought to have the privilege," agreed her sister and brother.

"Have your own way," I said, reluctantly. "It isn't my custom to allow myself to be hampered by tact, but perhaps you're right."

So when Mr. Hillier came, we had to suppress our enthusiasm, and I think we were all a trifle hysterical, excepting the baby. For once in my life, I answered Colonel Edgington's knock with genuine satisfaction.

"Weston," he announced, "I am the bearer of important tidings."

"Concerning me?"

"Concerning your master, foolish woman." I gave an ejaculation of surprise. "Ah!" he said acutely, "I thought the day would come when I should be able to startle you!"

CHAPTER XIX

It seemed to me that I should have to go to work cautiously in regard to the new scheme in my mind concerning The Croft. A policy of carefulness had grown up at Gloucester Place; for some time past accounts had been kept, accounts that had to balance or the expert young folk applied themselves to the figures, and ascertained the reason why. Mr. Hillier, as I knew, had been saving money since the loss of his wife (she, dear soul, never was able to acquire the useful trick) and once a man begins to hoard it is difficult to induce him to embark upon anything like adventure or risk. Also, I could not be sure to what extent their affection for the rooms in Gloucester Place might weigh; it was certain that the struggles and triumphs associated in their minds with Greenwich would count whenever a suggestion was offered of removal. Once, a casual reference had been made to the house in Tressillian Road, Brockley, where we had lived before going to Chislehurst; this idea appeared to be lacking in boldness. There was Katherine's little chap to be considered. We had the Park at hand, but I was fearful that as he grew up he might be playing with other children and—Well, I suppose, we people who have once lived in large houses remain snobs to the rest of our days.

I managed to find the auctioneer at his office in a comparatively leisurely mood, but he was a hustling sort of man, constantly looking at his watch and with the affectation of being over-crowded with engagements that deceives only the partially demented. He broke off more than once during our interview to ring people up on the telephone, and to impress me with the vastness of his business, and the importance of his dealings. The Croft, he admitted, was still unlet, but how long it would remain in this state of emptiness, he could not attempt to guarantee. Several folk were endeavouring to obtain it, and the matter was one of rent, and of rent only.

"You're wrong," he declared, when I mentioned that large houses were not now in great demand. "Absolutely off the main line. Never made a bigger mistake in the whole course of your existence. Try to put that idea out of your head, my dear madam, as soon as ever you can. By-the-bye,

I like to know who I am dealing with. Give me your name, and your full address."

I furnished him with the London Street address. It was no part of my scheme to give him the chance of calling at Gloucester Place, and blurting out information there.

"Good!" he said briskly. "I take it you are a lady of some property."

"You are safe in assuming that."

"My method," he went on, "is to be perfectly frank and straightforward. What I mean is, as frank and straightforward as business will permit. Now I don't mind telling you that I have two strong offers for the house, and at any moment one of these may decide to clinch the bargain."

"Your several, then, comes down to a couple."

"I'm telling you now," declared the auctioneer, solemnly, "the gospel truth. I can't disclose names, but if you are inclined to doubt my word, I can show you a part of communications I have received from these two parties."

I was willing to believe his statement on this point.

"Very well, then! You will understand, Miss Weston, that there is a reserve rental set, and my duty is—we can't afford to be sentimental, you know, in our profession—my duty is to get as near to that as I possibly can. Now, on this slip of paper I am writing the figures of the highest bid that has been made up to the present." He threw the note across the table. I crossed out the sum, and wrote an increased amount. "Right you are!" he said. "Come back here the day after to-morrow, and I may have something further to tell you."

Looking back, I really cannot be sure how far I intended to go in the transaction. It was, I knew, impossible for me to realise some of my investments and put the money down even for one year's rent; certainly I could not make myself responsible for taking up a lease; I fancy the idea was to carry on the preliminaries to a certain stage, and then go to Mr. Hillier and urge him to take the matter over. Meanwhile, in order to save myself from the risk of being caught in a net, I told Millwood to say, supposing anyone called at the shop, that I had gone. Nothing more; just that. Perhaps one had better not discuss the fairness of the proceedings. I wanted to see my people back at their old home, and I did not intend to be too particular about the means.

The haggling went on. I had to go to the auctioneer's office more than half a dozen times. I climbed the hill from Chislehurst station and went under the water tower so often that I became tired of seeing the Bickley arms engraven there. Then old Captain Winterton took a turn for the worse, and his wife began to fail; I gave all spare time to the ground floor. To my question, Mrs. Winterton answered that they had no relatives. At times, both rallied slightly, and I was able to assure them they would not finish their innings until they scored a hundred.

"I would like to live on for a few years," confessed the old lady. "I want to see that dear baby boy grow up."

Few incidents occurred in the neighbourhood that were not in some way or other communicated to me; for some reason, the striking case of Corporal Bateman of Royal Hill remained, declining to be evicted from my thoughts. Bateman represented to me, for a period, a type of the British soldier, and behaviour of the British soldier where matters of the heart were concerned. My Quartermaster-Sergeant had not, in all probability, encountered or heard of Bateman, and he little knew how much his home prospects were affected by the deportment of the Corporal. (Now, it seems to me that no excuse can be found for the way in which I allowed it to influence me; at the time, no excuse appeared necessary.)

Corporal Bateman had been what Greenwich called half engaged to his cousin; the two quarrelled over his enlistment (the cousin thought he should have first mentioned it to her) and when he left for France his mother only saw him off. Mrs. Bateman was one of the few elderly people unable to read or write; the joke in Royal Hill was that, to conceal this defect, she pointedly and markedly bought each evening a newspaper, and seated on a wooden chair at her doorway, affected to peruse it carefully, with ejaculations such as,

"Gracious me, what a war this is to be sure!"

And,

"You'd never think they'd have the face to do such things!"

And,

"Lay my boy is in the thick of it, although I don't see his name nowheres." By oversight, she sometimes gave these remarks to the advertisement page.

Corporal Bateman, after months in France, came home on leave, anxious to see again his old mother of whom he was genuinely fond, and all the more desirous because he had received no word from her. At the door, he loosened his equipment, and knocked. The cousin, appearing, straightway threw herself with some impetuosity into his arms.

"Oh Daniel," she cried, emotionally. "Home at last. Thank Heaven for this happy moment!"

Corporal Bateman disengaged himself, and looked around in a dazed manner. Glanced at the brass figures on the door.

"The number's all right," he said, perplexedly, "and the 'ouse looks correct, but I don't know you. Who are you, and what are you doing 'ere?"

"I'm your cousin," she replied. "Your cousin Phœbe, that you used to be so fond of."

"Haven't quite got rid of the effects of the gassing," he said, tipping back his cap, and rubbing at the top of his head. "I'd better have a stroll in the Park."

"You'll do nothing of the kind," declared the young woman. "Come inside at once, and wait till your mother comes home from the market."

"Have I got a mother?" asked Corporal Bateman, simply. "What's she like? Where's father?"

"I can't answer that last question, Daniel dear, because he drew his final breath years ago. Don't you remember the new suit you had for the funeral?"

"I don't remember nothing," he said, hopelessly. "Me mind's a blank."

He was anxious to stay outside the house until someone else arrived, but the cousin, an authoritative person, conducted him through the passage. On observing that he did not know where to find the row of hat pegs, she burst into tears; he regarded her with an increased aloofness, and asked the way to the best room. There she announced a desire to sit near to him, and to hold his hand, and to talk about old times; he remarked, in a confused mumbling way, that he made it a principle never to carry on with female strangers.

"Have you had your tea?" she inquired.

"I don't know," replied Corporal Bateman, absently. "If I have, I've forgot all about it. I forget about everything. Don't bother me, else I shall get worse."

She was in the kitchen preparing the meal, when Mrs. Bateman let herself in at the front door with a latch-key. The girl listened. "Good afternoon, ma'am," said the returned soldier. "Have you called to see mother? Because, if so, she's out!"

The two women consulted agitatedly later, endeavouring to find a plan for arousing the dormant intellect of the visitor. They counted it a hopeful sign that he remembered the name of the nearest public-house; Mrs. Bateman expressed the hope that a good supper would brighten him. As a result of their deliberations, the girl went softly into the room, where Corporal Bateman was now dozing, and gave him a modest and cousinly kiss; he awoke at once, and declared he would provide her with a coloured eye if she dared to do this again.

"A liberty," he said, aggrievedly. "That's what I call it. If it happens again, I go straight out of the house. You understand!"

Mrs. Bateman said she had read of such cases in the newspapers, and believed that at times a sudden shock had a remedial effect. The girl remarked that she knew what was in her aunt's mind, but hesitated to take the desperate step of making the announcement in question: she feared the stunning blow might send poor Daniel completely off his head, and then the blame would be hers, and the remorse hers, until the very end of life.

"He'll have to know one day," urged Mrs. Bateman. The girl shuddered.

"Let's put it off as long as we can," she begged. "Him coming home like this seems already like a judgment on me."

They found him looking through the family album in a casual, uninterested way; a year ago portrait of himself and his cousin, taken together, caused him to put the question, "Who are these two supposed to be?" He gave permission to his mother to take the nearest chair; the cousin, he said, was to sit at the opposite end of the room. As the pages were turned, Mrs. Bateman offered comments and explanations; he shook his head to intimate that he could neither confirm or deny the particulars.

"That's your uncle, my boy. The father of Phœbe, over there. He's took in his merchant service uniform. Quite a seafaring family, the whole lot of 'em. Excepting, of course, Phœbe, and she's made up for it by—" The girl at the other end of the room coughed; Mrs. Bateman accepted the warning. Corporal Bateman turned another page.

"Who's this good-looking sailor chap?" he inquired. "That," said Mrs. Bateman promptly, "is Phœbe's husband." The cough came too late this time. "Oh, my boy," she cried, self-reproachfully, "I 'ave been and told you something, and no mistake. The truth is, his ship was in dock for repairs, three weeks ago, and he came 'ome here, he did, and he married Phœbe, and you mustn't take on about it, my son, because what is to be will be, and everything's ordered for the best, and—Oh, don't do anything cruel to her!"

Corporal Bateman had risen and crossed the room. He took his cousin by the elbows, and gave her a sounding kiss.

"Hearty congrats, Phœbe, old girl," he said, in his normal manner. "It's a load off my mind. What I was afraid of was that you'd be wanting to make it all up with me again. How about us three trotting along to the first 'ouse at the Empire, up near the Broadway?"

The ingenuity shewn by Corporal Bateman caused me to gain the impression that the British Army, excellent in most ways, could in matters of sentiment, not be trusted implicitly. The moment was unfortunately chosen for my Quartermaster-Sergeant's blunder.

A square envelope came from Cartwright, and opening it, I found it addressed to "My dear Lily." Of course I ought not to have read on, but there are situations where etiquette cannot be strictly observed. It was an affectionate but not an extravagant note; the memory came to me of the statement of an officer, made early in the war, who censoring letters out at the front, discovered six from one youth, all in identical and loving terms, but with the Christian names of the girls different in each case. I could picture my dear Lily without trouble. A young girl, good looking, and probably occupied in some business that left her with more time than I had to exchange communications with a soldier friend at Seaford. I boiled with annoyance to think there was someone to whom George Cartwright was writing in these terms; I scorched with irritation to recognise that she was reading the letter intended for me. Towards the end there was reference to a wedding.

"It's the first time I trusted a man," I cried to baby, "and, my word, it shall be the last." The baby seemed under the impression that I was endeavouring to be humorous. "If he'd been kept out in France, he'd have been safe enough."

It has probably been written about already, and in any case I am not going to write about it here; I mean the trial a woman of my age endures when she discovers that her romance has gone. For a while, I lost interest in the matter of the Chislehurst house.

I had to run, with all my might, one afternoon to the doctor's house to beg him to come and see the old people on the ground floor; Katherine's little baby had been given to the care of a motherly servant next door. The doctor was on the point of leaving the house with his wife in his small two-seated car, and I threw the Gloucester Place key to him, gave directions, and started to walk back at a good pace. I noticed that, just inside the Park railings, a long soldier was lying prone on the grass. I took the view—it was just after half-past two—that he had been rather too busily engaged during the brief time of opening permitted to licensed premises. Glancing over my shoulder, I caught sight of the stripes on his arm. I found the nearest gate, and raced back.

"Cartwright," I cried, forgetting my grievance against him. "What's wrong, dear man? Pull yourself together. It's Mary Weston who's talking to you."

"Goo' Lord," exclaimed the Quartermaster-Sergeant, amazedly. "And here I've been mourning for you because I thought you'd gone to Heaven."

"It's not so bad as all that," I said. He jumped up, caught me in his arms, and kissed me until four children stopped to look on.

"Nearly all the worries in this life," he declared, "are about matters that don't exist. And I'm not a chap, in a general way, to go hunting around for trouble, but the information that reached me didn't somehow appear to give me much of a loop-hole."

"You army men get nervy."

"It wasn't that," he contradicted. "I got a relative of mine to call at London Street to inquire about you. There the answer was that you had gone, and my relation assumed it meant you had kicked the bucket."

I remembered then about the letter. "The news must have come as a relief to you," I said, coldly.

"Mary Weston, explain yourself."

"It isn't me that needs any explaining. It's somebody else, who'll find a bit of a difficulty in that respect. No doubt a soldier imagines it a great lark to carry on with three or four girls, and correspond with them; it's only when he gets a bit careless over envelopes—"

The Quartermaster-Sergeant looked serious. "Pride of Greenwich," he said, appealingly, "and Queen of Kent, I ask you, as a personal favour not to talk about that bloomer to anyone else but me. If it once reached Seaford, there's active minds there that would give it a touch of exaggeration, and the story would last for three years, or the duration of the war. Be a chum, and keep it to yourself." He held my arm; I shook him away.

"Out of mere curiosity," I said, "and for no other reason, I'd rather like to know what view your friend Lily took of the situation."

"Got frightfully excited about it."

"Don't blame her."

"Took a journey across country, at once, with the idea of finding you, and bringing you your letter."

"If I'd known where she lived, I'd have discovered her," I assured him. "And the conversation that would have taken place might have made your ear tingle."

"She's a sensible girl," went on the Quartermaster-Sergeant, "although she is my cousin, and, in spite of the fact that she's up to her eyes in needlework, and getting ready to marry my solicitor brother, she gave up the best part of a day in the attempt to make an exchange with you. What I blame her for is getting a wrong impression from your brother-in-law at London Street, and upsetting me to an extent that I leave you to imagine. It'll make a difference to the present I give her."

"Cartwright," I said, "ever since the affair happened, I foresaw as clearly as anything that you'd provide some emergency exit that you could slip through. I don't mind admitting your story does credit to your invention. It's a deal cleverer than I expected it to be. I regard it as a good piece of work, nicely put together, very well dove-tailed. Only drawback is that I don't believe it."

"You can look me in the eyes, and say that?" he demanded.

"I'll say it all over again if you like."

"Once is ample," declared the Quartermaster-Sergeant, resolutely. "I'll leave you now. And understand this, Mary Weston. I'm going out of your life, and so help my goodness"—he raised one hand impressively—"I don't come back to it unless you go on your knees, on your bended knees, to me." He strode away down the hill, taking no notice of the retort I made. It was intended to be effective, and later, I thought of several others that were even more stinging and determined. But it is of no use aiming words when a target does not exist.

To my relief, the doctor's car was outside the house in Gloucester Place, with the doctor's wife glancing at her watch, and clicking her tongue to indicate impatience. "Do hurry him up," she begged. "He takes such a frightful amount of time over his patients, unless they are on the panel."

I first called next door where Katherine's son was becoming slightly bored with the extravagant attentions paid to him. At our house, the doctor came out of the Wintertons' rooms as I turned the duplicate key.

"What has delayed you?" he demanded, curtly. "Sweethearting, I suppose."

"Quite the opposite."

"These old people are too ill to be left alone. If you can't see to them, we must find a nurse."

"I'm free now," I said.

It was a good deal like having three babies to look after instead of one, and, at any rate the occupation saved me from brooding over the finish of my engagement with Cartwright. I half hoped a letter would come from Seaford apologising for swift words and impetuous action, and I went so far as to draft an amiable reply, but the necessity for sending this did not arise. On the first Sunday I could manage to leave Gloucester Place, I hurried to Chislehurst, and ascertained the private address of the auctioneer. He answered the ring, and protested in a voluble way against interference with his one day of rest. His nose to the grindstone throughout the week, he declared, and here he was disturbed for the third time on the afternoon that he felt entitled to claim as exempt from the worries of business. I made as though to leave, but this procedure also failed to meet with his favour.

"Come in," he ordered, recklessly. "I'm a born slave, I suppose, and folk have got the idea that they're all entitled to act as my overseers." He flung open the door of the front room. "Uncle Tom's Cabin," he declared, "is nothing to it."

I glanced around. One of the chairs had a ticket, "Lot 240," still attached.

"I never saw Uncle Tom's Cabin," I remarked, "but if it was anything like this, the people had grounds for complaining."

"Most of the articles of furniture were bargains."

"No," I said. "Never were bargains, never will be bargains. It's all a muddle. Wonder to me is that you can live with it. I should go crazy if I were put amongst shoddy stuff of this kind."

"Tell me," he begged, "what you consider is wrong with the room."

There was little left when I had complied with his request, and he became increasingly submissive as I went on with the task. In going through the crowded mantelpiece I came across two cards that were seemingly intended to be placed out of sight. A kindly action is supposed to be its own reward, but here was something in the nature of a definite prize.

"My wife separated from me," he remarked, dolefully, "because she said I was not gifted with taste, and I argued that I was. Perhaps she was right. It's very good of you to take so much trouble."

"Don't mention it. I called about that house and property—"

"Afraid you're too late," said the auctioneer, resuming his quick business-like air. "The matter is not absolutely settled, but it is on the point of being settled. Two people, besides yourself, are making offers—perhaps I told you—and as I've seen nothing of you for some time, I assumed you had given up any desire to compete."

"I have!"

"Good gracious!" he cried. "But why?"

"Because Mr. Hillier, who has been calling on you, is an acquaintance of mine."

"Come, come!" he urged. "Friendship is all very well, but it needn't be carried to extreme lengths. Besides, he is only one."

"And your other caller, Colonel Edgington, I have known for many a year."

"That puts the lid on it," he cried, lapsing into slang. "This has absolutely torn it. I can only hope the two gentlemen are strangers to each other."

"Life-long friends."

"But," he pleaded, "you're not going to disclose the fact to them that each has been—"

"A woman," I said, rising to go, "can't possibly keep a secret."

I waited on Colonel Edgington, and took him back to Greenwich. From the time the bells rang for evening service, until the hour when people came back from church, he and Mr. Hillier and I threshed the matter out; the Colonel was indignant at the thought that anyone but himself should have hit on the notion of securing The Croft for the Hilliers, and particularly vehement concerning what he called my unwarrantable interference. At this Mr. Hillier took my side, and defended me, and when, to pacify the other, I pointed out that Colonel Edgington was the best friend the family ever had, Mr. Hillier suddenly burst into a roar that lasted minutes. It was the first time I had heard him do this since the war started.

"But for Aunt Weston," he said, wiping his eyes, "but for her, we two, Edgington, might have gone on bidding against each other for all time. I had determined, you see, to go back to The Croft."

"For my part, Hillier," said the Colonel resolutely, "I never let go of an idea, once I get well hold of it."

"Each of you will write now," I directed, "with-drawing your offer. No one but ourselves, apparently, wants the house, and in a week or two, Katherine—Mrs. Langford—will take it at a reasonable figure."

Colonel Edgington went across to the fire-place, adjusted his belt, glared at me, and turned to Mr. Hillier.

"Old friend," he said, "if there is anything in the flat in the nature of a beverage, I should like to give myself the pleasure of drinking this extraordinary woman's health!"

It was August again, and the Bank Holiday, a circumstance that jogged the memory, forcing one to think of the opening of the war two years before. (The banks were not closed, and few people took holiday, because we were still in the thick of the fighting, with good news from the British Headquarters, an excellent report from the Suez Canal, a splendid telegram from Petrograd.) The Croft looked just as it did then, and the countryside, which I once pictured as being over-run by the enemy, was peaceful, but for intermittent booming of guns that were being tested at Woolwich. The stationmaster told me cheap tickets had not yet been re-introduced, and I snatched at the excuse for not going down to Seaford, and there finding my Quartermaster-Sergeant, and, somehow or other, offering an apology to him; a card had reached me in July announcing the wedding of Walter Cartwright of Lincoln's Inn Fields to Lily Cartwright of Haywards Heath, and the last traces of suspicion had been forced to vanish. I might have written a long and explanatory letter, and I did try to do so, but the essays made appeared either too cringing or too haughty, and I persuaded myself that the first step ought to come from him.

Muriel had a week of leave from Gracechurch Street, and my nephew Herbert was staying at the cottage I had taken in Lower Camden, not ten minutes from The Croft; they were out together for the afternoon, with a tea basket for chaperone. Katherine no longer went to the City. She gave up the work reluctantly, but when the money came to her from the dear old Wintertons of Gloucester Place, I persuaded her, and Mr. Hillier assured her, there was no longer any excuse for attendance at the bank; I pointed out that she ought to make way there for some girl who was in need of the salary. So Katherine became the tenant in name, and in fact, of The Croft, and I went in and out of the house, and gave her a word of advice when there happened to be any difficulty with maids. "Why on earth," I overheard one of the servants say, "doesn't Mattie look about, and find a chap, and have the banns put up? She isn't too old, and there's plenty of tradesmen around here ready to wink at her, if she didn't give 'em the frozen face." When one is alluded to as Mattie, the adjective of Meddlesome is understood.

Katherine, and the baby, and I on the first Monday in August had tea on the lawn, and I carried the little fellow about, and picked daisies, and made them into a chain. A note had come from Katherine's husband; she read parts of it aloud to me, and I assured her it could not be long ere he came back, and she counted up once more the number of months he had been away. It occurred to me, in thinking of the space occupied by the war, that the one occasion I had felt annoyed with poor Lord Kitchener was when, quite at the beginning, he prophesied the war would last three years.

"I suppose, Aunt Weston," she said, "you are like Muriel. You intend to do nothing until peace comes. I mean in regard to getting married. Your Quartermaster-Sergeant. The one in the Guards. The tall, broad—"

"Oh," I remarked, indifferently, "that's all off. Didn't I mention it before? Yes, we found that we couldn't agree, and we decided it was of no use going on."

"But this is such a pity," she cried, anxiously. "Can't something be done? Surely, if there's been a misunderstanding it ought not to be a difficult matter to put it right."

"We're both of us obstinate, my dear, and I suppose we'd got too much accustomed to having our own way to be willing to give in to each other. He was in the habit of ordering people about, and I'd got hold of the trick of expecting everyone to obey me, and—and—"

Here, at a moment when I was talking cheerfully and light-heartedly, what must I do but break down. The maid, coming out to take away the tea-things, looked at me sympathetically, and, at my request, ran back to the house to find a handkerchief; Katherine patted my hand, and directed the boy to upbraid me, mainly by gesture, calling attention to an incident of the day before when he had been hurt by a naughty safety pin, and refrained from tears. He was told to urge me to be a soldier, and laugh it off. Mr. Hillier called from the workshop, asking me whether I had seen anything of a small screw-driver; the handkerchief came in time to enable me to offer, in replying, a composed and ordinary appearance. Edward and John arrived from some practice with convalescent soldiers near the West Kent Cricket Club ground, where the first had been playing, and the second—never more any games of the kind for him!—looked on. I slipped away to the tradesmen's gate, to avoid meeting them.

I had locked the front door of my small house in Lower Camden because, as it was a sort of a holiday, strangers might be about. The back looked up at the railway, and I always found it interesting to watch troop trains racing along the down lines with bunches of cheery faces at every window; it was less exhilarating to see the Red Cross trains going to London. There had come a long spell of hot weather, and in opening my gate I noticed that signs of melted tar had been brought from the roadway to the sill. With an exclamation of annoyance at the carelessness of folk, I opened the door, found a damp cloth, and returning, knelt on the mat to repair the damage. Absorbed in the task, I did not glance up when footsteps came.

"Fair maiden," said a deep voice. "Pray rise, and accept the pardon that is willingly granted."

"Cartwright!"

"Your own soldier laddie," he remarked, genially, "and none other. Called on the old people at Lewisham, and came on here, and been bombarding the door, I have, like a reg'lar Jack Johnson, and absolutely determined not to go back without seeing you. And now, Mary Weston, that you've apologised on your knees in the manner I some time since suggested, what about me coming in and having a glance round this nobby little domicile that you're getting ready against the time we finish off the war, and I retire from the British army?"

"Give those clumsy boots of yours a good scrape first!" I directed.